Sweet Like Whiskey

The Darling Brothers Book 1

Emmy Sanders

Beta Reading by Christie, Jen & Maxie of Smut Readers Society, and Lauren

Editing by M.A. Hinkle

Proofreading by Ky and Willow

Cover Design by Natasha Snow Designs

A special thank you to RJ Boerstler, KC Elle, and Blair Wynters for your help with Remi

ISBN: 9798989542055

Content Warning: This book contains casual alcohol use, minor on-page injury, and a character with chronic pain.

For everyone who loves slipping back into their cowboy boots, even if only within the pages of a book. Welcome home.

Contents

Note to Readers

First, the raccoon will be fine. I promise.

Second, this series includes a character who's Deaf and several characters who use American Sign Language. Please note ASL and English do not share the same grammatical structure. However, for ease of reading, ASL conversations are written using English grammar.

Chapter 1

ASH

There comes a time in life when a person has to decide whether they're going to continue down the same well-marked path they've been traveling for far too long or whether they're going to jump the guardrails and go offroad.

I've jumped the rails.

"This is fine," I say to myself, checking my navigation as yet another mile of empty road passes. "We're almost there. Everything is just *fine*."

It's so not fine.

"Me and you, right, Edna? We've got this."

My car sputters, and I let out an equally undignified squawk.

"Edna! Don't you dare crap out on me now. Stay strong, woman."

In response, there's a loud *clunk*, and my 2007 Honda Civic in tango red stalls out right in the middle of the road not two miles from my destination.

"This. Is. *Fine*."

With a little more force than necessary, I pull my keys from the ignition and step out of the car. There's no smoke or dramatic glaring signs telling me what's wrong when I pop the hood. In fact, I have no clue what I'm even supposed to be looking for.

Muttering a curse, I head back to the driver's side door and pull my phone from the holder on the dash. Naturally, I ring Virginia.

"C'mon, c'mon," I mutter, tapping my foot.

"Hey, baby boy," my closest friend and most favorite troublemaker says in greeting. Before I can admonish her for calling me *baby boy*—I'm thirty-five years old, thank you very much—she goes on. "Are you here?"

"I'm here," I confirm. "There's just been a *slight* hiccup."

"I'm listening," Virginia says, the din of conversation and the sound of clinking glasses accompanying her voice down the line.

"I broke down," I tell her.

There's a beat of silence, and then my friend laughs.

"Thanks so much, Ginnie," I groan. "So very helpful."

She snorts before her voice is back in my ear. "Where are you?"

"A couple miles away," I answer, peering around at the admittedly beautiful landscape. Trees dot the sides of the road, the tips of some of the leaves just beginning to yellow, and tall grasses spread like a blanket far and wide in every direction. In the distance, the mountains stretch toward the sky, their stony peaks blending seamlessly into airy blue. It's gorgeous. Like a postcard.

"Well, better get walking," Virginia says.

Somewhere in the recesses of my mind is a screech.

"I'm sorry," I say slowly. "I must have misheard. Did you just tell me to *walk*?"

"Baby, I'm already at work, and you're only fifteen minutes away. Put those pretty feet of yours to use and walk on down the road. I'll have a couple welcome shots ready for you."

Pretty feet?

"Oh, and Ash?" she says.

"Yeah?"

"Watch out for the donkey."

With that, my friend clicks off the call, and I'm left wondering what in the actual hell I've gotten myself into.

"It's fine," I say for the umpteenth time, popping Edna's trunk. I pull both of my suitcases out and set them on the asphalt. "This is the start of something new. An adventure. Nothing's going to get me down. *Nothing.*"

Slamming the trunk closed, I let out a breath. As I stand upright, the twinge in my back has me wincing, but I roll my shoulders, grab the handles of my suitcases, and put my *pretty feet* to work.

There's a reason I up and moved across the country on a whim. A reason I asked my friend if her standing invitation to crash on her couch was still good. A reason I drove my run-down car over 2,000 miles from Maine to the Wild freaking West, of all places, with no more than two bags in my possession and a conviction that it was the right thing to do.

My life was in desperate need of an upheaval. It's *not* because I'm having a midlife crisis at three-and-a-half decades, as my mom so kindly accused me of. It's not even because of my ex. At least, not directly.

I needed a change—for *me*. So am I going to complain about having to hoof it a couple measly miles at the end of my journey? Not a chance.

The navigation on my phone tells me The Barrel, the bar where Virginia works, is precisely 1.9 miles straight ahead. So, with determination, I set off that way, my suitcases dragging noisily behind me. After a while, I start to hum. Cat Stevens is welcome company on the trek, and when I remember Nicholas—*"don't-call-me-Nick" Nicholas*—isn't here to silently judge my song choices, I sing. Because why not?

Luckily, there's enough of a breeze to keep me from sweating through my shirt. For being the end of September, warm temperatures sure are hanging on.

Not so luckily, I'm only one mile in—or one mile away, depending on how you look at it—when one of my suitcases lists to the side and begins scraping against the pavement.

"No, no, no," I mutter, stopping and staring at the wheel that's now rolling slowly toward the grass on the other side of the road. "*Seriously?*"

A short honk has me whirling around, my pulse jumping. A rusted orange truck slows to a stop in front of me, its driver an older man with a big white beard.

Oh, Jesus. Please don't let me end up in some guy's basement freezer. I did *not* sign on for that.

"Need a ride?" the man asks, his window rolled down. The...is that a *goat?*...in the passenger seat bleats.

"Uh, I'm just heading into town," I tell him, well aware that doesn't answer his question.

"You own the car a mile back?" he asks.

"Yeah?" I hedge. "She's mine."

He nods. "We'll have Ratchet fix 'er up." Hitching a thumb over his shoulder, he says, "Hop in back. I'll drop you off."

"In...back?" I ask slowly.

"Misty's got shotgun."

Misty bleats.

I weigh my options for all of two seconds before deciding *screw it*. Suitcases in hand, I march forward and climb into the bed of the truck.

The man opens his rear window once I'm situated. "Name's Earl."

"Ash," I reply.

"Welcome to town, Ash."

Before I have time to formulate a response, Earl is gunning it. I brace myself against warm metal as the old, rusty truck ambles down the road. Misty hangs her head out the passenger window, and I bark a laugh.

In a matter of minutes, Earl is slowing down in front of what looks like the town center. It's the first time I've seen civilization in a good thirty miles.

"Where to?" he asks.

"Actually, you can just drop me here," I tell him, grabbing my suitcases. Earl keeps the truck in park while I jump down. When I get near the front of the vehicle, Misty bleats again, her head straining my way. "Can I...pet her?"

Earl nods, chewing something. Gum, maybe? Tobacco? "She's friendly."

Misty practically headbutts my hand when I hold it her way. I huff a laugh, rubbing over her head and behind her tiny stub ears. "She's cute."

"You got something to take down a number?" Earl asks.

"Oh. Sure?"

I pull out my phone, and Earl rattles off ten digits. "That's Ratchet's shop. Give 'im a call tomorrow for an estimate."

"Got it, thanks," I say, pocketing my phone. "And, uh, thanks for the ride, Earl."

He gives me a brisk nod. "Enjoy your visit to Montana. And Ash?"

"Yeah?"

"Watch out for the donkey."

I blink, and Earl pulls away, his truck rumbling as it takes a bend in the road. Shaking my head, I turn and face town.

And then I stop still.

Squat red-brick shop fronts flank either side of the gently sloping two-lane road, down which vehicles are parked, more than I'm expecting for early evening on a Tuesday. The mountains sit centered in the distance like a quiet sentinel, too far away for me to estimate their size apart from *huge*. Along the sidewalks are planters holding flowers in bright shades of pink and red and yellow, and awnings cover many of the businesses' front doors, creating a quaint, colorful visage. Small town charm at its finest.

But what captures and holds my attention is the large, swaying sign high above the street. Etched into the wood are four simple words. Four simple, monumental words.

Welcome to Darling, Montana.

I pull in a breath, fresh air filling my lungs. "We made it, Edna."

With a grin, I pick up my suitcases and head into town.

The Barrel isn't difficult to find, even without navigation. After passing a clothing store, a fudge shop, and an antiques market, I stop in front of a glass-front building flanked by two large casks. Like the other planters along the road, the wooden barrels are filled with flowers, brightening the exterior of the bar. "The Barrel" is stenciled on the window in front of me, and past it, I can just make out my friend.

Virginia lets out an ungodly screech the moment I push through the door, and every head inside the bar swivels in our direction. My tiny firecracker of a friend doesn't care in the least, all five-foot-three of her—five-*four* if you count the poofy brown hair—strutting my way. I have just enough time to drop my suitcases before Virginia is in my arms, squeezing me like I'm a lemon she's trying to juice.

"Jesus, Ginnie," I groan.

She squeezes harder. "Don't complain, baby boy. I haven't seen you in *three goddamn years*. I'm allowed to squeeze the stuffing outta you."

"Yes, Mom."

She drops down and swats me on the chest with a hand towel that had been tucked into her apron. I hiss, hand over my nipple as she turns to face the room.

"Everybody," Virginia calls, much to my mortification. "This is Ash. My best friend in the whole dang world. Be nice to him or you're cut off."

There are a few chuckles at that, a couple people wave, and a few others tilt their hats in greeting. I offer a quick smile before grabbing my suitcases and hustling after Virginia. As she makes her way behind the bar, I stuff my suitcases out of the way and slide onto a stool.

"Thanks for that," I mutter, brushing my hair off my face. "Just what I needed—everyone staring."

"Baby," Virginia says lightly, plunking a glass down in front of me. She fills it with water. "You're in Darling now. Ain't no such thing as a stranger here, so you better get used to it. Folks in this town are gonna be aggressively polite."

"That's...comforting."

She snorts before resting her elbows on the bartop. "You doing okay?" she asks seriously.

My stomach tumbles over, and I lean closer, speaking low. "Ginnie. Tell me I'm doing the right thing."

"You are," she says immediately.

"This isn't stupid? Coming all this way without a plan? Up and leaving everything behind?"

"Nothing you've done or ever will do could be stupid, Ash," she says before pausing. "Well, *almost* nothing. This is the right thing for you. I know it. You do, too. Trust that gut of yours."

I nod, deflating. "You're right. It's just... I don't have a job, a place to live, a working *car*."

"You're staying with me for now, and we'll figure out the rest," she says calmly. "In fact, I've got some leads on the job front. For tonight, just take a load off. Tomorrow, we'll get you sorted."

"Yeah, okay," I say, rubbing my temple. With a huff, I joke, "I don't suppose there are any men here? That would certainly help me take a load off."

Virginia's lips curve into a smirk as she reaches across the bar to grab my chin. She redirects my gaze out the window, where a couple guys our age are passing by. I nearly choke on my spit. From the big leather hats to the boots and belt buckles, they look every bit like real-life cowboys.

"Damn," I mutter. "They sure don't come like that in Maine."

Virginia chuckles, turning and plucking a bottle off the shelf behind the bar. She places two shot glasses down in front of me before twisting the cap off the bottle and pouring the deep amber-brown liquid with a flourish. "Darling Whiskey," she says with a wink, sliding the shot glasses closer. "Welcome to Montana, Ash."

With that, my friend walks off to tend to her customers, and I catch sight of my reflection in the mirror at the back of the bar. My hair is windblown, the blonde waves a mess, and my cheeks are still a little red from walking. But it's the smile on my face—the one that reaches my eyes—that has me doing a double take.

It's been a long time since I've seen that smile.

Giving myself a mental salute, I pick up a shot glass and bring it to my lips. The whiskey goes down smooth, pleasant oaky fire warming a path to my stomach. At the tail end is a hint of something that tastes almost like caramel.

With a happy hum, I exchange my empty glass for the full one.

Yeah. I think Darling and me are going to get along just fine.

Chapter 2

JACKSON

Loud, incessant knocking is the first thing to rouse me. The voice that follows has me sitting up with a groan.

"Jackson Darling! I know you're in there. Get your butt outta bed and answer this door."

"Jesus, Ma," I call, rubbing my eyes. "Hold your horses."

The knocking starts up again, and I swing out of bed, practically stumbling to my dresser. I pull on a well-worn plaid work shirt, step into jeans, and make my way toward the front of the house.

My mother's face greets me when I swing open the door, her fist held up in knocking position. It drops to her side as she gives me a sweet smile I don't much trust. "Morning, Jackson. We've got some things to discuss."

"It couldn't wait?" I ask, heading toward the kitchen.

My mom follows, not bothering to take off her boots. "It couldn't. You remember how I said it was time we found some help for the ranch house?"

I sigh, starting a pot of coffee and grabbing a thermos. "Mhm. I haven't had a chance to look."

"I know you haven't," she says, plopping down at the kitchen table. When I hold a mug up in question, she shakes her head. "Which is why I hired somebody myself."

I pause. "You what now?"

"Hired somebody," she says slowly. "Really, Jackson, it's like you're not listening."

I scrub a hand over my eyes. It's too early for my mother's antics.

"Name's Ashley," she goes on. "Arrived ten minutes ago."

"And you didn't think to consult with me first?" I ask, slamming the cupboard door a little harder than necessary.

"And why would I do that?" she snipes back. "Have you forgotten I still own part of this business?"

"No," I grumble, running my hands through my hair when I catch my reflection in the microwave. *Christ*, I look like a rumpled mess.

"What was that?" my mom asks loudly.

"Jesus, Ma. I said *no*, I haven't forgotten."

"Mhm," she hums, leaning back in her seat. "You may have taken over running the ranch, Jackson dear, but don't forget who made you. I brought you into this world. I can take you out of it."

I turn slowly, glaring at my mom. She smiles back at me. "You sound deranged."

"Maybe that's 'cause I had to tromp all the way over here to come wake you," she says.

I nearly huff. *All the way.* My house is less than a quarter mile from the main ranch house.

The coffeemaker stops spitting, and I pull out the carafe, emptying the contents into my travel mug. "You coulda called," I point out. "Who'd you leave the new hire with?"

"Your dad."

"Jesus," I groan, slamming the carafe back into place. "Why would you do that?"

"He's not that bad," she says.

I turn to look at her again. "Not that bad? Just the other day, you called him an old goat who had more stubbornness than brains."

"Well, that's true."

"And the day before that, you said his head was stuck so far up in the clouds, you wouldn't be surprised if he found Jack's beans."

"Well, yes," she says, sounding put-out. "I'm allowed to say that. I married the man."

"And divorced him," I point out. "Twice."

"Semantics," my mom says, waving me off. "The point is Ashley is waiting, so go brush your hair and say hello. You're doing the tour."

"Why me?" I ask, capping my coffee.

"'Cause I said so. I already gave the spiel. Cooking, cleaning, keeping things in line. Now's your turn. After all, you're the boss, ain't you?" My mom gets up, pushing her chair in noisily. "And Jackson?"

I heave a breath. "What?"

"Be nice."

"I'm always nice," I answer, affronted.

My mom laughs. Loudly. "Time's a tickin'," she says, heading for the door. A moment later, it slams shut, and I look up at my exposed beam ceiling, wondering what in the hell I ever did to deserve a mother like *that*.

I make a quick trip to the bathroom to tame my hair and piss—plus brush my teeth because I wasn't born in a barn—and then I'm out the door. The air is cool this morning but not as cool as usual for the start of autumn. Flowers are still blooming strong and the trees haven't yet let go of their green. There's time, of course. The seasons always change, and winter will be here before we know it.

Vehicles occupy the dirt lot in front of the ranch house when I arrive, many of them dusty or flecked with mud. I don't see any unfamiliar cars or trucks that could belong to Ashley. The house itself is expansive, two stories and built in a log-cabin style. Granted, it's more log-cabin *chic*. Big windows let in plentiful light, and a new metal roof shines under the sun.

I kick my boots against the mat before opening the front door. The ranchers are out working this time of day, as they are every dawn, breakfast having already been eaten. I would've been into my day already, too, if it weren't for the late night and extra shots of whiskey my brothers so helpfully shoved down my throat, courtesy of my birthday.

Forty goddamn years old. *Shit.*

The house is quiet when I enter, but it doesn't take long to hear my dad's voice coming from the kitchen. It sounds like he's lecturing our new employee on the differences between Holstein and Angus cattle. *Christ.* He couldn't give her a day to get settled?

I shake my head as I make my way down the hallway inside my childhood home, and then I come to a dead stop.

Two men are standing inside the kitchen. One is my father, dressed in blue sleep pants and a chunky oatmeal sweater, his glasses on top of his head. The other I'm not expecting in the least. He's taller than my dad, but not by much. His jeans are gray, and while his shirt certainly isn't inappropriately tight, the stretch of it doesn't hide the lean muscle he's sporting. His hair is a dark blonde, long enough to curl at the back of his neck, some pieces tucked behind his ear while others hang across his cheekbone. And his eyes... His eyes are a stormy blue-gray that widen in surprise the moment they land on me.

I'm so shocked, my tone comes out biting when I ask, "Who the hell are you?"

My dad blinks mildly, taking a sip of his coffee before saying, "This is Ashley."

My head cocks back, and I look at the man again. "You..."

Spinning out through the doorway, I stomp back across the house and throw the front door wide. I make my way to my mother's, the woman herself back behind the small cottage she now lives in directly next to the ranch house. She's snapping pole beans off the vine, the last of the crop, and dropping them into a bowl beside her.

"Ma," I call.

She looks up at my approach, not even flinching when the gate slams behind me. "Mm?"

"Ashley is *not* a woman."

My mom stands to her full height, an impressive six feet. She's a couple inches shorter than me, but it doesn't feel it as she stares me down. "And this is a problem why?"

"It's not a problem. You just said—"

"I never said Ashley was a woman," she cuts in.

"But..."

"Jackson Darling," my mom says, hands landing on her hips, her tone bordering on dangerous. "Surely my second-oldest son isn't implying a woman needs to be the one doing the cooking and cleaning."

"Of course not—"

"And *surely*," she goes on, "you don't have a problem with a man named Ashley being in your employ."

"What?" I ask, feeling turned around and upside down. "Of course not, I just—"

"Then I don't know what your problem is," she finishes, dusting her hands on her pants.

"I just... He just..."

With a groan, I turn on my heel and head out of my mother's garden. I hear her *mhm* following me, but I pay it no mind, my anger or surprise or I-don't-know-what slowly dissolving as I make my way back to the main house. I close the front door and let out a breath before striding toward the kitchen.

My dad and Ashley stop talking the moment I step through the doorway, the former raising an eyebrow, the latter giving me a cautious look.

"Sorry," I say, plunking my thermos down on the counter and holding out my hand. "Jackson Darling."

Ashley accepts my handshake. "Ash Alcott," he says, voice smooth and warm, just like his palm.

I drop it, nodding briskly. "Welcome to Darling Ranch, Ash. My mom said she talked to you about the job duties?"

"A bit," he says, tucking his hair behind his ear in a way that has me fighting a groan. "You need someone to cook meals for the...cowboys?"

His tentative question has my dad huffing a laugh. "I'll leave you boys to it," he says, patting Ash on the shoulder before turning to me. With his back to our guest, he waggles his eyebrows.

I fight another groan, shooing my dad away. The menace is laughing as he leaves the kitchen.

"Ranchers is fine," I answer. "You're not from around here, I take it?"

"What gave me away?" Ash asks, a mild smile on his face.

Everything.

"Nothing," I answer. "Why don't we walk while I go over the job? I can show you around."

"Sure," he says, setting his coffee mug down. It's still half full.

"Want a thermos for that?"

"Oh, uh..."

Stepping past the sink, I open a cupboard and grab a travel mug. Ash shoots me a grateful smile as I dump the rest of his drink into it. I simply grunt, handing it over and grabbing my own.

"So, we do a bit of everything around here," I explain as Ash and I head down the porch stairs at the front of the house. I lead him toward the pastures first. "Our main focus is the cattle. We run a dual beef and dairy operation. See that low red barn over there? That's for milking."

Ash nods, his eyes wide as he takes everything in. The cattle are out grazing, the sun not yet high enough for them to seek shade, although with the temperatures beginning to drop, that'll be less of a concern.

"They've already been milked," I tell him. "Five a.m. and five p.m. every day. Out further are the beef lot."

"Wow," Ash says quietly.

The astonishment in his tone has me following his gaze. Our land stretches far to the west, farther than the eye can see. Deciduous trees and pines dot the landscape, and cattle roam over still-green grass, like black-and-white ink blots on a spring canvas. To the left, a slow-moving river snakes toward the mountains towering in the distance, the surface of the water reflecting the bright blue of the sky.

I grew up on this land, and I've never once taken it for granted. But it's easy to forget, I think, the beauty in what you see every day.

It's not the first time a newcomer has reminded me of that.

Clearing my throat, I ask, "Where're you from?"

"Maine," Ash answers, giving me a smile. His bottom lip is fuller than the top, and there's a tiny divot in his chin that I have to forcibly tear my gaze away from.

"Come on," I say gruffly, heading in the opposite direction. Ash keeps pace at my side. "So we have about twenty employees who man the cattle. They come to the ranch house for meals. That's where you come in. Breakfast is at four—"

Ash makes a choking sound, and I pause.

"All right?" I ask.

He nods quickly. "Yep. Four a.m. Okay, what else?"

"Lunch at eleven. Dinner at six."

"Holy shit," he says before wincing slightly, presumably at the swear word. "That's a long day."

"The ranchers work in shifts," I tell him, stopping at the dirt drive that leads further into the property. "You will, too. We don't expect more than eight hours a day out of you, so you'll take time for yourself between meals. Plus, you're not expected to clean up after dinner. We'll handle that."

He nods, and I point toward the white barn at the end of the drive.

"Down that way is our petting farm," I explain. "We've got goats, a pony, and some chickens, although the chicks don't always like being pet. It's open to the public in the afternoons, and we have employees there, too."

Ash gives another nod. "Got it."

"We do trail rides on the weekends, as well. The brown barn? That's the stables. Some of the horses are for the employees' use only, but we have several with even temperaments who do great with kids."

Ash shakes his head slightly, that smile still on his face. "You weren't kidding. You're busy here."

"That we are," I agree, waving him back toward the main house. It's then I notice his shoes. "You're probably gonna wanna get some boots. Those won't hold up here."

He looks down at his feet, huffing a laugh. "Noted."

I sip my coffee as we walk. "Questions so far?"

"Uh, yeah," he says. "Who lives there?"

He's pointing at the cottages situated beside the ranch house. One is pink, and the other is blue. I heave a sigh as my mom waves at us from her garden.

"My mom lives in the blue house and my dad in the pink."

Ash looks at me in surprise. "They don't live together?"

"They're divorced," I say flatly.

His smile widens, and I find my gaze drawn to the angles of his cheeks and the way his eyes crease gently at the corners. "They're divorced, but they live ten feet apart?"

"You'll understand soon enough," I tell him, nodding my head toward the ranch house. "Come on. I'll show you around the kitchen. You staying close or outta town?"

"Oh, uh... I'm staying here."

My feet stutter to a stop, and Ash skids to a halt beside me. "Pardon?"

"Well, my car broke down on the way into Darling. Ratchet has it?" he says a little uncertainly.

"The mechanic," I mutter.

He nods. "Yeah, he's taking a look at it. But until I have a car again, your mom said I could stay here. She set me up in the guest room."

I shut my eyes tight and pinch the bridge of my nose. *Of course she did.*

"Is that...okay?" Ash asks, sounding concerned.

"It's fine," I tell him, opening my eyes and waving him forward. "Just fine."

Yep.

Everything will be *fine*.

Chapter 3

ASH

Jackson Darling is, in a word, trouble.

Or maybe, more accurately, I'm in so much trouble when it comes to him.

The man continues to show me around the kitchen, pointing out the mixer that's inside a low cupboard, but which pulls out and rises up on a moving platform so it's counter-height when in use. He points out where measuring cups are and whisks, of which there are three, and explains the general organizational system for the pantry. He even explains the different kinds of milk in the fridge because of course they use their own fresh pasteurized milk.

But the entire time Jackson is walking me through the job, my eyes are firmly on him.

If someone asked me to describe "cowboy in his prime," that would be Jackson Darling. He's rugged, his voice gravelly like he just woke up, a plaid shirt rolled to his elbows and worn jeans wrapped snug around his thighs. His hair is falling in a haphazard mess, pieces in front of his eyes like they just couldn't be contained. The brown is threaded through with the faintest hint of copper, the color a little more prominent in his close-shaven beard. And there's a roughness to the way he walks and the way he talks, the faint lines at the corners of his eyes speaking of a man who's seen a good few decades of life.

But those eyes, so crystalline blue, carry a softness I wasn't expecting.

Of course, when the man looks at me and grunts, "Did you catch that?" that softness all but disappears.

I hold in my smile. "Got it. Blue lid is whole milk. Red is buttermilk."

He grunts again, shutting the fridge door. "We've got some recipes in the book there," he says, pointing next to the utensil holder, "but you're welcome to cook whatever you'd like. We don't have any peanut allergies. No vegetarians. Ira is gluten-free, but he brings a bag lunch just in case."

"I can make gluten-free options. That's not a problem," I assure him.

He looks at me for a moment before humming, the sound short and to the point. "Let me show you the cleaning supplies. We don't expect you to keep it sparkling in here. It's a ranch house. It's gonna get dirty. But some basic upkeep when you've got time would be appreciated."

I nod along, following Jackson into the hall where there's a storage closet. The contents are pretty self-explanatory.

"And everyone eats together?" I check.

"Anyone who wants to eat," he says simply, waving me down the hall. "They come in if they're hungry. They know the time. It's not your job to feed the stragglers."

I huff a laugh, stilling when we step into a massive dining room at the back of the house. It looks like it might have been added as an extension, three of the walls made out of panels of glass that overlook the pastures. A porch wraps around the outside of the room, a few rocking chairs set atop the wood. Inside, a long, *long* table rests, easily able to fit the twenty or so workers the Darling Ranch employs.

"Where did you find a table like this?" I ask, stepping forward to run my hand along the wood. The outer edges are rough and uneven, like the bark on a tree. In fact, the entire piece looks as if it could have been made from a single vertical cut out of a massive tree trunk. Grain lines run along the top of the table, although they've been polished smooth.

Jackson grunts. "My dad made it."

"I'm sorry, what?" I say in shock. "Your dad *made* this? From scratch?"

He crosses his arms, expression neutral. "Mm. He has...hobbies."

"Jesus. My hobbies are reading and watching *Drag Race*," I mutter.

"What's that?" Jackson asks.

I shake my head quickly. "So meals are served here. And people stay for dinner? They don't go home to eat with their families?"

He shrugs, leading me back out into the hall. "Some of them do, but some of 'em stay. They're...a close group. You'll see."

I notice how he says *they're*, as if excluding himself.

"And you?" I ask. "What do you do around here?"

He pauses at the base of the stairs, hand on the railing. "A bit of everything."

With that, he heads up, and I huff a laugh, following. Jackson peeks inside the guest room Mrs. Darling—*Marigold*, as she insisted I call her—showed me earlier. My bags are propped inside. Two measly suitcases. Everything I fled Maine with.

Jackson walks further down the hall. "Your bathroom will be here," he says, motioning to a full bath with a stone-walled shower. "You'll be sharing it with my brothers."

"They live here?"

He nods, opening another closet. "Towels and laundry," he says before explaining, "Colton and Remi live in-house. Lawson, too, now that... Well, he's in the middle of a divorce. That's why we needed somebody looking after the ranch house. Lawson's wife had the job before you. She's a great cook. But she left the position six months ago."

"Who's been doing the cooking since then?" I ask, following Jackson back downstairs.

"My mom," he says. "My dad, too. Me, sometimes."

"You've all been busy," I note.

He hums, not disagreeing.

"Well, I'm glad to be here," I tell him truthfully. "I'm not formally trained, but I've always loved cooking, and I don't think I'm half bad at it. And, frankly, I needed a job. Badly. I hadn't planned on moving, I just kind of...did? But then my friend told me you were hiring, and I talked to your mom, and it's almost like fate, you know? The timing couldn't have been better."

And geez, Ash. Stop talking already.

Jackson grunts, staring at me. I offer a smile, but his gaze flicks down the hall, to where another man is approaching.

"Hey," the younger guy says. He has honey-brown hair and blue eyes, like Jackson's.

"Hey," Jackson replies, waving a hand my way. "Remi, this is Ash, our new cook-slash-keeper."

Remi shakes his head, tapping his chin just below his mouth, and Jackson nods, his hands starting to fly in purposeful motions. I watch, surprised, as he signs to his brother in what appears to be fluent ASL. Halfway through, Jackson speaks up.

"Ash, this is my brother Remington. He's Deaf, and he's not wearing the sound processor for his cochlear implant, so he can't hear you."

Remi holds up his hand in a clear hello. I mirror the gesture, adding my own "Hello" and a smile.

Remi signs something, and Jackson interprets for me. "He says, 'I'm excited to try your food. I'm sick of Jackson's spaghetti.'"

Jackson sends a gesture Remi's way, and based on Remi's responding laugh, I'm guessing it was impolite.

"Well, I'm happy to cook for you," I say. "Any favorite foods?"

Remi watches his brother's hands before looking at me and saying himself, "Biscuits."

I huff a laugh. "Biscuits. You got it."

Remi signs something else to Jackson, and the older man nods, adding his own, "Yeah, catch you later."

Remi gives me a wave, which I return, and then he jogs up the stairs to the second floor.

"He's quite a bit younger than you," I note.

Jackson rolls his eyes. "Yeah, thanks for the reminder. And he's twenty-eight. Hardly a kid anymore."

Still, I'd put Jackson closer to forty. That's a decent gap.

"I need to check on a few things before lunch," Jackson says, crossing his arms as he leans against the wall. "Can I leave you on your own?"

"You're going to throw me to the wolves on my first day here?" I ask, grinning. "What if I mess up lunch?"

"I think you can handle it," he mutters.

I don't know if he truly has that much faith in me or if it's a test of some sort, but I hop on the chance, eager to get started.

"Yep, I got this," I tell him, heading past into the kitchen. The time on the stove says ten, which gives me a good hour to figure out a meal.

I'm looking through the old recipe book when I feel Jackson's presence behind me. I glance over my shoulder, finding him standing in the doorway, a serious expression on his face.

"You need help, you tell me," he says simply.

My lips twitch into a smile. "Will do, boss."

Jackson frowns for a beat, but then he nods and turns from the doorway. His heavy boots tread through the house before the sound of the front door opening and closing reaches my ears.

I think grumpy Jackson Darling might just have a heart of gold.

"I'm so fucked," I say to myself, spotting a recipe for buttermilk biscuits. "Ah. Bingo."

I can hear people laughing inside the house before I can see them. Lunch is already spread out on the long dining room table, ready to go, so I grab the two pitchers of lemonade I made up and head that way.

Inside the dining room, there's a door that leads directly out onto the porch. It's open now, and a couple individuals are trailing in. A few others are already seated, excited expressions on their faces. They notice me quickly.

"Hey," I say, giving the men and lone woman a smile. "I'm Ash. The new guy."

"Well, shit," one of the men says. He takes off his cowboy hat as he pulls out a chair. "I didn't even know we had a new guy. What's all this?"

I set the lemonade down as I answer him. "The soup is chicken pot pie. I didn't have time to make a *real* pot pie, so that's what the biscuits are for. It's my first day. Cut me some slack." There are a few chuckles at that, and I grin, going on. "There's also strawberry poppy seed salad, sweet potato fries, and ham sandwiches. I honestly didn't know how much twenty people would eat. I might've gone overboard."

"Son," an older man says, pouring himself a glass of lemonade, "I think you've done just right."

"This looks great," the woman adds, giving me a smile. "And *shit*. Here come the rest of the vultures."

She hastily ladles herself a bowl of soup as several more people come through the door, all of them stomping their boots on the porch before stepping into the dining room. No one, I notice, takes off their footwear.

"Is Ira here?" I ask, looking around at the eclectic mix of young and old. I notice Hank, the elder Mr. Darling, come through the house-side entrance to the dining room.

"That's me," one of the older gentlemen says. I'd estimate him to be around fifty.

"The biscuits in the blue bowl are gluten-free," I let him know. "There's no flour in the soup, so you should be all set there."

His eyes widen. "Well, dang. Thanks for that."

"No problem," I say, stepping back as the plates, bowls, and silverware at the end of the table are picked up. The ranchers start dishing up their food, and a rush of warmth fills my chest as I watch them.

"So, uh," one of the newer arrivals says. "Who are you?"

I bark a laugh and reintroduce myself. The occupants of the table go around, doing the same, but I know it'll take more than one introduction for me to remember everyone's names. As I'm stepping back into the kitchen, figuring I'd better start cleaning up, my skin prickles with awareness.

"Checking to make sure I didn't burn the place down?" I ask, smiling to myself as I wipe flour off the counter into my hand.

"Just checking," Jackson answers, his voice rumbling through the space between us.

"Did you eat yet?" I ask.

"Not yet. Did you?"

"Sampled as I went," I admit.

He gives a gruff hum. "Once lunch is done, you should take some time to unpack. It's up to you when you wanna fit in your time off, but today, take the afternoon."

"Got it," I tell him, tossing a smile his way. His brusque delivery doesn't fool me one bit. He's not the hardass he pretends to be.

He nods but hesitates at the doorway.

"Something else?" I ask.

"No. Just...smells good," he practically grunts. And then he's off, disappearing from sight to join the lunch crowd.

"*Sooo* much trouble," I mutter under my breath.

It only takes forty-five minutes for the table to get picked clean. I start collecting empty dishes as the ranchers head back to work, many of them thanking me, a few others patting their bellies before shoving their cowboy hats atop their heads. A gentle breeze blows in the door as they leave.

"Was it enough food?" I ask Hank, the only person left.

"Oh, it was plenty," he tells me, nursing his glass of lemonade. "Dang good, too. They couldn't stop eating, otherwise we'd have more leftovers."

"I'm glad everyone enjoyed it," I tell him honestly, nodding to Remi, who walks in and snags a biscuit.

The younger Darling says a quick, "Thanks," before he's gone.

"You don't have professional experience?" Hank asks me, seemingly in no hurry to get on with his day.

"None. I thought about going to culinary school at one point, but it just never happened. Went a different route instead."

"Well," he says, a little smile on his face. "I think we lucked out, snagging you."

I huff a laugh, pleased. "Thanks, Hank. I think I lucked out, too."

The older man hums at that, reminding me of the absent Jackson. I finish stacking plates before heading back into the kitchen. When there's a thunk against the doorframe, I jump and look over.

"Shit, did I miss it?" a new face asks. He has the Darling-blue eyes Hank passed to his sons but darker hair than Jackson's. He looks a little younger, too, though not by much.

"Lunch? Yeah, you did, but I think there are a few scraps left."

"Thanks," the guy says, taking a step away before backpedaling. He comes fully into the kitchen and holds out a hand. "Colton."

"Ash," I tell him.

"Welcome, man. Shit, I bet my brother loves you." Before I can ask *which brother?* he lets my hand go and adds, "Sorry to run. It's just been a day, and I'm fucking hungry, you know?"

"Go," I tell him, huffing a laugh.

He does, giving me a quick salute as he leaves the kitchen. I stand there a moment longer.

Which brother?

And good grief, are all the Darling men gifted with damn fine genes?

Shaking my head, I get back to work. It's only a moment later when I hear, "Ah hell, this is good." I smile, glad Colton is enjoying his food.

Once the kitchen has been put back to rights, I head upstairs to unpack. My bedroom overlooks the west end of the property, where the mountains sit in the distance. I can see a few cowboys—or ranchers, whatever the difference is—riding amongst the cattle. It's picturesque, almost too stunning for words.

After unpacking my measly bags, I plunk onto the edge of my bed and pick up my phone. Virginia answers quickly, the background of the call quiet, telling me she's likely not at work yet.

"Hey, baby boy," she greets. "How was your first day at the new job?"

"Ginnie," I say slowly, standing back up and heading over to the window. I crank it open, inhaling deeply and feeling the breeze dance across my cheeks. "Have I got a story to tell you."

Chapter 4

JACKSON

"Ma."

"Oh boy," my mother says, standing up and brushing the dust off her jeans. "Here we go."

I stop at the edge of the goat pen. My mom is inside, a few kids of the goat variety dancing around her feet and bleating. It's late afternoon, the petting farm having just closed and the last of the visitors driving off behind my back.

"You invited him to stay," I bite out.

"Mhm."

"That man," I add, having no idea how else to describe him.

My mom gazes at me impassionately. "Well, I sure wasn't going to make him walk to work every day, now was I?"

"We have company vehicles," I point out. And she damn well knows it.

She simply hums, bending down to pet one of the goats vying for her attention.

"It won't work," I say.

"What's that, dear?"

"Whatever you're trying to do," I answer a touch hotly.

"And what's that?"

I huff a breath. "I understand why Dad divorced you," I tell her, walking past toward the barn.

She laughs loudly. "I divorced him!" she calls after me. "*Both* times."

I find Remi inside the shade of the barn, laying out fresh hay for the animals. They get plenty of pellets and treats throughout the afternoon, so their evening meal is light. I wave, getting my brother's attention when I notice he's still not wearing his processor.

'Did Mom tell you Ash will be staying in the house?' I sign, using a distinct name sign for Ash instead of spelling out the letters.

He nods. *'He makes good biscuits,'* he signs back.

I snort, and my brother grins.

'He's cute,' he signs coyly, to which I scowl. Remi laughs.

"The lot of you," I say, shaking my head. I add a signed, *'Pests.'*

Remi rolls his eyes. *'You love us.'*

I can't disagree with him. *'Will you be in for dinner?'*

My brother nods, and I give him a wave goodbye. He gets back to work as I head out of the barn. Snickerdoodle, our pony, kicks up her mane as I pass. I stop to give her a rub along her flank.

"How's it going, girl?"

She huffs against my side, headbutting me gently.

"Yeah, yeah. I'll bring some dates by later. How's that sound?"

She knocks against me again, and I pat her side before making my way toward the ranch house. The dairy girls are already inside for milking, the field closest to the house empty.

Some of the workers, those who arrived early morning, are gone. But others remain, finishing up their evening duties.

Never a dull hour on the ranch.

I run into Lawson, my older brother, as I step inside the house. He's standing in the doorway, staring at the coatrack where a few fall jackets and a couple hats hang.

"Law?" I ask. "You all right?"

He startles, as if he hadn't heard me come in. "Yeah, fine," he says, kicking off his shoes. Lawson is the eldest of us at forty-two. Like our mom, he has brown eyes. In fact, he takes after her in just about everything but disposition. Lawson is calm, like that river that cuts through our property. Whereas Mom, she's the sea.

"Have you met Ashley yet?" I ask.

"No, just got home. Who's Ashley?"

"The new cook. Goes by Ash."

The wince on my brother's face isn't a surprise. Lawson has been having a rough go of it ever since Laura asked for a divorce. Bringing up her replacement is surely knocking a few bad memories loose.

"Come on," I tell him, giving his shoulder a gentle squeeze. "I'll introduce you."

My brother nods and follows me down the hall. Ash is inside the kitchen, partway through dinner prep. Whatever he's making smells good enough to have my stomach voicing a rumble of approval.

"Ash?" I say softly, not wanting to startle the man. He turns with an expectant look on his face. "This is Lawson, my brother. He's a teacher at the combination middle-high school in town. Lawson, Ash Alcott."

"Nice to meet you," Lawson says, stepping forward to shake Ash's hand.

"Jesus," Ash says. "All of you."

"What's that?" I ask.

Ash huffs a small laugh as he drops Lawson's hand. "Nothing. You just all look alike. I hope everyone likes pasta. I wasn't sure what else to make because the fridge seems a little empty? But I found some chicken and figured I could spread the protein out using carbs."

"We're due for a grocery run," I admit, scrubbing the back of my neck as I think through tomorrow. "I'll have Colton go in the morning. If you want him to stock anything specific, just write it down."

Ash nods, looking between me and Lawson. My brother is staring off into space again. I clap him on the shoulder, steering him toward the door.

"We'll leave you to it," I tell Ash.

As our new houseguest turns back to the stove, my eyes, unbidden, skip down his body. First, to his exposed forearms and the blonde dusting of hair there. And then—despite my brain screaming at me to stop—to the swell of his ass beneath his apron strings.

My pulse kicks, and I grunt, turning swiftly away and following Lawson out the door. My brother is already halfway up the stairs, his gait slow as he takes the steps one at a time. I watch him go with a frown.

Once Lawson is out of sight, I hoof it the quarter mile home so I can clean up for dinner. Inside the shower, I scrub off the day's grime, using a brush under my fingernails and ignoring the way my cock tries to plump when I give it a cursory wash. I quickly banish thoughts of a certain round ass from my mind.

When I get back to the ranch house, it's six o'clock on the dot. The dining room is already filling up, my family present as usual, the remaining ranchers filing in through the door off the deck. Marty and Colleen are ribbing each other about their race back from the far fields, Marty claiming he won but Colleen denying it. My gaze catches on Ash as he comes in from the hallway, a large platter of rolls in his hands. His eyes find mine quickly, and he smiles, setting my heart off at a gallop.

"Ira is on the morning crew, right?" he asks, putting the rolls down near where I'm sitting.

"That's right," I answer.

"Good," he says in clear relief. "I didn't have time to make gluten-free rolls."

"You don't gotta do that," I tell him. "He's used to getting by."

Ash waves me off. "Please, it's not hard. I'll plan accordingly for breakfast and lunch. It's the least I can do."

Laura never bothered, but I don't tell Ash that. If he wants to cook gluten-free options for Ira, I won't stop him.

I simply hum in response, and Ash huffs a laugh, like I *amuse* him.

"Will you be joining us, Ashley?" my mom asks, taking a seat beside me. Her hair, threaded through with silver ever since she passed mid-fifty, is tied behind her in a loose ponytail.

"Sure," he answers. "I'll just grab the punch first."

Ash leaves the room, and Colton nudges my foot under the table. "Punch," he says, bouncing his eyebrows. I kick him in the shin, and he grunts.

"Boys," my mom says mildly.

Grabbing the platter of rolls, I take one and pass it along. Mealtimes at the Darling Ranch have always been chaotic. There's no waiting to begin, not with so many people coming and going around their work. If there's food on the table, it's fair game, which means, by the time Ash returns, the pasta has already been ransacked.

Ash takes a seat halfway down the table, seemingly happy, like usual. He's barely added a scoop of pasta to his plate when my dad asks, "So you ever seen a castration, Ash?"

Ash's eyes widen as my mom says, "What did I tell you about bringing up testicles at the dinner table, Hank? For Heaven's sake."

"It's a valid question," my dad shoots back. "Ball-handling is part of life at a cattle ranch."

Colton snickers, and Ash says, "I, uh. No, sir, I can't say I've had the pleasure."

My dad hums. "You will."

"Jesus," I groan. "Can we let the guy settle in for a damn day before y'all scare him off?"

Ash gives me a soft smile that feels much too warm, too *pleased*, so I return my focus to my dinner roll, slathering butter on top.

"Jackson can teach you about balls," Remi says, causing my butter knife to clatter to the table. *The little shit.* I shoot him a scowl, noticing his processor in place behind his ear. He grins at me as he adds, "He has plenty of experience."

"That he does," my dad says, completely oblivious to Remi's meaning. "He's been working this ranch since he was a toddler." He huffs a laugh before saying, "Shoulda seen him running through the milking barn in his birthday suit. Boy was always naked."

A few of the ranchers laugh as I groan.

Ash's eyes sparkle. "Does he still do that?" he asks my dad.

Lord.

"Nah," my dad answers. "Too old for fun, this one. He's all grown up now."

Ash's eyes slip down my torso as he says, "That he is."

Heat shoots square down my center, but I ignore it—and *everybody*—and take a big bite of my roll.

I choke a little when Colton says, "Well, there was that one time last year—"

"*Colt.*"

"—when he had one too many whiskeys and went skinny-dipping in the river," he finishes.

"I remember that," Colleen puts in from down the table, her voice full of amusement. "There were two full moons that night."

I hop up as the table erupts into laughter. "All right, all right," I grumble, grabbing my empty glass and making for the kitchen. Never mind that there's a pitcher of water at the table. I go to the tap and fill up my glass. After guzzling it down, I set the glass aside.

"Okay?" Ash asks from the doorway, apparently having followed me.

"Fine," I say, waving off his concern. *Why* he's concerned is a point I try not to think too heavily about.

"For what it's worth," he says slowly, his tone making me still, "I would've liked to see that."

I whip around and stare in shock as Ash exits the room, one question I hadn't even wanted to ask answered. Not that it matters one way or another who Ash is attracted to.

It doesn't.

Not even a little bit.

Not. At. All.

"*Fucking hell.*"

With a growl, I head back into the dining room. Fortunately, the rest of our meal passes without any more talk of testicles or full moons. Mom kindly shoos Ash when he tries to help clean up, telling him he's officially off the clock and that evening cleanup falls to the family. Ash takes a seat out on the porch as the ranchers head home. His chair rocks gently, the sun not yet starting to set, but it will soon.

"I think he fits here," my mom says quietly from beside me. Colton is carrying a stack of plates to the kitchen and Lawson is stacking glasses.

"Sure," I answer noncommittally. It's only been a day.

"Not everyone is your ex, Jackson."

I suck in a short breath, my muscles tensing. "Ma."

"I'm just saying."

"Yeah, well," I mutter. "You said he fit, too."

"And I was wrong," she says easily, even though I know the cost of her admitting that. My mom is stubborn. As unyielding as the mountains and just as hard at times. "He tried to fit, and that was the difference. He never sat outside and breathed the air."

"We've all gotta breathe."

"Jackson Darling, whatever am I going to do with you?" my mom says, not waiting for an answer before she walks off. A minute later, I hear, "Hank! Good Lord, man, you don't wash the glasses with the damn Brillo pad. Have you learned nothing?"

I shake my head, pausing when I see Lawson standing still at the end of the table. There's a collection of forks in his hand.

"Law?"

He startles.

"You sure you're all right?" I ask.

He grabs a few more forks. "I will be," he says simply before walking off.

Letting out a sigh, I head onto the porch. Ash glances my way before looking out over the land again.

"This place is beautiful," he says.

"Maine isn't?" I ask, taking a seat next to him.

He makes a soft, thoughtful sound. "It is. It's gorgeous there. The coast...it has its own kind of grandeur. The salty air. Blue as far as the eye can see. But this..." He shakes his head a little. "It's rough here. The land, the mountains, even the work you all do. It's like you've carved a life out of hardness, out of *harshness*. And I like that."

"You like hard work," I say, not quite a question. I already gleaned as much from the way he jumped in today, happily setting to his tasks.

His smile goes a little crooked on one end. "I like a challenge," he answers.

Clearing my throat, I look toward the west. The sun is nearly to the mountains now. "Do you have any questions? Like you said, I kinda threw you to the wolves today. But you did well."

Ash hums, precipitating me to look back his way. "You're a good boss, aren't you?"

"I try to be," I admit, although I don't particularly like the praise. Nor the way he's looking at me. "No questions?"

"Not yet," he says, rubbing absently below his lip. "Can I do the shopping once I get my feet under me?"

"Of course."

"Who cooks on the weekends?"

"We do," I answer. "You're welcome to join us for meals."

He nods, his chair rocking softly, squeaking against the wooden deck. "I think I'm going to like it here."

With my heart beating a little too fast for reasons I'd rather not identify, I stand.

"Jack," Ash says, causing me to come to a halt. "Where do you live? If everyone else is here, where are you?"

"Just down that way," I say, pointing without meeting his eye. "At the end of that unmarked lane."

"You're still on the property?" he asks.

"I am."

"But alone," he adds.

A pause. "Mm."

He hums softly. "That tracks. Night, then, Jackson Darling."

I pull in a breath. Expel it. My chest barely moves an inch. "Night."

I walk away without looking back at Ashley Alcott, trying to convince myself it has nothing whatsoever to do with what I might see on his face.

I almost believe it.

Chapter 5

Ash

Waking at three in the morning is nearly my undoing. *Nearly.*

But I buck up, get my feet out of bed, and work the kinks out of my body as I head down to the kitchen. I can hear others stirring before long, the house coming alive as I cook bacon, eggs, and French toast, including a gluten-free option for Ira from bread I baked last night.

At four o'clock on the dot, the early shift ranchers start to arrive, a flood of sound coming in from the dining room at the back of the house. There's some laughter, feet stomping, chairs screeching across the floor.

The sun is still asleep, but the animal folk are wide awake and ready to work.

People are well into their food by the time I bring the last of the eggs to the table. Ira, I see, found the smaller plate of French toast I left with a little toothpick on top labeled "GF." He shoots me a quick grin, pouring maple syrup over his entire breakfast plate, eggs included.

"Morning," Jackson grumbles, coming into the room. A few *mornings* are tossed back his way. His eyes meet mine briefly before he takes a seat.

I pour myself a cup of coffee and snag a piece of bacon, not yet hungry enough for more. That doesn't seem to be a problem for the ranchers who are blazing through hearty portions. Colton comes into the room before long, seemingly half asleep. Remi, too, although he's more awake. He waves a quick hello before grabbing three bacon strips and heading off. I saw Marigold's light turn on from the kitchen window, but neither she nor the elder Mr. Darling are here for breakfast.

It took me a minute to get everyone straight, but I think I have it now.

Marigold and Hank Darling are divorced for the second time but are—I'm pretty sure—still madly in love, considering they live mere footsteps away from each other. They're both in their mid-sixties, and while Hank is a subtly handsome man who's aged finely, Marigold is plain stunning. There's a grace about her that's mesmerizing and a bluntness I appreciate. I adored her immediately. And Hank, well... He's endearing in the way a child who doesn't know better is.

And then there are the Darling brothers, four of them. Lawson, age forty-two. Jackson, who's forty. Colton, thirty-seven. And Remington, twenty-eight. All handsome in their own right. All unattached—as I've learned—apart from Lawson, who will be soon. They're a close-knit family, that much is clear.

Jackson, though. He's the one I'm drawn to. I'd like to say it's simply a matter of lusting after an attractive man, but I'm fairly certain it's more than that. There's something about him that intrigues me. The loyalty he has toward his family and this ranch. The way he's a little growly and rough around the edges but clearly a good man. How he tries so hard to keep his stoic mask in place, which only makes me all the more eager to see it slip.

I can't help but wonder what it would take to make the man unravel.

As the ranchers start heading off, their plates cleared, I watch Jackson. He takes his own plate and silverware out of the room, seemingly cleaning up after himself, before reappearing with a thermos in hand. Without a word, he steps out onto the back deck. Curious, I follow. It's still dark, not yet five in the morning, but the big red barn is lit up and the cows in the nearby field are walking that way. Do they know it's time to be milked?

Jackson approaches the fence line, his voice ringing loud and clear. "Get. Get on, now. Go."

His tone isn't mean, just...*forceful*, and the cows who'd been lying down get up and trot off toward the barn. I shiver, fairly certain it has nothing to do with the morning chill.

Heading back inside, I get started on cleanup. Colton is the only one still sitting at the table, his head in his hand.

"Not a morning person?" I ask.

He swings his gaze my way slowly. "Nope."

I huff a laugh. "Me neither."

Although I have a feeling that's going to change, whether or not I want it to.

I grab the nearly empty coffee carafe and plunk it down in front of Colton, smirking when he jumps. "Buck up, partner. The day has just begun."

His laughter follows me out of the room.

"Hey, Mom."

"Ashley, honey. Did you make it to Montana? Are you with Virginia? I still think you're making a mistake."

"I'm here," I tell my mom, ignoring the last part of what she said. "I'm not with Ginnie right now. I got a job, actually. I'm on a ranch."

My mom is quiet for a moment, clearly digesting that, and I look out over the land from my spot on the back deck. It's midafternoon, and I just finished cleaning the floors inside the house. I've been enjoying the shade since, as well as the view. The sky is bright but dotted with clouds, and I'm fairly sure I can see Jackson far off on horseback. I squint a little harder.

"A ranch," my mom says after what feels like an eternity. "Ashley..."

"Mom, please," I cut in, not wanting to hear another diatribe about my choices. My mom made her thoughts perfectly clear before I left. "I don't need mothering right now, okay? I could use a friend."

She sighs. "How are you liking it?"

"Honestly? It's amazing here. I'm cooking for the employees and staying at the ranch house. They have cows. And actual cowboys."

"Sounds...quaint," she says.

I snort. "There's dirt on the floor. You'd hate it."

I can practically hear her cringe. "You're safe? These are good people?"

"They are," I assure her. I may not know them well, but I know that much. Plus, Virginia vouched for them, and I trust her with my life.

"Do you know when you're coming home?" my mom asks.

I let out a slow breath, not sure how to tell her I might not *ever* be coming back. To visit, sure. But I don't think Maine is home for me, not anymore. Maybe it never was. I don't know if Darling could be that, but I want to find out.

"Not sure yet," I say. "I'll let you know."

"Please be careful, Ashley. I'm allowed to say that as a friend, too. I just... I love you," she says quietly. "I never want harm to come to you. So please, look out for yourself. And don't forget to listen to your body."

I nearly roll my eyes. I'm a grown-ass man who's been taking care of himself for a long time, but I don't remind my mom of that. "Love you, too, Mom."

"Say hi to Virginia for me," she adds.

"Yep. Talk soon."

When I click off the call, I set my phone down on the table next to me, right beside my glass of lemonade. With nothing pressing to do, I kick back and enjoy this little slice of country life I seem to have found myself smack dab in the middle of.

It's some time later when I hear the approaching sound of hooves. I blink my eyes open, not having realized I'd shut them, and watch as Jackson comes riding up on a jet-black horse.

Hoo, boy.

He's wearing plaid again today, but I swear the man wears it better than anyone I've ever met. His eyes are bright yet brimmed in shadow underneath his hat. His *cowboy* hat, despite him telling me he's a rancher, not a cowboy. His jeans are tight, legs hugging the horse, and he moves with an ease that speaks of longtime experience in the saddle. He was probably riding horses the same time I was learning to swim.

I sit taller in my seat as he pulls on the horse's reins, making a gentle "whoa" sound. The horse, who I can tell is a boy after a quick glance, comes to a stop, but not before spinning in a tight circle twice, as if he has energy to spare.

"Howdy," I say, smiling brightly.

Jackson grunts in response. "Have you been over to the petting farm yet?"

"I have not."

"I can show you now," he offers. "Unless you have something else to do?"

"Nothing better than you," I mutter.

"Hm?"

"I'd love to," I say louder, standing and pocketing my phone.

Jackson nods, jumping down from his horse in a fluid move I follow greedily with my eyes. He holds the reins out in front of the horse, which I take to mean he's going to walk.

"What have you been up to today?" I ask, falling into step next to him but keeping a bit of distance between me and the horse. I have no clue if I might spook him.

"Mm. Bit of everything. Surveyed the fences, checked the local milk deliveries, ordered supplies. Did Colton get the groceries you need?"

"He did," I say. "But hold up. You guys hand-deliver milk?"

"Couple times a week," he says. "We bring it out to stores and a delivery service that runs it to folks' homes."

I stop still, and after a moment, Jackson stops, too.

"What?" he asks a little warily.

"Your town has a fresh milk delivery service?" I repeat. "Like, bottles that get dropped off at people's doorsteps?"

"Yes?"

"Holy shit," I mutter, immediately wincing. "Sorry."

Jackson snorts, the closest he's come to a laugh since my meeting him. "You can swear 'round here. It's not gonna bother anybody."

"Good to know," I mumble, getting my feet under me again. "Milk delivery. Geez."

Seriously, what is this place?

It doesn't take long to reach the petting farm. Jackson ties his horse's reins to a post near a water trough back behind the barn where people aren't allowed, and then we walk up front to the visitor's entrance. I immediately make an *aww* sound I'm not the least bit embarrassed by. Because *good grief.* Baby goats.

I hustle inside as Jackson explains to the attendant who I am. I make a mental note to say hello before I go, but right now... I sink to my butt in the middle of the fenced-in petting farm, and, immediately, I'm swarmed.

I laugh as a goat tries to nibble my ear, another climbing onto my leg and nearly slipping off again. A third pulls at my shoelace, a few others nearby bleating.

"Oh my God," I breathe, doing my best to pet each and every one of them. "You look like little goat bunnies."

"They're Nubians," Jackson says from behind me. He walks around to where I can see him before adding, "The breed is lop-eared, like rabbits."

"They're adorable," I say, petting one of the goat's long, dangling ears. "You're the cutest, aren't you?"

Jackson hums. "You're one of those, huh?"

"One of what?" I ask, scratching a goat on his or her haunches.

"The talking-to-animals-like-they're-babies type."

I look up at Jackson's loosely crossed arms and flat expression. "Why yes, I am," I coo, petting the goat in front of me but staring at Jackson. "Because he's a good boy who deserves it, isn't that right?"

Jackson clears his throat, gaze skipping away, and I smirk to myself. When there's a tug on my hair, I turn my head to the side, only to come face to face with a long nose and hair-covered eyes.

"Snickerdoodle," Jackson says, passing in front of me to reach the pony. "We don't eat the guests."

Snickerdoodle backs up a step, her body and mane, as one might expect from her name, a golden tan. She whinnies, sounding as if she's arguing.

"Nuh-uh," Jackson says. "Doesn't matter if he looks good enough to eat. He's off limits."

Was...was that a joke? Did Jackson Darling just make a joke?

"Now who's talking to the animals?" I tease.

Jackson simply scoffs, leading the pony back a couple more steps. "At least I don't baby 'em."

"Sure, you don't," I say, turning to the goat who's nibbling my sleeve. "He's a meanie, isn't he?"

"Jesus," Jackson grumbles. "Day two, and he's already got lip."

I huff a laugh, fairly certain my boss isn't upset about that fact.

"Yeah, well," I mutter, "these lips have gotten me out of plenty of trouble, so I think I'll keep them."

Jackson looks sharply my way, his nostrils flaring. It reminds me, momentarily, of a bull, and I can't help but wonder if he sees the green flag I'm waving.

Jackson clears his throat before looking away. "My, uh, brothers want to throw you a welcome party," he says, hand running down Snickerdoodle's long neck.

"That so?"

He grunt-hums. "I've got a bonfire out behind my place. Tonight if you're free, since it's Friday. There'll be whiskey," he adds, like he's not sure whether or not that's a good thing.

"And you?" I ask. "Will you be there?"

He makes that short, rough sound again. "Yeah, I'll be there."

"All right," I say with a smile. "Sounds good to me."

"Good," he says, and then, "You wanna feed 'em?"

"The goats or your brothers?" I joke.

He doesn't bother answering me, just walks off toward the attendant as I chuckle to myself.

When Jackson returns, he has a small pile of baby carrots cupped in his palms. He holds them out my way. "Here."

The goats crowd me as I take the carrots from Jackson's work-roughened hands. Their tiny hooves step all over my legs, leaving little dusty prints.

"You're gonna be a mess if you stay down there," he points out.

"I don't mind," I reply, letting one of the goats snag a carrot. "Getting dirty can be fun."

I don't look up to see what Jackson's expression is doing this time, but I swear he tenses just the tiniest bit. I give another carrot away as a voice inside my head questions what it is I think I'm doing, flirting with my new boss. I ignore it.

I came here looking for something new, didn't I? A fresh start. An adventure.

Well, Jackson Darling could certainly be all that.

When the carrots are gone and some of the goats have left my side to beg other, newly arrived guests for treats, Jackson holds out his hand. "Ready?" he asks.

I clasp his palm, sun-warmed and steady, and let him tug me to my feet. "Ready," I say, immediately pulling in a breath when a muscle in my back protests the sudden movement. I roll my shoulder as I drop Jackson's hand. "Thanks for showing me around."

He frowns at me. "All right?"

"Fine," I tell him. "Let me ask you this. The whiskey we'll be having tonight. I don't suppose it's Darling Whiskey?"

"You've had it?" he asks, walking with me back toward the gate. A few chickens scatter as we pass, their feathers ruffling.

"Oh, I've had it," I answer. "It's good. Potent."

"Dangerous," Jackson adds at a mumble.

I try to keep my amusement hidden. "Does that mean we'll be seeing a full moon tonight?"

Jackson scowls. "Not a fucking chance," he grumbles, pushing through the petting farm gate. It slams behind him, and he stalks off, heading in the direction of his horse.

"Oh, we're in trouble all right, aren't we?" I ask the goat that's trying to escape. I give him or her a gentle nudge back before exiting the corral and following after Jackson. "Yes, we are."

Chapter 6

JACKSON

I don't know why I thought this bonfire would be a good idea.

Actually, correction. I *didn't* think it sounded like a good idea. But I went along with it anyway.

Ash has a beaming smile on his face as he reclines in his Adirondack chair, another of my dad's projects from years back. He's laughing at whatever story Colton is telling, but I don't hear a word of it.

I'm too caught up in *him*.

Bad fucking idea, that's what this is. The whiskey sure isn't helping, even though I'm sipping slow. I need to keep my distance and my head. I need...

"Wait, wait," Ash says, his tone capturing my attention. "The Darling Donkey, as in he belongs to the town?"

"That's right," Colton says.

"And he just...wanders?" Ash asks. "Like, he goes wherever he wants?"

"No one's gonna tell him no," Colton says. "But he's got a bell to warn you when he's coming."

Ash lets out a laugh that sounds incredulous. "Jesus. Is he really that bad?"

"Worse," Lawson answers, looking more aware than he did earlier. More like his usual self. I'm glad to see it. "He bit my arm when I was sixteen. Still have a mark."

Lawson tugs up his sleeve to show Ash in the low light of the fire. A crescent-shaped scar mars the outside of his forearm.

"Holy shit," Ash says. "Wait, sixteen? How old is this donkey?"

My brothers all pause, seemingly doing the math.

"Thirty-two," I answer.

Ash's wide eyes swing my way. "Thirty-fucking-two?" he repeats, apparently over his concern about swearing. "How long can donkeys live?"

"Forty or so is a pretty standard upper limit," I tell him.

"So there's a senile donkey terrorizing the town, and you're all okay with that?" Ash asks, sounding amused now.

Colton shrugs. "He earned his due. Saved little Marjory Bell when he was just a foal."

"The donkey saved a girl?" Ash asks.

Remi smiles, the tale a favorite of his, but it's Lawson who speaks up. "The story is legendary around here. The Bells are an old family in town. They own the distillery. When Marjory was three, she wandered off while the family was having a picnic. No one could find her until the Darling Donkey came trotting down the road, braying wildly. Curious, a few folks followed him to where, half a mile away, little Marjory had fallen into a sinkhole."

"Holy shit," Ash breathes.

"So, yes," Lawson says before taking a sip of his whiskey. "He's an asshole, but he's *our* asshole."

For some reason, Colton looks at me and grins. I flash him my middle finger.

"That's wild," Ash says, shaking his head. He's leaning back in his chair, looking utterly at ease with his legs splayed comfortably and his whiskey tin in one hand. The other runs through his hair, causing the strands to fall messily around his eyes before he tucks them back behind his ear.

I swallow down my groan.

"What about you, Jackson?" Ash asks, startling me, even though I'm looking right at him. "Any wild stories? Other than the midnight skinny-dipping, of course."

Colton snorts. "Jackson doesn't *do* wild."

"What does that mean?" I gripe.

"C'mon, bro. You're too dependable. Too *mature*."

"You say that like it's a bad thing," I mutter. If anything, Colton's the one who could use a little more *maturity* in his life.

My brother shrugs. "It's not. But name the last time you went and let loose."

Silence falls around the campfire.

"He needs to get laid," Remi says.

I sputter, staring at my traitorous brother. He just smiles back at me. "Jesus fucking Christ. I don't know why I put up with this shit."

"Come on, Jackson," Remi says evenly. "Otto left—"

"No," I cut in.

"—over two years ago."

"It's time to move on," Colton adds gently, like he's talking to a spooked horse.

"Really?" I ask that particular brother. "You're talking to me about moving on? What about Noah King?"

Colton immediately scowls. "Did you fucking see this?" he asks, shifting around enough to pull something from his back pocket. He unfolds what appears to be a small newspaper clipping. "Look at this. 'King Farrier Service, the best shoeing in three counties.'" He slaps the paper closed before shoving it back in his pocket. "*Three counties*. What a fucking dick."

"You keep that in your pocket?" Remi asks.

"He's just trying to get back at me," Colton goes on. "This is a direct attack on the ad I put out last month."

"Where you claimed to be the best farrier in town," Lawson says.

"Well I am," Colton counters, tone hot. "You telling me I'm not?"

"Oh boy," Lawson says evenly.

As my brothers start to bicker, I toss back the rest of my whiskey. Ash's eyes catch mine from across the fire, and there's something in his expression I'm not expecting. It takes me a second to place it. *Sympathy*. It's the last thing I want.

I set my tin cup on the ground before standing. "'Scuse me," I say to nobody in particular.

The trek to my back door is short, the long grasses and weeds crunching underfoot as I walk. I tug the door firmly closed behind me before pacing into the bathroom and bracing myself against the sink.

Otto.

"Goddamn it," I mutter, pushing off from the basin. I piss, zip up and wash my hands, and then step back into the hall. I come up short when I see Ash leaning against the back door.

He followed me. *Again*.

"Nice place," he says casually, looking around. From the back hall, he can see a good portion of the house. The hallway is short, just my bedroom on one side, the bathroom on the other. Further in, the space opens up, high ceilings covering the living area off to the left and the kitchen to the right. Wooden posts and beams are exposed throughout, and cream-colored walls keep the place light.

"Thanks," I mutter, crossing my arms. Unless I want to go through Ash, it appears I'll have to wait.

"The...full moon incident," he says. "Was that because of your ex?"

Fucking hell. How did he guess that?

I don't say anything, but Ash nods, as if he gets it. How could he?

"What are you doing in here?" I ask, my tone harsher than I intend.

He shrugs lightly. "They started talking about him again, and...it didn't feel right hearing it without you knowing."

"Why?" I ask, at a loss.

He shrugs again. "Exes are personal."

This conversation feels dangerous, as if we're teetering on the edge of a precipice I'm not yet ready to face.

Ash must be able to read it from my expression because he shoots me a soft smile. "Bathroom?"

I push the door next to me wide, and he nods, stepping forward. Before I can move, he's slipping past me into the bathroom, his arm brushing my chest. I hold my breath, not moving a muscle. But I swear—I *swear*—he slows down, making the contact linger. His eyes meet mine, stormy, stormy gray, and then he's past.

I walk down the hall, not bothering to wait for Ash before heading outside. The fire flickers a couple dozen feet away, my brothers' laughter ringing through the night air.

I move forward, my feet following the less perilous path.

When I wake, it's midmorning, the sun shining brightly and accosting my eyes. *Damned whiskey.*

I take my time getting out of bed. Technically, it's my day off. But that doesn't mean much. I work seven days a week, regardless of whether or not I should, according to my family.

The morning crew will already be hard at work this time of day, but my own business isn't pressing. So I take a shower, brew a pot of coffee, and sip it from a mug while catching up with a few online reports. By the time I make my way over to the ranch house, it's nearly noon.

I hear singing when I step inside the door, and it's so unexpected, I stop still to listen. It's a Neil Young song, if I'm not mistaken. "Heart of Gold."

Ash's voice is smooth as he sings about getting old and searching for love or maybe just companionship. Whatever it is, he feels it, the words soft and sweet and full of an aching melancholy that makes my own chest constrict. Not wanting to interrupt, I stand inside the doorway for long minutes, just listening. Until a soft throat clear comes from nearby.

My mom gives me a knowing smile from the doorway to the mudroom. She must have come in that way while I wasn't looking. "Sure is pretty, don'tcha think?"

I grunt, ignoring her soft laughter as I head down the hall. Ash has switched to humming by the time I reach the kitchen, and despite girding myself for it, the sight of him still sends a jolt through me.

"Hey," he says, noticing me immediately. He's standing in front of the counter, an apron draped over his neck and tied around his waist as he kneads dough. His hands and forearms are dusted in flour, the smooth planes of his face lit by the midday sun that's shining in through the south-facing window.

"What're you doing?" I ask gruffly.

He wings up a blonde eyebrow, sparing me the briefest of glances before refocusing on the dough. "What does it look like I'm doing?"

"It's your day off."

"Yeah, well, I really wanted to get a loaf of gluten-free bread made up for Ira's sandwiches this week. Figured I'd do it now. Sounded like fun."

I make a sound, and Ash gives me another look.

"What is it?" he asks, tone patient.

"You should be relaxing," I get out, knowing my mom would call me a hypocrite for saying so. But he *just* got here. I don't want him run ragged from the start.

I don't want him running off...

"Jackson," Ash says mildly, interrupting my unwelcome thoughts, "this is the most relaxing job I've ever had. I get to cook for a bunch of people that enjoy my food, clean up a little, and then sit around in one of the most gorgeous places I've ever been. Believe me, I'm plenty relaxed."

He does look it. Even though he's working the dough rhythmically, his body is loose, not tense. He's smiling, for Christ's sake. He looks *happy*.

"Fine. Just... Don't work too hard."

He snorts at that. "What's that saying about the pot?"

I roll my eyes, turning around.

"Meet kettle!" he calls.

"Jesus Christ," I mutter, heading back down the hall. When Ash starts humming again, I stop and close my eyes. I open them to find Remi standing right in front of me and jerk back. "Not a fucking word," I warn quietly.

He locks his lips and tosses the imaginary key before walking off.

My ringing phone is a distraction I welcome. "Yeah?"

"Hey, boss. Slight problem," Archie says. He's my manager over on the dairy side of things. "We got a call from Plum's. They had a refrigerator malfunction overnight and lost a decent chunk of product."

"They need more milk," I deduce.

"That's right."

"I can run it," I tell him. "Have it ready for pickup in ten minutes?"

"You got it. Thanks, boss."

As I slip my phone back in my pocket, Ash's voice comes from behind me. "Problem?"

I turn, finding him hanging halfway out of the kitchen doorway. "Nothing major. Just a supply run."

He nods a few times, lips pursed.

"What?" I ask slowly.

"Can I come?"

"You wanna deliver milk?" I ask, not sure I heard that right.

He nods, looking damn eager. *Christ.*

"Fine," I grumble.

His grin widens. "Just let me cover the dough real quick and wash up."

Ash disappears back into the kitchen, and I walk out onto the front porch, wondering what in the hell I'm doing. *You know*, a little voice in my mind whispers. I punt it far, far away.

Ash joins me before long, all cleaned up, his apron gone. "Ready," he says.

"Let's go," I reply against every one of my better judgments.

Archie has the supply of milk ready by the time we arrive. I load it into our refrigerated truck, and Ash jumps in the passenger seat like he's going to a lobster boil, or whatever it is they do over in Maine.

I turn the ignition. "You buckled?"

Ash doesn't say a word, so I look over at him. He's biting his lip. It pops free when he says, "Yes, Jack. I'm buckled."

I grunt. For reasons unknown, Ash laughs as I pull out onto the drive.

When we get to Plum's Grocers, my tagalong is all business. Without being asked, he helps bring the crates of milk in through the back door. When I remind him he's supposed to be taking it easy, he snorts while pointedly eyeing me up and down, and then he grabs another crate. My argument dies on my tongue.

Ash talks to Jenna, one of the employees, as Russ signs for the delivery of the milk. Jenna laughs brightly, touching Ash's arm. He doesn't seem to mind.

None of your damn business.

"Think the temps will be dropping anytime soon?" Russ asks. He's an older gentleman who's been managing Plum's since I was a child. His father held the position before him.

"They always do," I mumble, distracted as I take the tablet back.

He nods, setting his hands on his stomach. "Suppose so. Been a strange start to fall, though."

I glance Ash's way again. He's smiling wide. "Sure has been."

I say my goodbyes to Russ and give Ash a little wave to follow. He extricates himself from Jenna's company and heads my way. "Hey, mind if I grab a couple things before we go?"

I grunt. "Fine."

Ash gives my arm a slap before walking past the refrigerated units into the main part of the store. I follow after him, feeling like a damn dog.

Ash grabs a handheld basket and picks up shampoo, conditioner, and body wash. Then he heads toward the snack aisles. When his basket gets full, he shoves a box of crackers at my chest.

"The hell?" I grumble, snatching it before it can fall to the floor. "What am I? Your pack mule?"

He stacks a bag of chips on the crackers in my hands. "Do you like complaining for the sake of it?" he asks, tone light.

I falter, wondering when this man decided it was okay to *tease* me. "I don't—"

"Arguing for the sake of it, too," he says, taking a step that puts him at my side. He leans close, fingers brushing against my waist. "It's okay, Jack. Your secret is safe with me."

Ash is halfway down the aisle before my brain kicks into gear and I whirl around. "The heck you talking about?"

He looks over his shoulder and winks. "Wouldn't be a secret anymore if I told, would it?"

Jesus fucking Christ.

I shake my head, boots thudding as I follow after him. "Whatever you say, sunshine."

Silence follows, and *ah, shit.* Ash is staring at me like I just handed him a golden ticket.

"Come on, darlin'," he shoots back, a husky sort of chuckle in his voice. "Let's get home."

Ash walks off, an effortless swagger to his steps. I manage to pull my eyes off his ass long enough to register what he said.

Darlin'.

Home.

Fucking hell. I don't think I was prepared for Ashley Alcott.

Chapter 7

ASH

I wince as I get out of bed, my body sore and muscles tight. It's not a surprise. I've been neglecting my routine while getting settled at Darling Ranch, not the wisest decision on my part. At least today is Sunday, so I'll have some time to recoup.

I stop by the empty upstairs bathroom before heading downstairs to the kitchen. The breakfast crowd is long gone by now, the house relatively quiet. I can hear some activity upstairs, but I'm not sure which Darling brother it is.

I'm just sticking my rice-filled heating pad in the microwave when there's a shuffle of feet behind me. The teen in the doorway stops still, head cocking as she looks at me.

"Um, hi," I offer.

"You're new," she says, crossing her arms.

"I am. Ash Alcott, the new cook."

She tentatively accepts the hand I hold out her way, shaking once before letting go and refolding her arms. "Wendy Darling."

"Wendy Darling?" I repeat. "As in Peter Pan?"

The teen immediately scowls, reminding me so much of Jackson that I have to bite back a laugh. "Go ahead," she says. "I've heard it all."

"No, it's a great name," I assure her.

She rolls her eyes. "Have you seen my dad?"

For a heartachingly long second, I wonder if I *am* looking at Jackson's daughter. Not that it would matter one way or another. Would it? But then Lawson stops outside the kitchen, and his expression is so fond and full of pride, there's no doubt in my mind who Wendy's parent is.

"I thought I heard you," he says, smiling as he steps forward to tug the teen in for a hug. Wendy's own face softens as she hugs her dad back. "Did you meet Ash?"

"Just did," Wendy says.

Lawson kisses the side of her head before letting go.

"*Dad*," Wendy grumbles, raking a hand through her hair, although I swear she looks pleased.

"Ready to head out?" Lawson asks her.

She nods decisively. "Yep. See ya, Ash."

"Nice to meet you," I reply.

Wendy leaves the kitchen, but Lawson lingers, maybe having sensed my curiosity. "We're going trail riding," he explains.

"How old is she?" I ask.

"Sixteen."

"I didn't know you were a dad."

He nods idly, picking at the wooden door frame as he says, "Yeah. It's been...hard with the divorce. Wendy has been staying with her mom."

"Well, go," I say, not wanting to keep him. "Enjoy your day with your daughter."

He gives me a grateful smile before disappearing from sight.

These damn Darling brothers. Could they be any sweeter?

Getting back on track, I set the microwave for two minutes. I'm just pulling the heating pad out when I hear a grunt.

My pulse jumps, and I reflexively place a hand on my chest as I look over my shoulder. "What is it with people popping up in this doorway?"

Jackson frowns at me. "Something wrong?"

"Yes. You scaring the crap out of me."

"No," he says, waving a hand at the heating pad. "That."

"Oh." I huff a laugh as I shut the microwave door. "No, I'm fine."

His frown deepens. "Clearly, something is the matter if you're using a heat pad. What is it?"

I raise an eyebrow. "I'm fine, honestly. Just sore."

"From working too hard?" he asks.

It takes everything in me not to roll my eyes. "Not exactly. I just have...issues. With my back. It's not new."

"You should get that checked," Jackson says, following me out of the kitchen.

"I have," I say, working to keep my voice even. "Many times."

"And?"

"*And*. It hasn't helped."

He tsks. "Well, there must be something the doctors—"

"Jackson," I say, stopping and whirling around on the stairs. He halts abruptly, looking up at me in surprise. "I'm going to stop you right there before you start mansplaining my own healthcare to me. I've seen many doctors. Over a dozen, okay? I've been poked and prodded and run through MRIs. I've done multiple rounds of physical therapy, osteopathic manipulation, and tried all sorts of alternative therapies. It's better than it used to be. It is. But the pain doesn't go away, and it might not ever. I've gotten used to it."

He doesn't say a word, staring at me with a look of intense concentration on his face.

"Okay?" I check.

He nods.

I turn and finish walking up the stairs. He follows.

Jackson stands in the doorway to my bedroom—the *guest* bedroom—as I plop the heating pad on the bed.

"Are you just going to stare?" I ask.

"How long?"

"How long what?" I say around a sigh. Maybe I shouldn't be so short with my employer, but he's the one barging uninvited into my room, so he can deal. I climb onto the mattress and lie down with my shoulders on the heating pad, letting out a groan. It's almost too hot, but I relish the temporary burn.

Jackson clears his throat. "How long have you had back pain?"

I think that through. "Five years, give or take?"

He's quiet, so I turn my head to look at him.

"What is it?" I ask.

"Is it from something? An injury? Or the symptom of a bigger problem?"

My lips twitch despite myself, and I let my arms drop wide. "Damn it, Jack. You just can't help yourself, can you?"

"Can't help what?" he asks briskly.

"Your mother hen thing," I answer, smiling when Jackson scowls.

"I don't do that."

"Mhm. Whatever you say, darlin'."

Jackson's reaction is instantaneous. I don't know if it was me throwing his words back at him or the *darlin'*. But his chest rises and his eyes sharpen, and *oh*, do I want to push. I want so badly to make his control snap.

"You didn't answer the question," he says gruffly.

Sighing, I turn my head back toward the ceiling so I don't get a crick in my neck. "I don't know what it's from," I tell him truthfully. "And neither do the doctors. It started slow and got worse. For a while, it was pretty bad. I had a lot of accompanying neuropathy. Tingling in my hands, pins and needles in my feet when I walked, numbness, that sort of thing. But they ruled out just about every diagnosis under the sun. Physical therapy helped. Stretches and heat help. It's gotten better, and now, I'm managing."

"But it doesn't go away," he says, his tone rough enough to have me looking his way again. "In five years, it's never gone away."

"No," I confirm.

He looks incredibly upset by that.

"It's not so bad most of the time," I say, wanting that damn look off his face. "On an average day, the pain is minimal enough that I can ignore it. I haven't been doing my regular upkeep since I got here, so it's my own fault I'm having a flare-up. I'll be fine in a day or two."

He chews on nothing for a moment, reminding me of the cattle he tends to. I manage to keep the thought to myself.

Finally, he says, "Do you need anything? Water or...a snack?"

Oh Jesus.

"Jackson," I say seriously, "if you want me to back off, you're going to need to stop being so thoughtful."

He looks almost alarmed, but I'm pretty sure he knows exactly what I'm talking about. I'm not surprised when he whirls away, his boots thudding down to the first floor. I *am* surprised when, less than a minute later, those boots stomp right back up the stairs.

My heart gives a great big *thump* as Jackson storms through the door. He sets a glass of water and a bottle of acetaminophen down on the nightstand and takes a step back. "Doesn't mean anything," he says.

A smile curls my lips. "Sure."

"Doesn't."

"Okay," I repeat, smiling wider. "Whatever you say."

He grunts impatiently before turning, but he stops at the doorway. "Text me if you need something."

And then he's gone, and I'm left staring at a wide-open door, a stupidly big grin on my face.

You've done it now, Jackson Darling.

Get ready.

Sunday marks the beginning of Virginia's weekend, the first of two days she has off from the bar. She picks me up late morning, a big pair of sunglasses perched on her dainty nose. Even with the shades on, I can tell she's tired.

"Ginnie," I say, stepping out onto the porch before closing the door behind me. "You look rested this morning."

And *uh-oh*. She bristles.

"Really?" Virginia says, spinning and stomping down the porch steps. "This is the first time I've seen you since you arrived, and that's what you have to say to me?"

"Ginnie—"

"Nuh-uh, Ashley fucking Alcott. You damn well know Saturdays are my longest shift of the week. Plus, I woke up late and had to scramble to get your sorry ass, so I haven't even had my coffee yet. I am not in the *mood*."

By the time I catch up to Virginia, she's standing in front of her car, hands on her hips and a frown marring her face. It's cute, but I don't dare say so. I pull my friend into a hug, ignoring her responding squawk.

"I love you so very much," I tell her seriously. "You are gorgeous and smart, and I adore you from the top of your head to the bottoms of your feet. And the fact that I'm close enough to do this?" I squeeze her a little harder for emphasis. "Makes me ridiculously happy. I'm sorry, okay? I didn't mean anything by it."

"Goddamn it, Ash," she mutters, hugging me back. "I'm glad you're here, too."

"I know," I say gently. "So where can we go in Darling that has coffee? My treat for behaving like an ass."

"The bakery," she says with a huff, stepping back. She gives me a shove before rounding her car, not quite ready to let me off the hook. I head for the passenger seat with a chuckle.

Darling's bakery is right in the center of town, not that far from The Barrel. Its awning is pink, and the smells of chocolate and bitter coffee hit me the moment we walk through the door. I'm impressed by my friend. She waits until we're seated, a latte in front of her and a croissant in front of me, before she pounces.

"Spill."

My lips quirk. "Ginnie... I'm pretty sure I'm in love."

Virginia lowers her sunglasses slowly, pulling them off her face and revealing skeptical hazel eyes. "Ash, I know you tend to move fast, but it's been four damn days. I think you're confusing good dick with actual emotion."

I huff a laugh, slapping my friend's shoulder. "I meant the *town*. Or the job. Take your pick. Not...*that*."

"So you haven't..."

"No, I haven't," I say.

She hums and sips her drink. "Is it because of Nick? Has he called?"

It doesn't escape my notice that she called my ex *Nick*, when she knows he hates it. Virginia is nothing if not loyal...and a little vindictive.

"He called once," I admit. "I didn't answer. And don't give me that look—he's not so bad."

"He wasn't good for you," she counters.

"I'm not denying that. But he's not a bad guy, Ginnie. Just..."

"Anal-retentive. Stuck up. Lacking a funny bone," she lists, ticking the points off on her fingers. I have no doubt she could keep going if she wanted. "I never understood what you saw in him, Ash."

I fiddle with the flaky edge of my croissant before shrugging. "He was really supportive with, you know..."

Her face softens, and she curses quietly. "I know, and I'm sorry. I forget sometimes how bad it was."

Nicholas was one of my physical therapists. I'd been seeing him on a professional level for three months when he asked me out. I switched therapists after that, but Nick... At the time, I appreciated how much he looked after me. Now, having hindsight and the experience of years with the man, I can admit to myself I think he saw me as broken. As someone he could fix and take care of. He liked that more than he ever loved me.

"It's beside the point," I say, waving a hand. "We're done. It's in the past. Moving on."

"Good," she says. "So when are you gonna move on to Jackson Darling?"

I groan, even as a smile pulls at my lips. "I regret telling you about him."

She makes a *psht* sound. "Please. Like you'd be able to keep your feelings a secret from me. You're an open book, baby boy."

I can't refute that.

"He's my boss. It's a bad idea," I say, even though I don't believe it. Despite me working for Jackson's family, I'm not the least bit concerned about the dynamic between us causing issues. He's not even the one who hired me. Marigold is.

Virginia sees through my flimsy attempt to skirt her scrutiny. "Mhm. Try again."

"He's hot," I admit.

She grins, her dimples appearing. "Uh-huh."

"And a total sweetheart," I add. "Even though I'm fairly sure he'd deny it to his last breath."

She waves for me to go on.

"And, fuck, Ginnie, he came galloping up on a horse the other day, and I damn near popped a boner. I didn't realize I have a thing for cowboys. Especially *grumpy* cowboys."

My friend doesn't even try to hide her amusement. "So you're going after him?"

"I am," I tell her. Why even try to deny it?

Virginia squeals under her breath.

"You really want me past Nicholas, huh?" I say with a chuckle, popping the last of my croissant in my mouth.

Virginia puffs out a breath. "That's not it. Or, well, not *all* of it. Maybe I just want you to have a reason to stay, all right?"

I reach across the table and give her hand a squeeze. "I'm not going anywhere anytime soon," I assure my friend. It feels too soon to say *or ever*, but I can admit to myself the idea of returning to Maine doesn't feel right.

Darling? It feels right.

Virginia and I hang out for a couple hours, playing catch-up long after her coffee is gone. Some of the more touristy businesses in town are closed today, but she points out the food options, including a sandwich shop and a restaurant that serves an eclectic mix of cuisine. After that, we amble through the antiques market. I end up finding a small figurine of a cowboy on a jet-black horse. Virginia snorts when I buy it, but she looks secretly pleased.

Virginia drops me back off at the Darling Ranch when our afternoon is up. "You know," she says almost fondly, looking through the window of her car, "I used to come here when I was a kid. Went trail riding a time or two. Visited the petting farm a lot."

Virginia grew up here in Darling. She traveled to the east coast for college, which is how we met. But she moved back several years ago. It bummed me out at the time, but seeing her at home like this...it fits. I can understand now why she wanted to come back.

"You should stop by sometime when the petting farm is open," I tell her. "We can cuddle the baby goats together."

She huffs a laugh. "It's a date. Now get outta my car. And don't forget to tell me every goddamn detail of what happens with you and Jackson."

"Every detail, Ginnie? Really?"

"Every. Single. One. Until I get my own cowboy, I'll be living vicariously through you."

I give her cheek a kiss, making no promises one way or another, and get out of the vehicle.

As Virginia pulls away in a small cloud of dust, I jog up the porch stairs of the ranch house. I've just toed off my shoes and am rounding the corner into the hall when the man of the hour appears.

Jackson stops at the other end of the hallway, looking flustered. If I didn't know better—although *how* I know better is a mystery—I'd think he was angry.

"Where've you been?" he asks, tone tight.

"Enjoying my day off," I answer, the little cowboy figurine tucked in my hand. I step closer, stopping at the bottom of the stairs, just a foot in front of him.

He eyes me up and down, as if checking for injuries. "So you're fine?" he practically grits out.

I smile. "More than."

He grunts, skirting past me.

"Jackson?" I call before he can get far.

He stops and turns, eyeing me warily.

I open my hand and hold up the little cowboy for him to see. "Look what I found in town. Kinda reminds me of someone." I close my fist before adding, "I think I'll keep him near my bed."

The emotions that pass over Jackson's face move almost too quickly to follow. But I don't miss the naked *want*. It's there, plain as day, before he hides it away behind a mask of indifference.

It's all the confirmation I need.

Jackson doesn't voice a response. He simply nods, once, and walks off.

I clutch the cowboy tighter in my hand.

I think I have my work cut out for me when it comes to Jackson Darling.

Chapter 8

JACKSON

Fall hits swiftly.

One day, it's sixty degrees out and sunny. And the next, the temperature is dropping into the low forties and it's spitting rain, dampening the fields and making everybody, cattle included, miserable.

Everybody but one person, it seems.

"God, that's gorgeous," Ash says, standing in front of the big windows at the back of the house. The dining room has already cleared out, the lunch crowd having gone back to work. There's a mop in Ash's hand, but the mud on the floors seems to have been temporarily forgotten. "Don't you think that's gorgeous?"

It takes me a moment to move my focus off of *him*. Outside, the rain has cast a haze over everything, field and skyline both. "It's...gray."

I grunt when Ash whacks me on the chest.

"Gray can be gorgeous, too," he says, shaking his head.

The brief flash of his smiling eyes is proof I can't argue with.

When I turn around, trying to focus on the reason I came back here in the first place, Ash says, "Your hat is in the hall. It was hanging on your seat, but I set it aside when I flipped the chairs up to clean. You guys are a mess, you know that? Not that I'm complaining. Just stating a fact."

Surprised he knew what I was looking for without my asking, I nod and head out into the hall. The hat is right where Ash said it'd be, on the old worn hutch. I plop the slightly damp material on my head and walk back through the dining room.

Before I can reach the door, Ash says, "You're quiet today."

I stop and look at him. "I'm always quiet."

His lips twist. "No, you're not. Short isn't the same as quiet."

He ignores my grunt.

"Is it the rain?" he asks, spinning the mop handle in his hands. His hair is curling more today, maybe because of the humidity. There's a piece hitting his cheek, and for a second, I wait for him to tuck it back behind his ear. He doesn't.

"Nobody's in a good mood when it rains," I point out.

His grin challenges that. "Sure," he says easily. And then, "You look good wet, though."

I pull in a breath.

Ash laughs as I storm out the door. He follows me, standing just inside the doorway as he calls, "Think we'll get a rainbow later?"

I flick my hand over my shoulder.

"Have a good rest of your day, darlin'," he yells.

The door thuds shut, and I shake my head, ignoring the stutter in my chest. Days. It's been *days* of this. The flirting. The...*darlin'*.

I should tell him to stop.

I damn well should.

"He's gone too far this time!" comes a shout.

I whirl around in alarm, finding Colton striding my way. "What?" I ask. Surely my brother isn't talking about...

"Noah fucking King," he says, brandishing his phone and coming to a stop in front of me. "He stole another client right out from under me. I just got off the phone with the McGregors. Their horse, Belinda, *loved* me, and Noah undercut my prices and *took* 'em."

I let out a sigh. "You know that's how business—"

"Oh, I think not," Colton says, his blue eyes spitting fire. "It's personal with him. It's *always* personal."

"You two need to let bygones be bygones already," I mutter, heading toward the horse barn.

He lets out a *pft*, keeping in step next to me as the rain comes down, more like a mist than falling drops. "There's no rationalizing with that man, Jackson. He's had it out for me since the beginning."

"You don't help."

He lets out an affronted sound.

"You don't," I reply, despite his obvious ire. "You two are like dogs, yapping at each other through the fence. One day, that fence is going to crack, and one or both of you are gonna get bit."

He looks at me in what might be confusion or possibly shock before shaking his head. "We're not *dogs*. And I'm not the problem."

"Sure," I say.

"I'm *not*."

I don't argue it further, and Colton is quiet beside me as we reach the barn. I expect him to stew about his rival for a few more minutes before heading on his way, but he sticks close, trailing me to the tack room.

"By the way," he hems in a tone I don't much care for, "did I just hear Ashley call you darlin'?"

Oh Lord.

"No," I lie.

"It's cute," he says, grinning like a fool. "He's keen on you."

"You sound twelve," I grumble.

"What twelve-year-olds do you know that say 'keen?'" he asks. "It's okay to like him, you know."

I open my mouth to respond—with what, I don't know—but I don't have time before my brother thumps me on the shoulder.

"Later," he says, walking off just as succinctly as he arrived. I assume I'm alone—*blessedly*—but a soft sound to my left alerts me otherwise.

"Jesus, Remi," I say, switching to ASL when I see he's not wearing his processor. *'Stop sneaking around.'*

He snorts, hands moving fast. *'Not my fault you were in your head and didn't notice me.'*

"Yeah, yeah," I mutter, shaking my hand to wave him off. Turning, I start collecting some tack that needs repairs. There's a leatherworker in town who does the work for us.

Remi makes a soft sound, drawing my attention. *'Can I ask you something?'* he signs, a contemplative expression on his face. *'Serious question.'*

Fuck. As if I can deny my brother.

I nod.

'What do you see for yourself, Jackson? You and Otto were talking about marriage before he left.'

Remi's reminder is like a punch to my gut, but he goes on, his hands and arms relaxed but moving swiftly.

'Do you want to build a life with someone? Or did he take that away from you?'

I scrub my hands over my eyes, stalling more than anything. A year ago or certainly two, I would have said *no*, that I didn't want that anymore. That he'd crushed that dream under his boot as he walked out of my life.

But now? Time really does heal. It heals broken hearts, fractured memories. It heals those places in us that feel endlessly gaping and painfully raw. Maybe it's because we forget. We can't hold on to those fragments like we once could. But in the end, I'll take getting older and forgetting over hanging on to the sharp edges of my past.

'I want that,' I finally sign.

My brother nods once. "You'll get it, Jackson," he says, sounding so sure.

A part of me wants to believe him. A part of me is scared to hope.

'And you?' I sign. *'What do you want?'*

It's easy to look at Remi and see only my baby brother, but he's nearly thirty. He's not a kid anymore, and conversations like this remind me of his age and the fact that he likely has his own dreams that could very well extend beyond these boundary lines.

Remi shrugs, a loose, casual motion. *'I'm happy with where I am,'* he signs. *'If I meet someone... They'd need to fit into that. Not change it.'*

I clasp my brother's shoulder, squeezing once. *'I love you,'* I tell him, the words shaped with my hand as well as my lips.

Remi rolls his eyes, but he returns the sentiment with crossed fingers, emphasizing the meaning. I swear he mutters something that sounds an awful lot like "big softie," but I probably just heard him wrong.

My brother goes back to tending to the horses and mucking empty stalls as I collect the tack to bring into town. Despite my best efforts, I can't get his—or Colton's—words out of my head. All day, they stay with me like the scent of livestock, sticking to my clothes and my skin and burrowing under my very fingernails. I pick at them for hours, trying to loosen their hold, but they don't budge.

I *do* want someone to call my own. But I'm under no delusions of that being an easy task. I live on my family's ranch at forty, my job is demanding and can be, at times, a twenty-four/seven commitment, and I'm not exactly a honey-coated treat. I'm set in my ways, abrasive, downright difficult.

It took time for Otto to find my charms, buried and few as they are. And in the end, even he didn't judge me as worthy. He came, and he left, and now I'm still here, picking up the pieces of the life I thought I'd live, trying to mash them into a recognizable shape again.

Like Remi, I could be happy on my own. I know I could. But I do want more. I *dream* of it, even though I long ago told myself to stop.

I want warm skin pressed against mine at night. I want to dig my fingertips into muscle and hear the sounds of someone unraveling because of my touch. I want to see that look in their eyes that lets me know I'm seen, I'm heard, I'm loved.

Goddamn it, I want love.

And it feels like the worst fucking thing.

I miss dinner hour at the ranch, not returning home until long past eight. My dad waves at me from the rocker outside his cottage as I drive past. I slow to a stop and roll down my window.

"You're soaking wet," I call.

"It's raining," he answers. I stare, and he says, "What? Were we not stating facts?"

I shake my head, flicking a quick goodbye as I roll up the window. No point in trying to understand that man. When I get to my house, I kick off my muddy boots and carry them inside to be washed later. Unlike my dad, I do my soaking in the shower, washing off the day's grime and lingering for a few minutes, letting the hot water soothe my tired muscles.

My thoughts, much to my consternation, return to Ash.

I never would've guessed that the sunshiny man who's invaded my life is living with chronic back pain. He sure doesn't show it. Apart from the time I caught him with the heat pad and maybe a wince here or there, he's always smiling, always happy. Is it fake? It doesn't feel it.

I've had my fair share of aches and pains, of course, and part of that, I'm certain, simply comes with aging. But it's not every day. It's not *every single day.*

Goddamn it. I don't know why I even care.

I shut off the shower and step out of the tub in a swirl of steam. As I'm drying off, I hear what might be a knock. Detouring to my bedroom, I pull on underwear and jeans, and then I head for the door.

I'm not expecting Ash to be the one standing on my porch, but there he is, hair dampened from the rain and eyes widening as he takes me in, his gaze running over my bare torso for far longer than is polite.

"Need something?" I grunt, not liking the way that gaze feels. Not liking the heat in it. How it has my blood sizzling in response.

Ash huffs a small laugh before meeting my eyes. "Hi," he says breezily. "So you missed dinner, and everyone assured me it wasn't because you were eating elsewhere, so here." He shoves a tinfoil-covered plate at me. "*And...*" He pulls a bottle of Darling Whiskey out from behind his back. "I brought this as a bribe so you'd let me join you. So... Can I join you?"

I look at the whiskey in Ash's hand. At his earnest expression and the painfully beautiful face I've tried so hard to ignore. At the blonde hair breaking like waves over his temple and around his ears. At his broad shoulders and straight nose and those stormy eyes that are begging me without words.

No, I want to say. *Yes*, my brain whispers.

Ash looks victorious as I take a step back. He sweeps inside, carefully removing his shoes and walking into my house as if he's already comfortable in my space. His hand drifts along the edge of my couch as he passes through the living room, a slow, tortuous process.

"You'll probably want to reheat the food," he says, not even looking back at me. He's in my kitchen now, opening cupboards. He makes an *aha* sound as he finds the glasses, grabbing two in one hand before he heads to my table. "Coming?"

Everything about this man is dangerous. Yet I find my feet carrying me forward anyway.

Deciding my safest bet is to focus on the food, I remove the foil and place the plate in the microwave. When I turn around, Ash is pouring a couple fingers of whiskey into each of the glasses. He takes a seat, utterly relaxed, his foot propped up on the edge of his chair and his arm hanging loosely over his knee. His eyes rake down my torso again as he takes a small sip of the amber-brown liquid, and I'm reminded of the fact that I'm not wearing a shirt.

The microwave beeps, and I turn away, heart thudding.

Ash is quiet as I take a seat near him. His closeness unsettles me. The *man* unsettles me.

"It's good," I tell him after a minute.

"Glad you like it."

"Mm."

We go quiet again, and Ash twirls his glass in one hand, the liquid shifting like a gently rolling sea.

"How's, uh...your back?" I ask.

His smile grows slightly. "Better. Thanks for the medicine you brought."

I nod, and Ash's lips twitch, drawing my eye down to the small divot in his chin. Such a masculine feature on such a pretty face. It'd be the perfect spot for my thumb to grab a hold of while I—

Fuck.

I avert my gaze, cheeks hot, my body coming to life in a way I haven't experienced in so very long. I grab my whiskey in an attempt to drown out the images in my mind, but it doesn't work. They only burn brighter, the alcohol lighting a fuse as it forges a path across my tongue.

I feel reckless.

I don't like it. And I crave it.

"Jackson," Ash says, his foot moving from the edge of his chair to the top of my thigh. I freeze, everything in me drawing tight. "Are you open to being propositioned?"

Jesus Christ. The candidness of this man.

I can't answer him. I don't know what I'd say. I'm afraid if I open my mouth, the answer will be *yes*.

I grab Ash's ankle, intent on pushing him away. Somehow, my grip only tightens.

Ash notices. Of course he does. He leans forward, his gaze holding mine, challenging. "I propose," he says slowly, "that we kiss. Because see? I have this theory about you, and I want to know if I'm right."

I can't think. Can't remember why I thought this was a bad idea.

"Jack," he says softly, his toes curling against the top of my leg.

It's my name—that single syllable spoken with so much longing—that does it.

I tug Ash's ankle. His eyes widen for only a fraction of a second, and then he's moving, following my pull. Our mouths clash as Ash grabs hold of my knee to steady himself, his fingers digging in. My hand grips his jaw tight, keeping him in place or—I don't know—maybe trying to bring him closer. For a moment, it's chaos, frantic and precarious, like a newborn foal.

But then Ash pushes forward again, abandoning his chair and climbing onto my lap. His hands thread into my hair, tugging, urging me to settle, and *fuck*. I subside, letting him control me, letting him lead me like *I'm* the damn foal. His lips brush mine, softer now, coaxing me open, his tongue sending a shock through my system as it greets my own.

Dangerous. So fucking dangerous.

He doesn't let me up for air, not for long minutes. I'd forgotten how good it feels to *kiss*. To be connected to someone in this way. To feel lust and want coalescing like possibilities I want to chase.

I wasn't expecting this. Any of it. Ash came into my life like a sudden easterly wind, with a smile brighter than the sunlit sky, and now he's in my lap, his mouth and mine learning each other's language. He's kissing me like he wants to know me, or maybe like he already does.

It's glorious. It's terrifying. I don't want it to ever end.

Ash's sigh against my mouth is what finally has my rationale returning. Because it feels like he's surrendering, too. And damn it all, I'm not prepared to have that kind of control over this man. Not yet.

He must feel me tense because, slowly, he pulls back. I regret it when his lips feather away from my own.

"Mm," he hums, his hair tickling my face as he kisses my cheekbone once. His voice settles close to my ear. "Exactly like I thought. So. Very. Sweet."

I pull in a shaky breath as Ash lets go of my hair and climbs off my lap. He picks up his drink, finishing the whiskey in a neat gulp, and then he sets down the glass with a soft thunk.

"I'm going to have you, Jackson Darling," he declares with all the confidence of a man who already knows he's won. "When you're ready, I'll be waiting."

With that, he walks out my door, leaving the memory of him branded like whiskey on my tongue.

Chapter 9

ASH

There's a smug smile on my face the entire weekend after my visit to Jackson's. Every time I catch the man around the property, he blushes. *Blushes*. Like the memory of my lips on his own is enough to have him running hot.

Needless to say, I'm on cloud nine. Which is why I'm humming to myself when Marigold comes into the kitchen late Monday morning.

"You're in a good mood," she says, seemingly happy herself. She's wearing a light flannel today, the blue the same color as the sky.

"Hard not to be on a sunny day," I reply, skirting the real reason as to why I'm feeling so darn giddy.

I like Marigold, but there are certain truths she doesn't need to hear from me. Like the fact that I'm lusting after her son.

"By the way," I add, "we're running low on flour and a few other things."

"If you write up a list, I'll have somebody make a run," she says, picking up the empty coffee pot and bringing it to the sink to wash. "Unless you'd rather do it yourself?"

"You don't have to clean that," I tell her. "I was getting there."

She *pfts*. "It's still my house. I'll clean if I want. The groceries?"

I don't bother arguing with her, having a feeling it'd be futile. "Yeah, I'll do it, if that's okay?"

"Sure is," she says happily. "I'll get keys and a credit card to you after lunch. Now what in the heavens..."

I follow Marigold's gaze out the window. Hank is walking past with a large white mesh hat tucked under his arm. It looks like...

Marigold throws the latch on the window and hoists up the pane. "Hank! Tell me you did not buy *bees*."

A beekeeper's hat, that's what it is.

I cover my mouth as the elder Mr. Darling stops, looking toward the house. "Well now," he says loudly, "I would, but I know you don't like it when I lie."

I sputter a laugh as Marigold says, "Bees, Hank? Really?" She slams the window down and hastily dries her hands. "I swear to God, that man has more ambitions than sense. Excuse me."

Mrs. Darling storms gracefully from the room, and I watch out the window as she catches up to her ex-husband. Hank sets the beekeeper's hat on his head and holds his arms wide, as if to say, *see?* Marigold pinches the bridge of her nose.

I chuckle before getting back to work. It isn't long before I'm setting lunch out along the table in the dining room. Like usual, I leave the dishes stacked near one end, and the ranchers help themselves as they come in. The increase in chatter, the stomping of boots, even the soft scrape of chairs moving in and out has become a soundtrack I'm familiar with.

Colleen, one of the second-shift ranchers who starts work post sunup, gives my arm a soft nudge as she passes. "Morning, Ash. This looks great."

"Thanks," I answer with a smile, taking my own seat. Lunch isn't anything fancy, just tomato soup from scratch, grilled cheese with some gruyere thrown in, and a few sides. But a simplified version of this meal was my favorite as a kid, especially in the fall. Something about warm soup and cold, wet weather has always made me feel cozy.

It's nice to share that with these people.

As I'm loading my plate with a grilled cheese sandwich, my senses prickle. I look up just in time to catch Jackson walking into the room, his hat held down at his side. He's wearing the same worn jeans and plaid shirt I saw him in earlier, but there's a streak of dirt near his temple that wasn't there before. I can't help but wonder what he did to earn it.

Jackson takes a seat across from me, his eyes meeting mine for the briefest of moments before he starts plating up his food. I'm debating an icebreaker that doesn't involve his lips on mine when Colton plops into the seat next to me.

"Hey," he says, reaching across the table to grab two sandwich halves. He drops them on his plate, followed by another, and then practically takes out my eye to reach the soup.

"Jesus, Colton," Jackson grunts. "Watch where you're putting your limbs."

"Sorry," Colton mutters, falling back into his seat and shooting me an apologetic smile.

"It's fine," I tell him, even as Jackson shakes his head. I wonder if he even realizes how often he parents his siblings.

"*God*," Colton groans around his food. "That's good."

Jackson grumbles what I think is supposed to be an, "Mhm."

Colleen clucks her tongue from a little further down the table. "I sure hope you offer him more praise than that from time to time, boss. We'd like to keep this one around, you know."

Jackson's cheeks immediately start to redden, and I simply can't help myself.

"Oh, he's plenty sweet," I say, holding my smirk in check. "Isn't that right?"

Colton snorts. "Sure. *Sweet.* That's our Jackson."

Jackson keeps his gaze on his food, but his chest rises and falls in steady bursts. He's not as unaffected as he pretends to be. What would he look like coming utterly and wholly undone?

I want so badly to find out.

Conversation continues, countless threads carrying on amongst the near twenty lunch-goers. There's no Remi today, but I've noticed it's somewhat of a crapshoot on whether or not he and Colton attend meals. Lawson is generally absent prior to dinner, seeing as he's at the school. And Marigold and Hank come and go as they please.

Jackson is the constant. He's here at nearly every meal-time. I have a sneaking suspicion it's for his employees' benefit. To show up. To be present and a part of their workday.

I admire that.

When lunch wraps up, the ranchers go on their way. There's an auxiliary bathroom attached to the back of the house that most of them use on their way in and out, especially to wash their hands before eating. The family, on the other hand, frequently wander the house itself. Which is why it's no surprise when I cross paths with Jackson on my way into the kitchen. He's filling up his canteen with water.

"Ah, so you do drink something other than coffee," I say, stacking some plates in the sink next to him.

He huffs, which I take to mean *duh*.

"Can I ask you something? It's not personal," I add when Jackson gives me a cautious look. "Just a question I have about the ranch."

He twists the cap onto his water and settles against the counter. "Sure."

"The whole feeding the employees thing," I say, waving a hand back toward the dining room. "Who started that? I've never heard of something like that outside of maybe a camp or resort, where everyone is stuck on site. But here, it's a given—breakfast, lunch, and dinner, for whoever wants it."

Jackson nods, looking lost in thought for a moment. "To be honest, I can't recall if it was my dad or my mom who first suggested it, and they'd probably both try to take the credit. But one way or another, it began when I was around ten. I remember 'cause it was the year the addition was built on the house."

I hum, having wondered about that.

"It's...not just about food," he says slowly. "It's a morale thing. It's comradery. We're not moving herds through the mountains anymore, not like my grandpa used to. But this job, it ain't always easy. Conditions are harsh, and it's not the right fit for everybody. But we've had far less turnover in the past few decades than we used to. Maybe it's not because of shared mealtimes. Maybe it is. I dunno. But it's a tradition we've kept."

"You've kept," I say.

"What?" he grunts.

"It's a tradition *you've* kept. I know you're in charge around here, Jackson. It's obvious."

He makes a throaty sound, like he's disagreeing with me. "My parents are still involved in the business."

I huff a laugh. "Sure. In name, maybe."

He makes that sound again, but I power on.

"I like it, Jack. That's what I'm trying to tell you. You're a family here. A really big one. And *you* are the person keeping everyone together. Thanks for—" I shake my head, a little embarrassed. "Thanks for welcoming me into that family, too. It means a lot."

Jackson doesn't seem to know how to respond to that. Not at first. "Everybody's happy you're here," he finally says.

My smile returns. "You, too."

He rolls his eyes. "Now you're fishing."

"Can't say that's ever been my sport," I admit. "Maybe I should learn to ride before picking up the rod."

Jackson blinks at me. "You've never ridden a horse?"

I shrug. "Nope."

He stares at me blankly for exactly two seconds before spinning and flicking on the faucet. "Come on. Let's get these dishes cleaned. You need a damn lesson."

My grin is out in full force now. "That so?"

"You're working on a ranch, Ash. Of course you needa know how to ride. Jesus."

His disgruntled tone has warmth pooling in my gut. I let my arm brush his as I take the plate he rinsed. "If you say so, darlin'."

"*Christ*. None of that," he grumbles under his breath. "And for the record, I'm not *sweet*. I don't know where you're getting that."

"Sure, Jack," I reply lightly, loading the dish into the washer.

He shakes his head, making a put-upon sound, but he keeps handing me dishes, and in no time at all, we've worked through the mess from lunch. I run upstairs to grab a light jacket before the pair of us head outside.

Jackson leads me across the ranch toward the stables. "So, here's the short of it," he says, all business. "Never stand behind a horse. That's just asking for trouble. Meet them head on, like you would a person. Be gentle. Respectful. The ones we have here know what they're doing, so trust 'em."

"Trust the horse. Got it."

"Loose reins to hold steady," he says, slowing down as we reach the entrance to the barn. "You tug and they'll slow, stop, or eventually back up. Squeeze your legs and dig in your heels and they'll pick up the pace."

I cough a laugh, my mind dropping right into the gutter. Jackson looks at me in concern, until understanding lights his eyes.

"It's not *that* kinda riding," he intones.

"Hey, you said it, not me."

He heaves a sigh, but I swear there's a smile on his face. A tiny one. "This is Shorty," he says, stopping in front of a stall.

I look in. And then up. And then up some more. "Good grief, Jackson. Don't you think that's false advertising?"

He snorts before opening the stall door. Holding out his hand, he clicks his tongue. Shorty, the tallest horse I've ever had the honor of meeting, snuffles his palm. Jackson pats his—or her? No, definitely his—neck before looking back at me.

"Shorty is a gentle giant. He'll treat you right."

I can't help but smirk. "Sounds like a good time to me."

That blush returns to Jackson's cheeks, but he doesn't take the bait. "Come on. Let's get 'im saddled outside, and then you can hop on top." He stills. "Not like *that*."

I hold up my hands placatingly. "Hey. Top, bottom, I'm fine with either. Sides are good, too. You know, for that record we're keeping."

Jackson closes his eyes, taking in a slow breath. "What am I gonna do with you?" he mutters, following quickly by, "*Don't* answer that."

I wave him forward, battling my laughter. "After you and Shorty."

Jackson leads the beast of a horse out of the stall and into the open before looping his lead around a post. Then he leaves me with the horse while he collects gear.

I eye Shorty and hold out a hand the same way Jackson did. He's a pretty horse, all shiny brown with a white stripe running down the center of his nose. Shorty, presumably having deemed me worthy, greets my palm, his breath puffing hotly against my skin. The tickling sensation has me chuckling. "You're not so bad, huh?"

Jackson returns, a saddle and some other items in his hands. If he caught me talking to Shorty, he doesn't mention it. He explains the various pieces of equipment he's holding and how to dress a horse. First, he removes the simple halter Shorty is wearing and puts on a more complicated bridle. Next, he lays a saddle pad down on the horse's back, followed by the leather saddle, which he cinches under Shorty's belly. He adjusts the length of the stirrups for my legs and goes over the proper way to hold the reins in one hand. And then he waves me forward.

"Hold here," he tells me, putting his own hand on the horn of the saddle. He taps the stirrup closest to us. "Then put your foot in here and pull yourself up."

"Just like that?" I ask.

"Just like that."

"All right," I mutter, getting into place. Jackson steps out of the way, watching as I ready myself. I pull in a breath, then another, and then I hoist myself up.

I don't make it.

Jackson rushes in as I stumble backwards, his hand holding tight to my hip as I regain my balance.

"That went well," I say mildly.

He huffs a laugh, which has me grinning. "You're green. It's to be expected. Try again," he says, letting go and stepping back.

I stick my foot in the stirrup and look over my shoulder. "Maybe I need a boost."

"You don't need a boost," he says flatly.

"I think I do," I hedge, well aware my jeans are pulling tight against my ass in this position. "What harm could it do?"

"Plenty, I'm sure," Jackson mumbles.

I flash him my winningest smile. "Please?"

Jackson eyes me for an extended beat, and then, much to my surprise, he steps forward, plants his hand on my ass, and says, "Lift."

I jump, and he pushes. This time, my leg sweeps cleanly over the top of the horse, and Jackson lets go as my butt hits the saddle. My pulse sprints like I just ran a mile. *Well, then.*

Jackson clears his throat. "There. You're up."

"On top," I clarify.

"Jesus," he groans. But he dutifully helps me get my feet positioned in the stirrups. I shift a little, testing the sturdiness of my position.

"Out of curiosity," I say slowly, unable to help myself, "which do you prefer when you're...riding? Top or—"

"I'm not answering that," he cuts in, scooping up the reins and handing them over. "Here. Pull left to turn the horse left. Right to go right."

"Easy enough," I mutter, bracing myself as Jackson gives Shorty's bridle a gentle tug. He eases the horse around and leads us out toward a clear area of grass, where the ground is slightly trampled and there are no obstacles for us to hit.

"Keep a loose hold on the reins," Jackson reminds me, walking Shorty in a large circle. "Knees wide. Once you have a feel for the motion, I'll let go."

"*Knees wide.* Like I have much of a choice," I point out, giving Shorty's neck a gentle pat. "But we like 'em thick, don't we? Yes, we do."

"Christ," Jackson mutters, turning his face away. "There you go again, babying the animals."

I snort, pretty sure that's not what has him so rattled. Leaning down, I whisper to the horse, "Don't listen to him. You're a good boy. Even if I'll be walking funny later, thanks to you."

Jackson coughs, letting go of the reins. "Think you're set."

I nearly squawk, gripping the thin strips of leather tightly. Shorty's head comes up, and then he takes a step back. "Shit, shit," I mutter. "I'm in reverse."

I'm fairly certain Jackson is laughing his head off, but I'm too focused on not coming to an equine-related end to check. I loosen the reins, and Shorty stops, his ears flicking once. *Okay.* Crisis averted. Now to go forward... I squeeze my legs, but nothing happens.

"Like you mean it," Jackson says.

I look over at him, lifting an eyebrow. "Shorty likes it rough?"

His lips twitch, but, otherwise, he doesn't react. Arms crossed, he says, "He's a horse. You're a tiny human."

"Excuse me? Tiny?"

"Squeeze 'im like you mean it."

"So many things I want to say," I mumble. I squeeze my legs, getting my heels involved. After a single stutter step, Shorty starts walking. "Holy shit."

This time, Jackson definitely chuckles. "Try turning."

Gently, I pull the reins to the left. Shorty turns that way, moving in a wide arc.

"Good," Jackson says. "Ready to gallop?"

"What?" I nearly shout.

He booms a laugh, and it's so unexpected and, frankly, mesmerizing, that I stare at him. He never put his hat back on after lunch, so I can see the crystalline blue of his irises in the sun. And his cheeks are pulled into a grin, enhancing the subtle lines at the edges of his eyes.

It's gorgeous. *He's* gorgeous.

"The great Jackson Darling," I say in wonder. "Making a joke. I never thought I'd see the day."

"Yeah, yeah," he says, flicking a hand toward me and the horse. His smile, however, doesn't quite falter. "Why don't you try having him stop. Just stop, not reverse."

"Har har," I answer, pulling gently on the reins. Shorty slows, and once he stops completely, I let go and turn to Jackson. "How'd I do?"

"Pretty good, sunshine. There's hope for you yet."

I grin, my insides hotter than that sun beating down against the back of my neck.

Oh, there's hope, all right. Plenty of it.

Chapter 10

JACKSON

Ash makes a few loops with Shorty, getting more comfortable and confident with each passing minute. Watching the way his legs shift, the way his fingers hold the reins and how his ass sways with the slow movement of the horse is a distraction. One I'm doing a poor job of ignoring.

It doesn't help that he's smiling wide, that infectious enthusiasm bursting from him like goddamn rays of light. I wonder if he's an angel. An angel sent to torment me.

You can have him, a little voice whispers. *He's waiting for you to make a move.*

I nearly groan.

"There you are," my mom says, effectively dousing me in cold water. I turn just as she reaches the edge of the field. "Here. These are for Ashley." She passes over a set of truck keys and a credit card. "Mind showing him where the vehicles are?"

"Sure," I mutter, pocketing the items.

Her gaze shifts over my shoulder, a smile on her face. "He's a natural, isn't he?"

I turn back around, watching as Ash guides Shorty to a stop at the far end of the field. He glances behind the horse before tugging the reins again. Shorty starts to back up, and Ash makes beeping sounds.

I snort a laugh, quickly covering it with a cough as my mom looks over at me.

"Ah," she says slowly.

"Nuh-uh," I counter, not liking that gleam in her eye. "Don't go getting any ideas."

"What ideas could I possibly have, Jackson Darling? Please, do enlighten me."

"You think you're so clever."

She chuckles, unperturbed. Looking at Ash, she says, "Almost like he was meant to be here. Funny, that."

My mom walks off, and I let loose a few choice words before refocusing on Ash. He and Shorty are walking over now.

"Was that your mom?" he asks, coming to a stop in front of me.

I reach up, giving Shorty's neck a pat. "It was. Ready to turn in?"

"Probably a good idea," he says. "I still have a few things to take care of before dinner. Thanks for the lesson, Jackson."

"Don't mention it," I murmur, giving Shorty's bridle a tug and leading the pair back toward the barn. "Next time, we can do a trail ride, if you want. It's a good way to get comfortable in the saddle. Nice and slow."

Ash hums. "Sure," he says, the word more suggestive than it has any right to be. "I can take it slow."

"Can you?" I find myself asking.

He chuckles, a throaty sound. "I can sure try."

I ignore the heat coursing through my body and pull the pair to a stop. "Down you go."

Ash lifts an eyebrow. "Just...down?"

I nod. "Down."

A little awkwardly, Ash holds the horn of the saddle and swings his leg over Shorty's back. His foot stays tangled in the stirrup on his way toward the ground, so I grab him before he can hit the dirt. My heart thumps wildly as Ash's back collides with my chest, my hand planted firmly on his stomach to hold him steady.

He turns his head to the side, eyes full of mirth as he meets my gaze. "Hi."

Clearing my throat, I shove him upright, *not* thinking about the way he smells or how he felt tucked up against me so damn perfectly.

Ash simply chuckles, brushing his hair back, that smile still on his face. "Well, I'd say I nailed the landing. What do you think?"

"We'll work on it," I mumble.

He snorts, turning to give Shorty a pat. "Thanks, Shorty. I'll probably be icing my ass later because of you, but I appreciate the ride."

Jesus.

"Here," I say, pulling the keys and card from my pocket. "My mom brought these for you."

"Perfect," Ash says, accepting both and twirling the keys around his finger.

"Gimme a minute, and I'll show you to the truck."

He nods, following me inside the barn as I get Shorty settled in his stall. It doesn't take long, considering the horse didn't work up enough of a sweat to need more than a quick brush. By the time I'm done stashing the riding gear, Ash is standing back near the doors of the barn. His arms are behind him, hands clasped together as if he's stretching.

"All right?" I ask, heading his way.

He nods, unclasping his hands and shaking out his arms. "Fine. You know, I used to work in an office."

"Yeah?" I say, not sure what precipitated the statement.

"Mm. I did public relations for this sports agency? Not important," he says, shaking his head. "I was just looking at this view and thinking how vastly different my life is right now from what it used to be. And I thought I liked it. Back then, I mean. I *did* like it well enough. I liked my job. My...partner."

My gut does something akin to a nosedive. "How long were you together?"

"Nearly three years," he says, squinting against the sunlight. "That's wild, right? Such a long time. How long were you with Otto?"

I chew the inside of my cheek before answering. "Almost two."

Ash nods, wincing slightly, like he gets it. I guess he does. "It was such a long time," he says again, sticking his hands in his back pockets. "A long time to lose myself."

"What d'you mean?"

He rocks on his heels, looking out toward the mountains. "Have you ever woken up one day and realized you weren't where you wanted to be?"

My heart starts to pound, but Ash doesn't wait for an answer before going on.

"I have. I woke up and realized I was lost. Just...*lost*. I'd lost myself in my relationship. In the easy, planned trajectory of my life. I'd gone down this path that was...*fine*. It was fine, but I wasn't excited to greet the sun each day. I wasn't excited about *life*, period. I don't know how it happened or when, exactly, but it's like... I woke up, and I knew. I had to get out."

My hands shake, so I hide them behind my back.

"I broke up with Nicholas," Ash says, tone almost flat. "Quit my job. I packed two bags, put the rest of my stuff in storage, and I came here."

"And...now?" I ask, grateful when my voice comes out even.

He lets out a sigh, his eyes closing for a second or two before he looks over at me. "Now I'm excited to greet the sun, Jack."

I don't know what to say to that. Don't know how to tell him I'm happy he found some joy in life. Don't know how to explain what it feels like to know he found that *here*. Don't know how to tell him I've heard this story before. That it didn't end well for me last time.

So I say nothing at all, and Ash looks back out toward the mountains. "Ready?" he asks.

"Yeah," I say a little gruffly.

I lead Ash over to the lot near the milking barn where the company vehicles are parked. A few clouds come out on the way, blocking the sun. I do my best not to shiver.

"Try your keys," I tell him once we reach the short row of heavy-duty trucks.

Ash pulls them from his pocket, pressing a button, and the truck on the leftmost side lights up. "It's not a manual, is it?"

"Automatic," I assure him. "You can keep it parked up near the house for however long you're using it. No need to drive it all the way back here between trips."

He nods, popping open the driver's side door and peeking inside.

"Fill up gas on the card," I tell him. "Try not to hit anything."

He snorts. "Noted."

"Did you ever hear anything about your car?" I ask, realizing he hasn't mentioned it.

"Um, yeah," he says, smiling a little sadly. It's the first time I've seen his smile twist down that way, and I find myself not liking it. Not one bit. "I guess the cost of repairing Edna is more than she's worth, so Ratchet suggested I scrap her. I know it's the smart decision. I just…"

He trails off, and I cut in. "There's no rush. We've got the extra vehicles. Might as well make use of them."

His lips turn up the tiniest bit. "Thanks, Jackson."

I grunt. "Uh, Edna?"

His expression shifts to part fondness, part mischievousness. "Mhm. She was a good ol' girl. Pretty, too."

"Never took you for a cougar hunter."

Ash's mouth opens slowly. "Jackson Darling," he says, causing a jolt of *something* to hit my gut. "Two jokes in one day. You better watch out. I hear they'll revoke your grump card for that."

"My…" I shake my head and grunt. "Jesus. Get going already."

He laughs, hopping up into the truck. "See you at dinner?"

Nodding once, I step back.

He gives me a two-fingered salute and shuts the truck door. The engine rumbles to life a second later, but Ash doesn't pull out. He rolls down the window instead. "Hey, Jackson?"

"Yeah?"

He rests his arm on the open window frame, looking me square on. "I've had homes, but I've never felt *at home*. I know it doesn't make sense, but here? In this place? I feel at home. So I'm not running. I'm not going anywhere, okay? And I know there are no guarantees in life, but when it comes to this? I'd really like to find out what the two of us could be. Because

I think it could be something. Something good. I hope you'll give us the chance to find out."

I nod stiffly, at a loss for words. This man isn't Otto. Whatever parallels they may share, Otto was never this transparent with me. He never left me knowing, without a shadow of a doubt, where he stood. Where *we* stood.

"This weekend, I'll have some free time," I say, my heart doing its best to beat right out of my chest. "Wanna go trail riding?"

Ash's smile is slow. Serene, almost. It's a lazy afternoon spent outside with nothing but the sun above and the dirt below.

It's scary how familiar that smile feels.

"Yeah, Jack," he answers. "I'd love nothing more."

"All right then."

He inhales a breath and lets it out. "For the record, you're wrong. You might just be the sweetest man I've ever met."

With that, Ash rolls up his window, backs out of his spot, and drives off down the dirt road, leaving me staring after him. I stare until the dust settles.

The rest of my afternoon passes in a blur of activity. It's not until nearly six o'clock that I realize I haven't seen my youngest brother all day. Remi is naturally quiet, always has been, but that's not the same as being *absent*.

He doesn't respond when I text, so I head to the main house, peeking into the dining room first. Dinner is laid out, and a few of the ranchers are seated already, as well as my dad, but no

Remi. Ash gives me a smile when he sees me in the doorway, but I hold up a finger to let him know I'll be a minute. He nods, looking a little concerned by whatever he sees on my face.

Heading upstairs, I make my way to Remi's room. The door isn't shut, but I still knock once before easing it open the rest of the way. As I'd worried, Remi is lying in bed, the lights off and his drape drawn shut. Colton is with him, sitting against the wall, his hand soothing over Remi's back. There's a pillow in front of Remi's face.

"Migraine day?" I ask Colton, knowing Remi won't be wearing his processor right now.

Colton nods, frowning. "Bad one."

"Does he need a new ice pack?"

"Yeah, if you don't mind."

"Not at all," I say, easing back out of the room and heading downstairs. As I'm pulling an ice pack from the freezer, Ash walks into the kitchen.

"Hey, everything okay?" he asks, grabbing a pitcher of water from the counter.

"Remi has a migraine," I tell him.

He makes a sympathetic sound. "That happen often?"

"Unfortunately, yeah. Ever since he was a kid."

"I'm sorry to hear that," Ash says, and I think if anyone could understand what it's like to deal with pain you can't always control, it's him. "Anything I can do?"

I'm about to shake my head when I reconsider. "Maybe biscuits tomorrow morning?"

He smiles gently. "Consider it done."

I give a quick nod of thanks and leave the kitchen. When I get back upstairs, neither of my brothers has moved. Remi doesn't even open his eyes as I gently pull the pillow away to switch out his ice pack. I wrap the new one in the same towel and set it against his forehead, but Remi lifts a hand to tap the back of his neck. I move it there before placing the pillow back over his eyes.

"Thanks," Remi says quietly, his voice muffled.

"How long have you been up here?" I ask Colton.

He shrugs, careful not to jostle Remi too much. "Couple hours?"

"I'll bring you some dinner."

His smile is appreciative but tired.

The dining room is buzzing when I get back downstairs. I grab a plate, loading it for my brother. My mom catches my eye from down the table and signs Remi's name, a question on her face. I give her a nod, and she touches her chest. She knows what it's like for him.

Deciding to eat upstairs with my brothers, I make up a second plate and head back to Remi's room. Colton thanks me when I hand him his dinner, and I sit down on the floor in front of the bed, not wanting to dirty my brother's sheets with my jeans. We're quiet as we eat. Remi shifts once, turning onto his other side. Colton moves the ice pack for him.

When there's a soft knock on the door, I expect to see my mother. Instead, it's Ash.

"Hey," he says quietly. "Can I come in?"

I give him a nod, and he steps inside the room, a small basket in his hands. He stops in front of me, crouching down and speaking quietly. "I'm not sure what your brother usually does for his migraines, but I made up some ginger tea in case it might help. It's in the thermos there to keep warm. There's also a bottle of water and a can of pop. You know, for the caffeine. Plus some chocolate because I swear it works miracles."

"Thanks," I say, my throat tight.

He nods once, handing the basket over. "The peanut butter cookies are for dessert. There's one for me, too, if I can have a seat?"

My swallow feels rough. "Sure."

Smiling, Ash sits down next to me, his knee settling against the outside of my leg. He plucks a cookie from the basket in my lap and takes a small bite, humming. I pick out my own before passing the basket back to a smirking Colton. He puckers his lips, and I flick his shin, ignoring his responding hiss.

As Ash and I eat our cookies, Colton rouses Remi as gently as he can, explaining what Ash brought and asking if he wants anything. Our younger brother sits upright after a minute, leaning against the wall with his eyes mostly shut. He doesn't say a word about Ash's presence, only raises an eyebrow my way before accepting the ginger tea. He sips it with a gentle sigh.

The four of us sit in companionable silence for quite some time, long enough for Remi to lie back down and fall asleep. No one seems to be in a hurry to be anywhere else. And when Ash's hand finds a tentative, questioning home on my knee?

I don't make a single move to discourage him.

Chapter 11

ASH

"Too much?" I ask my reflection, checking over my hat and boots in the standing mirror at the corner of the room. I can't decide if I look ridiculous or like a real Montana cowboy.

Deciding maybe the hat is one step too far—*for now*—I leave it on my bed and make my way downstairs.

It's cool today, and I'm grateful for the lining in my jacket as I head across the grounds to the horse barn. Jackson texted me not long ago to say he was there getting the horses ready for our trail ride. I've had butterflies in my stomach ever since.

He didn't call this a date, not exactly. But I'm fairly sure that's what it is. Especially considering Jackson told me we'll be going out on our own, not with either of today's scheduled trail-riding groups.

Definitely a date.

I try not to swallow my tongue as I step into the barn and set eyes on Jackson himself. He's hefting a saddle onto the black horse I often see him riding. The man is fine. *Painfully* fine. His jeans fit him well, his jacket is open, gifting me with a view of his shirt that's ridden above the line of his belt buckle, and his short beard looks freshly shaved, the reddish-brown strands giving him a rugged appeal not unlike the landscape around here.

It's a shame to look away, but seeing Shorty saddled up and ready to go, I head his way and give a low whistle. "My main man, look at you."

Jackson's head pops up, a bewildered expression on his face before he realizes I'm talking to the horse. I keep my laughter to myself as I greet Shorty, petting the stripe on his nose and letting his nostrils tickle my palm.

I step Jackson's way next. "Afternoon, Jack."

His responding, "Afternoon," sounds like a grumble.

"You look good," I tell him.

It takes Jackson a second to register that I'm talking to him this time. He grunts, tightening his horse's saddle.

"Can't take a compliment," I say, shaking my head as I offer my hand to the black horse to sniff. "He's pretty. What's his name?"

"Starlight," Jackson says, straightening up and giving the saddle a testing wiggle. "Don't ask. Remi named him when he was eight."

"Which makes Starlight how old?"

"Twenty."

I hum, fingers drifting over the white shape on Starlight's forehead. It does look almost like a star.

"What's that?" I ask, noticing Jackson heft two leather bags onto Starlight's back. They're connected with a strap such that the bags sit on either side of his spine. Saddlebags, maybe?

"Supplies," he says. "Just in case."

"And how treacherous are these trails?" I ask, only half-joking.

Jackson huffs. "Not bad, so long as you stay where you're supposed to. This is just... It's nothing."

Well, that's not suspicious.

"Okay, Jack," I say slowly. "Keep your secrets. For the record, I like surprises."

He shakes his head, lips twisting.

Once Starlight is ready to go, Jackson instructs me to lead Shorty out of the barn. I grab his reins, feeling like a seasoned pro. That is, until it's time to get up in the saddle.

"Go ahead," Jackson says. "You first."

"Are you going to feel me up again?" I ask, sticking my foot in the stirrup. I bounce on my toe, getting ready.

"I didn't feel you up," he says, sounding put-out.

"Oh, you did."

"I didn't—"

"Did."

"Christ. Get on the damn horse already," he gripes.

Huffing a laugh, I pull myself up, the motion easier now that I know what I'm doing. My leg makes it over Shorty's back, and I let out a triumphant, "Aha!"

Jackson shakes his head, although there's a smile quirking his cheek as he checks my stirrups. He stills as soon as he notices my boots.

"Do you like them?" I ask, twisting the heel his way.

"They'll hold up better than what you had," he allows, giving my leg a pat that has a *zing* traveling up my body. He rounds the horse to check my other stirrup.

"You can tell me I look good in my new boots, Jack."

"You're impossible," he mutters. He fixes my second stirrup before declaring me good to go.

I'm about to fire off a retort—*why yes, I'm always good to go around you*—when Jackson grabs his horse's saddle and swings up into riding position in a motion so seamless and fluid, I don't even remember seeing him leave the ground. I blink, my breath suddenly coming short.

Ho boy.

"Ready?" Jackson asks, gathering the reins in his hand.

"Ready and raring," I rasp.

Jackson clicks his tongue, and Starlight sets into motion.

I stare at the man's ass for a moment. "Good grief," I mutter, getting Shorty moving after him. Speaking louder, I ask, "How far are we going?"

"However far we want," Jackson answers. "We've got a few different trails marked out. The longest ones reach the base of the mountains."

I look off in that direction. The mountains are closer here than in town, but they still seem so far away.

"Does anyone ever get lost?" I ask.

Jackson huffs what might be a laugh. "No. We know these trails. And guests aren't allowed off on their own."

That's reassuring, at least.

Jackson leads me to the tree line at the back of the property and then directs his horse through a break in the vegetation, me at his heel. We settle into a leisurely walk along a well-trodden dirt path, the sun intermittently blinking through the leaves of the trees. It's quiet. Just the soft sounds of birds and the occasional moo accompany the clomp of the horses' hooves.

I look around, content to enjoy the scenery and the gentle side-to-side sway of riding horseback. I also can't help but enjoy the gentle sway of Jackson's ass. I'm only human.

It isn't long before there's a split in the path. Jackson goes left, sticking close to the tree line. I catch sight of someone out in the pastures, but they're too far away to tell who it is.

"You can talk, you know," Jackson says after a while.

"Oh, you're giving me permission, are you?"

He glances back at me, a subtle roll of his eyes visible before he faces forward again. "Like you need permission. I just mean—I won't mind."

I hum to myself. "I was enjoying the view."

He looks over his shoulder again.

"Very nice trees," I say with a smile.

And truthfully, they are. The leaves have started changing color, some of the foliage more yellow now than green. There's even some red and purple. I bet, in another week or two, it'll be an autumnal masterpiece.

Jackson grunts an, "Uh-huh," clearly doubting which views I happened to be enjoying.

Never one for subtlety, I add, "Your ass is nice, as well."

"There it is," he murmurs.

I huff a laugh.

I'm not sure how far we go distance-wise, but we ride for a good hour before Jackson leads us up a gentle incline. The path isn't as wide here, and lower vegetation brushes my legs as we move. When Jackson stops in a small clearing, I do the same. He jumps down off Starlight's back and walks my way, not even tying his horse to a tree or anything. I guess he trusts him.

"Am I getting down?" I ask.

Jackson nods, standing just behind my leg and grabbing hold of my hips. For a second, I stop breathing.

"You're gonna swing this leg over the horse," he says, patting my far hip, "until you're standing in the air. Support your weight with your arms, and then let this foot"—he pats the other hip—"out of the stirrup and slide down. Less chance of tripping that way."

"I didn't trip," I say hoarsely. "It was a calculated fall."

"Mhm," he grunts. "C'mon."

Jackson gives my hips a little squeeze to encourage me, and I'm powerless to do anything other than follow his directions. He keeps his hands in place as I swing my right leg over the back of the horse. He gives me another squeeze to stall me once I'm upright.

"Now lean your weight on the horse. Yep, like that. And take your foot out of the stirrup."

I close my eyes and try *really* hard not to focus on the fact that I'm bending over a horse with Jackson's face quite near my ass. Not wanting to get a boner against poor Shorty's side, I pull my left foot out of the stirrup and let my weight pull me down. Jackson's hands stay on my hips, guiding me, until my feet hit dirt.

It takes a second, but Jackson lets go. "Good," he says gruffly.

I nearly groan. He should not be saying that word in *that* voice.

Jackson heads back toward Starlight, and I shake out my legs, trying to let the simmering heat from Jackson's touch fade away. "I'd say that was a ten out of ten dismount. What do you think?"

He shoots me a look. "Don't get cocky now."

Snorting, I stretch my back and look around. I'm a little stiff, but I'm sure that's to be expected after sitting in the saddle for so long. "Why'd we stop?" I ask.

Jackson grabs Shorty's reins and leads him next to Starlight, securing both horses to a nearby tree. "Wanted to show you something."

"Cryptic. You didn't bring me out all this way just to get rid of me, did you? Because I have to tell you—that seems like a lot of work."

He stares at me blankly. "Why would I possibly do that?"

"Oh, so you *do* like me."

He blinks before shaking his head. "Impossible."

Huffing a laugh, I follow Jackson as he heads up a short hill. "It's okay, Jack. I won't tell anyone you want to suck my face..."

The word *off* puffs out of me as I reach the top of the hill. We're standing on a natural overlook, not terribly high up but high enough for a breathtaking view. Pastureland stretches as far as the eye can see, black-and-white cows dotting the landscape. The river cuts through the fields, water glistening blue in the late afternoon sun. Far away is a fence line, so small it's barely visible.

"Is this all yours?" I ask, voice hushed.

Jackson hums. "It is, and then some. Look. There's Marty."

He points at a speck in the distance, and I laugh. "How can you tell?"

"Just can," he says.

I shake my head and glance behind us. I didn't realize it as we were heading through the woods, but we're at the base of the mountains now. They seem impossibly tall, towering above the tops of the trees. Quiet, but imposing. I can't even imagine all these mountains have seen.

"It's gorgeous here," I tell Jackson, not for the first time.

When I turn back around, I find him watching me instead of the scenery. He hums, and my pulse kicks. But then Jackson blinks and looks away.

I follow his gaze back toward the cattle, clearing my throat. "Your dad says you have a hybrid herd."

Jackson nods. "Mm. We've found a Holstein-Angus cross works best for our operation. Holsteins are good milkers, and Angus is a standard for beef. The hybrids are good for both, so we crossbreed and split 'em accordingly."

"Did you always know you wanted to be a cowboy?" I ask, Jackson's seriousness making me smile.

"I'm not—"

"Jack. You're not just a dairy farmer," I point out. "And yes, you run a ranch, so rancher is appropriate. But how is calling you a cowboy in any way incorrect?"

He simply grunts.

"Well?" I prod.

"I suppose, *technically*, you could call me a cowboy," he concedes, although it seems to pain him to do so.

I grin, and he huffs a breath.

"And yes," he says, sounding salty, "I always knew I wanted to do this. It's not just 'cause of my family. Lawson went his own way."

"Teaching," I say.

Jackson nods. "But for me... This life is part of who I am. I'm not sure I could ever leave it."

"I get that," I say softly.

He looks over at me again, gaze almost sharp. "Do you?"

"Yeah, Jack. You say this life is a part of you, but I think it's the other way around. I think you're a part of this place. Asking you to change that would be like...like trying to uproot these mountains. Although, frankly, I think you might be the more stubborn of the two."

Jackson doesn't laugh at my joke. He continues to stare at me in a way that's focused and almost unnerving. Just when I'm about to break the silence, he asks, "You hungry?"

"You're...not planning on catching me a fresh cow, right?"

His lips twitch. "No. I brought food."

My smile is a slow, *slow* thing. "Jackson Darling, did you pack us a picnic?"

He immediately scowls, making me laugh. "'Course not."

"No?" I say, following after him as he heads down the hill. "I hate to break it to you, but unless you also packed a table in those tiny bags on Starlight's back, we're eating on the ground. That, cowboy, is a picnic."

He shakes his head, his movements jerky as he opens one of the bags. "My mom packed it for us," he grumbles so quietly I nearly miss it.

I stop. And stare. After a moment of silence, Jackson glances my way.

"Not a goddamn word," he says tightly. "I didn't wanna hurt her feelings by refusing. And I thought, well... Everybody's gotta eat, right?"

I bite my lip. "You didn't want to pack me food yourself, Jack?"

He goes still. "That's not... I didn't mean..."

"I mean, *damn*. I wasn't expecting flowers or diamonds. But I cook you food all the time. Every *day*."

His eyes widen, and *oh*, he's too fucking easy.

"The least you could do," I continue, pitching my voice dramatically, "is make sure I don't starve out here in the wilderness. I guess I should be grateful *someone* cares. I'll have to find a way to thank your mom, huh?"

"You're fucking with me," he says, deadpan.

I shrug, keeping a straight face. "Maybe I *should* try cougar hunting, after all."

"Ash."

"No, no. I see how it is. I'll just take Shorty and be on my way. Don't you worry about little old me."

"You're not going anywhere," Jackson rumbles, stalking after me as I head in Shorty's direction.

I pick up my pace, all but grinning now. "It's *fine*, Jack. I'm sure I can find my way back to the ranch by my—"

"You're not going *anywhere*," he repeats, backing me up against Shorty's side.

My breath puffs out of me, pulse thundering. "No?"

"You're. Impossible," he says again, his sharp blue gaze flicking between my eyes and mouth.

"No," I counter, giving him a smile as my heart kicks. "I'm right here."

Jackson's lips are on mine before I can take a full breath. He presses forward, his body pinning me between him and Shorty. His kiss is brutal, and I'd almost think it angry if I couldn't feel the desperation behind every movement. The scrape of his stubble and the nip of teeth. The way he groans low in his chest and how he grabs my jaw like he doesn't want me going anywhere if it's not with him.

I could tell him he has nothing to worry about, but speaking isn't possible.

So instead, I grab Jackson's jacket and urge him closer. His hips meet mine, and a flash of heat soars down my spine as I feel the very obvious evidence of his arousal through the denim of his jeans. I'm about to see what Jackson will let me get away with out here in the woods when the surface at my back shifts. I don't know if our weight pushed Shorty to the side or he simply decided he'd be a cockblocking asshole, but both Jackson and I stumble as the horse moves a step away, our kiss coming to an abrupt end.

Jackson doesn't let me go as the pair of us catch our breath. His hands stay fisted in my jacket, his face resting against the crook of my neck. He's in my lungs, smelling like the wild, like this place. A sharp breeze and fallen leaves. Crispness and comfort. The smallest hint of sweet caramel.

He's the first to step back, his cheeks flushed as he averts his gaze.

"So," I cough out, tugging my jacket back into place. "There was talk of a picnic?"

Jackson lets out a small breath, nearly a laugh, as he returns to the open saddlebag on Starlight's back. "Are you gonna be a shit about it?"

I feign offense. "Me? Give you trouble? Jackson, I'm offended. Truly."

He shakes his head, lips pressed tightly together. "Come on," he says, heading back up the hill with our food. I follow. Of course I do.

"Hypothetical question," I throw out, stepping over an exposed tree root. "Is riding horseback with a boner uncomfortable?"

Jackson groans. It's the answer I expected.

Ah well. Worth it.

Chapter 12

JACKSON

Ash has a smile on his face as we exit the tree line at the start of the trail. His hair is ruffled and his cheeks bright, and I can hardly look away from him.

Him or those smiling lips.

"That was fun," he says, breaking my trance as our horses walk side by side toward the stables.

I grunt, and he snorts.

"You had fun, too," he says.

I don't deny it.

"Pretty sure I'll be sore tomorrow, but I don't even care," he goes on. "If your ass isn't feeling it after a good ride, you're not doing it right."

The latter was clearly a joke—one that has my pulse skyrocketing—but his comment about being sore makes me pause. "It wasn't too much, was it?"

He nearly rolls his eyes. "No, it wasn't. I'll be fine."

He'll *be* fine. Not that he *is* fine.

I try to hold my tongue but can't. "What d'you do? For your back, I mean. You said you have stretches?"

He holds my eye for a moment before nodding. "From my physical therapists mostly. Just a few things to keep my back muscles loose and my spine in alignment and all that."

"And you, uh, do those every day?"

"Unless I forget," he says slowly. "Why?"

I shrug. "Just curious."

"Mhm."

"And, uh... How often do you needa do the heat pack thing?"

"Jack," he says, tone warning.

"What?"

Ash's expression is stern. "Don't, okay? Don't start thinking of me as weak. I know what I can handle, and a little pain isn't going to stop me from living my life. I don't need you treating me like glass. I've had enough people in my life do that."

I pull Starlight to a stop, and a moment later, Ash stops, too.

"I don't," I say seriously. "I don't think of you as weak, Ash. Quite the opposite. I just wanna know how you cope, all right? I wanna know what you do, so if there's a way to help, I can do it."

He looks at me for the longest time, his eyes raking over my face. Finally, he nods once and kicks Shorty back into motion. I catch up quickly.

"It varies," he says. "Couple times a week on the heat is typical. I have a low-dose muscle relaxer I take at night if it's really bad. It helps reset things. Maybe once a month for that. I used to get massages, too, but I don't know if you have anyone close by that does that?"

I shake my head. Not that I'm aware of.

He shrugs. "So that's it. It's...maintenance, you know? Just part of my everyday routine. Like eating or sleeping or jerking—"

His words come to a swift halt, and my body flashes hot. *Jerking off.* He was going to say jerking off.

Fucking hell.

"There's literally no way to recover that," Ash says around a laugh. "So I'm not even going to try. Here we are."

Ash is the first off his horse, dismounting with barely a hitch. He's a fast learner; I'll give him that. I stare after him as he leads Shorty inside the barn, telling the horse what a good job he did today, *yes, he did.*

I can't quite get my breathing to even out.

By the time I catch up, Ash is working through how to take off Shorty's saddle. I help him out, showing him where to put the saddle pads for cleaning and how to store the tack. After that, we spray and brush down the horses, Ash laughing all the while.

I still can't breathe.

Ash ends up half-soaked by the time we're done, but he doesn't seem to mind. He's all smiles as we return the horses to their stalls, clean and mostly dried. I show him where the various pellets and grains are and how to read the horses' feed charts on the outsides of their doors. He scoops the right amounts while I refill their hay.

By the time we're done, it's nearly seven in the evening.

"I think I'm due for a shower," Ash says, picking at his shirt, which is clinging wetly to his skin. His jacket is waiting on a straw bale nearby.

I nod, not trusting my voice enough to speak. My heart keeps pounding, and I can't stop looking at Ash's mouth. At his smile.

He wings up an eyebrow, catching my staring. "Unless... Do you want to join me?" he asks, brazen as ever.

Yes.

"I don't...know if that'd be a good idea," I say, not sure why I'm still holding back.

Why am I holding back?

Ash's expression softens. "Okay, Jack. Walk with me?"

I nod, and Ash grabs his jacket. The two of us take off.

Most of the weekend employees are gone at this time of day. The dairy cows are outside again, having already been milked for the evening. Their diet is different from that of the beef lot, but they still spend plenty of their time grazing. In the other direction, Remi is closing up the petting farm, Snickerdoodle trailing after him.

"It's so peaceful here," Ash says.

I hum.

"Not quiet, exactly," he adds. "Just...nice."

"Yeah."

Ash huffs a laugh. "Like someone else I know."

It takes me a second to connect the dots. "I'm not nice."

He straight up barks a laugh. "Sure, Jack."

"Christ," I grumble, ignoring his audible amusement.

By the time we reach the ranch house, my palms are sweating and my nerves are jumbled. I feel like a teenager after a first date, not knowing what to say or do. My eyes keep falling to Ash's lips, no matter how hard I try to stop it.

"I had a good time today," Ash says. "Thanks for taking me out."

I nod a bit jerkily.

"And tell your mom thanks, too," he adds, mouth twisting into a smile. "You know, for that food you just couldn't refuse. Because it's so incredibly hard to say 'no thank you.'"

I rub the back of my neck, and Ash huffs a laugh.

"Night, Jack," he says softly.

Ash heads up the porch stairs, and I hold my hand up in a goodbye. After sending me one last smile, he disappears inside.

The entire time I walk to my house, my thoughts war. As I shower, I can't stop thinking about Ash's mouth and his laugh and the feel of him pressed against me as we kissed. Once I'm dry and dressed, I pace, thinking about the ginger tea he made my brother and the way he looked up at the mountains as if awed.

I think of his golden hair and stormy eyes and that god-damn dimple in his chin.

I think of the way he told me, "I'm right here."

I think of every possible outcome, the good and the bad, and how, in the end, there's only one way to find out for certain what we could be. If, like Ash said, we could be something good. Something *real*.

My pulse is racing as I walk the quarter mile back to the ranch house. The sun is set now, having sunk down beyond the mountains. I don't falter as I head through the front door, kicking my boots off inside. I don't stop as I walk down the hall and take the stairs up to the second floor. I don't think or hesitate. I knock on Ash's door, and I wait.

He opens it after only a few seconds, his eyes widening in surprise. His hair is wet, and there's a towel draped over the edge of the bed. "Jackson?"

I step in, taking Ash's face in my hands. There's a question stuck in the back of my throat that I can't get out, but Ash must read it on my face because he nods in my grip.

"Yeah," he breathes, permission freely given.

I move forward, and the pair of us turn in tandem, rounding the door as my mouth comes down on his. Our momentum pushes Ash into the wood, the door thudding shut in the process. He moans against me, a noise I hastily swallow down before tugging him in the opposite direction, all too aware of those in this house who could hear us. Ash's hands grapple with my shirt as we move, his fingers finding skin, our lips never parting.

When I bump against the dresser at the far wall, I spin him into the furniture. He grunts, legs spreading wider to make room for me to crowd in close. I can't stop kissing him. Can't stop touching. His abdominals tense as my hand drags down the front of his shirt, a groan leaving his mouth, his hunger just as evident as my own.

Ash's breaths are loud when I drop my lips to his neck, tasting clean man on my tongue. His groan this time is louder—*too* loud—so I cover his mouth with my palm. He makes an affronted sound, tugging my hand away, even as he arches into my touch.

"You can't just—"

"Shh," I tell him.

"Jack—"

I cover his mouth again, holding his gaze as I lower to my knees. He gets the hint, his eyes rolling up before snapping open again. Slowly, I let go of his mouth to open his jeans.

"Fuck," he mutters, helping me along, shoving his pants down as soon as I have them unzipped. He grips the edge of the dresser, breathing ragged.

I don't make him wait, too impatient myself, wanting this too damn much to drag it out even a second longer. I tug down his briefs, run my nose up the length of his cock, and then take him into my mouth.

Ash nearly shouts, and I shift my gaze up just in time to catch him biting the side of his hand to muffle it. His eyes are half-lidded and electric. They struggle to stay open as I slip my lips down the length of him, tasting clean man again, but also something more. Something uniquely him.

"Jack," he groans around his hand.

I suck, dragging my lips upwards, swirling my tongue around his crown as I grip the base of his dick. His hips jerk, cock throbbing in a blatant display of arousal. It's heady, knowing I'm affecting him so. Knowing he was hard for me the moment I sank to my knees.

I want to make him come for me, too.

I pump his shaft as I mouth the sensitive head of his cock, so smooth against my lips and tongue. His breathing hitches when I lick his slit, and I'm rewarded with a salty hit of precum. I can tell Ash is trying to keep his noises in check, but he's not very successful. Deep groans reverberate out from his chest, accompanying words spilling from around his makeshift gag. There's *Jack* and *fuck, your mouth is sweet* and *if you stop, I'll die*.

I have no plans of stopping. I take more of Ash's cock into my mouth, replacing my hand with my lips as I work him over. His skin is hot, his cock impossibly hard and swelling further. Ash's hand slaps against the dresser as he gets close, his other gripping my hair tight.

"Fuck, Jack. Fuck, *fuck*."

I clamp my hand back over his mouth, and he doesn't try to stop me. His hips hitch off the dresser, his cock so deep in my throat I'm taking nearly all of him. I can feel the moment Ash starts to come. Can feel it against my tongue, against my lips, against my palm as his breathing stutters. I suck hard, pulling my lips toward his tip, and *there*.

Ash floods my mouth as his teeth clamp onto the meat of my palm. I stroke him through it, something in the deepest parts of me stuttering and restarting like his breath. His hand leaves my hair as his orgasm wanes, instead covering the hand I have pressed against his mouth. His teeth release their grip, his lips pursing in what feels like an apologetic kiss.

"Fuck," he murmurs again, pulling my hand down to his chest as I softly clean his cock with my tongue. He grunts, a satisfied sound I can feel against my bruised palm. "Jack."

I meet his eye, unprepared for the softness I find there. He gives me a tug, trying to pull me to my feet. I let him.

My heart pounds as Ash drags me close, uncaring about his half-clothed state. His hand grips my ass over my jeans, slotting us together, his other in my hair again, thumb beside my ear. I feel...*exposed.*

"What is it you want, Jack?" Ash asks, his lips feathering along my cheek. They drift over my lips before trailing along my jaw.

I don't think he's asking about right this instant, but I can't answer that. I hardly know myself.

"I don't need anything in return," I croak out. "I didn't expect—"

Ash clucks his tongue, leaning back enough to see me. "Jackson Darling, must you be so stubborn? I didn't ask what you need. I asked what you *want.*"

I pull in a breath, and Ash's hand runs down my jaw, his thumb brushing my bottom lip.

"We *need* air," he says, fingers skimming down my neck, over my pulse. "We need food. Water. Sleep. But I want to know what you *want.* What it is you ache for. What you'd ask for, right this very minute, if you could choose. What, in the most selfish parts of you, are you greedy for? What is it you *want?*"

"You," I answer without a thought.

Ash's grip stills on the side of my neck before tightening. "Fuck. I knew you'd be trouble."

I don't have time to decipher that before Ash's hand is sliding down between us, landing on my crotch like a brand. His lips touch my ear, so soft.

"You have me, darlin'."

My heart gives a great big thump as Ash shoves me gently backwards. He drops to his haunches in front of me, tugging my jeans down with zero finesse. I flail for a single second before grabbing the lip of the dresser, bracing myself over Ash's form as he pulls me swiftly from within my boxer briefs.

He shakes his head slightly. "Of course you're perfect," he mutters. And then he licks the head of my cock.

My breath punches from me, but I can't look away, can't tear my eyes off the sight of Ash taking my cock into his mouth. He sinks nearly all the way down before reversing course, his hand encircling me as he pops free.

"We're going to work on you talking to me," he says before licking me in an almost kittenish manner. His hand continues to work my base, the familiar tug and squeeze feeling so much better than it has any right to. It's been too long. *So* long since I've had this. And this is *Ash* crouching at my feet. His hand on my dick. His tongue coming out to swipe at my crown.

Fuck.

"You're going to learn you can trust me," he says, eyes flitting up to meet mine. "You can trust me, Jack."

"Ash," I groan.

"I know," he says, a small smile on his face. "I've got you."

He ducks his head again, and I miss the sight of that smile. But then his mouth is back on my cock, and his hand is sinking inside my underwear to grasp my balls. Ash cups them, rolls them, his fingers sliding back against my taint. I about shoot to my tiptoes as those fingers rub and rub and *rub*, the suction of his mouth never ceasing.

Just like that, I lose it.

I call out Ash's name as my muscles tense, my fingers blanching against the top of the dresser. He doesn't pull off, even as my release coats his tongue. For the briefest of moments, I feel out of my body. I'm washed in sensation, in the euphoric waves rolling beneath my skin. In the pull of my balls emptying in blissful relief. It's all-encompassing, threatening to pull me under and sweep me away.

But then, there's the pressure of Ash's hand on my hip. His mouth soothing my cock. The hum he lets out that seems to travel straight up into my chest. He's there, grounding me as I catch my breath, as I try to wrap my head around the fact that I had sex for the first time since Otto, and it felt...*good*. It felt good and right, and I don't think I realized until right this instant how terrified I was that that wouldn't be the case. That maybe he'd truly broken me. That—*maybe*—I wouldn't ever be able to have this again.

But he didn't take that from me, did he?

A soft kiss against my hip has me glancing down. Ash's hair is a mess, half-covering his eyes as he looks up at me. His cheeks are red, and his lips look slick.

"Okay, Jack?" he asks quietly.

I turn and sink down beside him, my ass landing on the floor. Ash takes a seat, too, kicking his legs out in front of him. Our softened cocks are still hanging out, and I have no doubt my face looks as utterly wrecked as his. But none of it matters.

"I'm all right," I tell him honestly. I'm not sure how he seems to know something is going on in my head. Maybe I'm just not that great at hiding it. Or maybe he's simply looking.

Ash rests his head against the dresser, gaze softly assessing as it travels over me. "You're not going to walk out that door, right?"

I shake my head slowly. "No. Not yet."

He nods, seemingly satisfied with that. Facing forward again, he closes his eyes, an almost serene smile on his face. "Fuck," he mutters.

"Fuck," I agree, still trying to catch my breath.

Ash lets out a small chuckle. And then another. And then he's laughing outright, his chest shaking and a grin on his face.

Without quite knowing why I'm doing it, I laugh along with him.

Chapter 13

ASH

When I wake, the sun is just starting to rise, casting soft light into the room and giving the walls a hazy glow. I stretch for a minute, working out the ever-present kinks in my body. Even though I'm sore, I feel good. Refreshed, even.

A smile spreads across my face as I remember the man who's at least partially responsible for my good mood. I wouldn't be surprised if Jackson is already up and moving around the ranch, even though it's the weekend. He's probably grumping about, overthinking what happened between us last night. But somehow, I know he's not regretting it.

The look in his eye as he left was proof enough of that. His gaze had been pinned on me like he didn't want to go. Like he was afraid I might slip through his fingertips given the chance.

I get it. I don't know the whole story of what happened between him and his ex, but Jackson has clearly been hurt. He's wary of that happening again. The best I can do is show him I have no desire to be a cause of more pain.

When I fling off my comforter and transfer my weight to the ground, there's a moment where the bottom of my feet sting. Peripheral neuropathy. It's worse when my back is acting up, the nerves in my body affected by the inflammation connected to the pain. It's like a shitty chain reaction—pain leads to more pain. But I walk through it, and by the time I reach the hall, the pinprick sensation has mostly passed.

I take care of my business quickly and head downstairs, finding a half-full pot of coffee in the kitchen. I fill up a mug and make my way to the back porch to enjoy the morning view. The air is cool, cutting through the sweater I put on, but the sight of the mountains lit pink in the early morning sun is oh so worth the chill.

It's idyllic here. Beautiful in a way I'm not sure I could ever get sick of.

I'm startled from my thoughts by a voice saying, "Morning."

Huffing a laugh, I turn around. "Morning, Lawson."

The eldest Darling brother is sitting in a chair, his own mug of coffee in hand. I take a seat next to him, looking out over the dairy girls, as Jackson calls them. They're gathered in small groups, and I can't help but wonder if they form friendships like we do, or if it's simply prey instinct keeping them drawn together.

Lawson clears his throat softly, as if he's warming up his speaking muscles. "You settling in all right?"

"Yeah, I am," I tell him. "Honestly, it's been a really easy transition. If anything, that's the odd part."

He nods. "You think you're sticking around then?"

Ah. So this is about a certain grumpy cowboy we both know.

"I'm not going anywhere," I assure Lawson, not begrudging him looking out for his brother. Nor surprised he caught on to what's happening between me and Jackson.

He nods again, turning his gaze out over the ranchland as he sips his coffee. "Otto did a number on him," he says quietly.

I let out a breath. "I don't think that's something I should hear from you, Lawson. No offense. It's just...he'll tell me when he's ready."

He looks at me again, gaze serious, his brown eyes—so like Marigold's—setting him apart from his brothers. "People leave," he says simply. "Sometimes, they leave."

My chest squeezes tight. I don't think he's talking about Otto or even me. "Your wife?" I ask as gently as possible.

His eyes widen, surprise flashing before guilt sets in. So...not his wife, then.

Before I can find out who walked out of Lawson's past, Hank comes into view. He has a gallon of pink paint in one hand, the color streaked down the sides of the tin, and his beekeeper's hat is on his head.

I huff a laugh as he waves our way. "You know what that's about?"

Lawson shakes his head. "Not a clue. One of his hobbies, I'm guessing."

Hank passes, and Lawson stands. He turns to me with a sigh.

"Ashley, maybe it's not my place to say anything, but I love my family. Colton would tell Jackson to simply let loose and have fun for once. He thinks it's that easy. But what he doesn't understand about our brother is that his heart has always led first. Jackson doesn't know any other way. So just...be sure, all right? It won't be casual for him."

I nod, my pulse beating swiftly. Maybe Lawson's words should scare me, but if anything, they have the opposite effect. The man himself nods back before walking around the corner out of sight.

I think I just got the big brother shakedown. I feel...strangely honored.

When my coffee is gone and the sky has turned an airy blue, I return my mug to the kitchen and grab the yoga mat I bought in town. My exercise routine isn't strenuous by any means, and usually, I do it in my room. But there are fewer employees about this time on a Sunday, so I head to the back deck again and enjoy the scenery as I run through the paces, loosening the muscles between my shoulder blades, those in my neck and down my spine, a few out through my arms, and, finally, my hamstrings. I'm near the end of my stretches when I feel a presence off to my right.

I nearly laugh. "Morning, Jack."

Jackson's footsteps thunk up the wooden stairs, an unreadable expression on his face as he approaches. He looks good. Handsome. But he always does.

"Are we back to being quiet?" I ask.

"No," he answers, voice a little rough around the edges. "Just..."

"Enjoying the view?" I tease.

He grunts what might be a begrudging affirmative. I sit upright, crossing my legs in front of me as Jackson takes a seat in a rocker, the furniture shifting slightly with his weight. He props his elbows on his knees and looks off in the direction of the cattle.

"Did you want to talk about last night?" I ask, wondering if that's why he's here.

He looks at me almost sharply. "We did, didn't we?"

This time, I do laugh. "I'm not sure the words that came out of either of our mouths could be classified as *talking*."

Jackson's cheeks pinken slightly at that, a damn endearing sight.

"Do you want it to happen again?" I ask, praying like hell I haven't read him wrong.

After a moment, he nods once, and I breathe a sigh of relief.

"Jack... Are you out at work? Because if you're expecting this to stay a secret, I think we've already failed."

He huffs. "'Cause *somebody* is damn loud."

"Excuse me," I say, chuckling at his brusque delivery. "I'm not the only one who was loud. You're welcome for that, by the way."

He scrubs a hand down his face, but I swear he's smiling. "I'm not..." He blows out a breath and tries again, his eyes aimed away. "I'm not gonna ask you to be a secret, Ash. I don't play games, all right? That's not what I want. Everybody here knows I'm gay. It's not a problem."

I let loose a breath, and Jackson looks over at me almost warily.

"What is it?" he asks.

"Nothing. It's just... That was a damn good answer, Jack."

He grunts, glancing away again, self-conscious or nervous, maybe. The man is like a porcupine, all squishy soft beneath his quills.

"Christ, you're cute," I mutter.

He looks affronted. "I'm not *cute*."

"Mhm."

"I'm *not*."

"It's a compliment, Jack," I assure him, standing and rolling up my yoga mat. "Want to have lunch with me today?"

If he's surprised by the offer, he doesn't show it.

"Are you gonna keep calling me cute?" he asks.

"Might," I admit.

He hangs his head, grumbling in a way that has me grinning. Before he can give me an answer, my phone rings. I pull it out and check the screen.

"My mom," I tell Jackson, accepting the call. "Hello?"

"Hey, honey," my mom says. "How's the ranch?"

"Great," I tell her, glad to hear a distinct lack of judgment in her tone compared to the last time we talked. "I'm loving it here. The job is perfect for me, and everyone has been really welcoming."

Jackson looks off toward the petting farm, giving me some semblance of privacy, but I don't miss his pleased smile.

"That's good," my mom says, tone shifting. "Ashley, honey, I heard something from Linda at the country club this morning. You know Linda, Nicholas's mom's neighbor?"

"I believe so," I tell her, my stomach twisting. "What'd she say?"

"Nicholas is on his way to Montana."

For a second, her words don't compute. "What? *Why?*"

"Well, apparently you haven't been returning his calls," she says.

"Because we broke up."

Jackson's gaze snaps back my way, his expression hardening into something cautious, almost wary. I give him what I hope is a reassuring smile.

"I know," my mom says in my ear. "But I guess he has some things to say."

"And he couldn't wait for me to call him back?" I wonder aloud, scrubbing over my eyes before I let out a groan. What could he possibly have to say that's so important it warranted a trip out here? "Thanks for letting me know, Mom."

"Of course. Call me soon, and we'll catch up."

"Sounds good. Love you."

"Love you, too."

When I hang up, Jackson is watching me. Waiting. It's a simple thing, really, but I like the fact that he wants to know what's going on. That he isn't running.

"My ex is coming," I tell him. "Because I wasn't answering my phone."

His brow pinches. "That's..."

"Rash?" I supply.

He grunts, and I huff a laugh. Shaking my head, I pull up Nicholas's number and hit call. It rings and rings and then goes to voicemail.

"Of fucking course," I mutter, just as there's a beep. "Nicholas, give me a call, please. I'll answer."

I hang up and switch over to my text thread with Virginia.

Me: Nicholas is on his way here. He doesn't know my address, so he might head to your place. Keep an eye out?

Jackson clears his throat. "Is there any chance of you two—"

"No," I say immediately, meeting his gaze head-on. "We're done. Completely."

He nods, brow furrowed. My phone pings.

Virginia: No need, baby boy. I have my eyes on him right now. He's here.

"Well, shit," I puff out. "I guess I'm going for a ride."

"We," Jackson says definitively, standing up.

There's a stutter in my chest. A sway and a settle that reminds me distinctly of being on Shorty's back. "Is that so?"

"Mhm," Jackson grunts. "We can get that lunch while we're in town."

My lips quirk. "Jackson Darling," I say slowly. "You better watch out."

"For what?" he asks a little warily.

I give him a smile, tucking my yoga pad underneath my arm. "You keep saying stuff like that, and you might not ever see the end of me."

He does his best to look put-out, but I don't miss the satisfaction in his eyes. "So long as you stop calling me cute."

"I make no promises," I answer. "Now, come on. Better not leave fate waiting."

Jackson drives us into town in his truck. He's quiet on the way, and I leave him to his silence, my own thoughts occupied with why Nicholas flew all the way across the country just to speak to me.

He never once tried to stop me from leaving.

Jackson pulls into an empty spot in front of The Barrel and shuts off his truck. Virginia told us to meet them inside, seeing as her apartment is within walking distance and the bar will be closed for a few hours still. Good neutral ground.

I grab the door handle, but something stops me from getting out.

"All right?" Jackson asks, voice low and rumbly in the confines of the cab.

I nod. "Think so. Maybe? No." I let go of the handle and turn to face him. "Do you know what he said to me when I told him I thought we should split? He said, 'okay.' Just *okay*, as if I'd told him I was running to the store for milk. He didn't care, so why is he here? What did he come for?"

Jackson's brows draw in, but his face remains otherwise impassive. "He wants you back."

I huff. "How do you figure?"

"Why wouldn't he?" he shoots back, the words nearly punching the breath from my lungs. "He made a mistake. So he's here to fix it."

"If that's the case, I don't want to fix it. I know I made it sound like our break was sudden, but we'd been drifting apart for well over a year before we separated. There's nothing left to fix."

Jackson nods slowly, seemingly lost in thought. "And you're sure?"

"Positive," I tell him.

His eyes meet mine again, searching. And then he swiftly exits the truck.

I stare after him for a beat before jumping into action. "Jackson," I hiss, shutting my door and rounding the vehicle.

He tugs the front door of the bar open, disappearing between the giant barrel planters. I jog to catch up.

When I get inside The Barrel, I spot Virginia first. She's sitting at a table in the center of the room, posture stiff and one leg crossed over the other. Her eyes soften when they reach me, but it's clear she's not happy. My gaze shifts to Nicholas next. He stands quickly as Jackson and I approach, his eyes sweeping past Jackson and landing on me. He looks happy to see me, and, honestly, it catches me off guard.

Jackson reaches the table first, coming to a stop a couple feet away from my ex. I catch up a second later, huffing a breath.

"Ashley," Nicholas says, giving me an almost apologetic smile. "Sorry for turning up like this, but I need to talk to you."

Jackson shifts a little, drawing Nicholas's gaze.

"Uh," my ex says, clearly thrown by the extra company. Even so, he holds out his hand politely. "Nicholas Murphy. Sorry, but who are you?"

Jackson wraps his arm around me, ignoring Nicholas's outstretched hand. With his fingers curled against my hip in a possessive hold, he declares, easy as can be, "I'm Ash's partner."

Nicholas's eyes widen. *Virginia's* eyes widen. In fact, the only one of us who doesn't look gobsmacked is Jackson himself. He's staring my ex down evenly, as if he didn't just drop a bomb inside the room.

Holy freaking shit.

My grin is slow but steady as I turn to face my ex. "Yeah. What he said."

Chapter 14

JACKSON

The tension inside the bar is rife, the silence heavy before Nicholas utters, "Partner?"

"What are you doing here, Nicholas?" Ash asks, ignoring his ex's question and curling his hand over the top of my own.

My heart is pounding so heavily I can hear it in my ears.

Nicholas's arm falls back to his side, his eyes swinging between me and Ash. Finally, he focuses his attention Ash's way. "Like I said, I need to talk to you."

"Okay," Ash says slowly. "So talk."

The guy looks Virginia's way, like maybe she might rescue him. But she doesn't move a muscle, her face a blank mask. Looking back at Ash, he says, "Could we go somewhere private?"

"We can talk here," Ash says, giving my fingers a quick squeeze before he heads toward the table.

I quickly follow, grabbing the seat next to him as Virginia stands. "I'll grab drinks," she says, walking off.

Slowly, Nicholas retakes his seat, angling his chair Ash's way. "You left quickly," he says.

I nearly wince. Strike one for the ex. Starting off with an accusation.

Ash stiffens next to me, and I give the back of his neck a squeeze, fingers sifting through the soft hair at his nape. There's a distant part of me wondering what in the hell it is I'm doing, but the voice is easily ignored.

"That was my choice to make," Ash answers calmly.

"But we didn't get a chance to talk things through," Nicholas responds, placing his palm flat on the table, almost like an offering. His eyes flit to me again before he says, voice low, "Does he have to be here?"

Ash's lips tip up the tiniest bit, his smile sharper than usual. "You can ask him to leave if you want. I don't control him."

Nicholas's eyes flick to me. "Could you give us some privacy, please?"

"No thanks," I answer.

Ash huffs a laugh beside me as Nicholas frowns.

"Nick," Ash says before making a soft sound and starting again. "Nicholas, I suggest you say what you came here to. I'm here. I'm listening. But I'm not feeling very patient."

Nicholas lets out a breath. "I want you to come home."

My hand flexes against the back of Ash's neck.

"It's not my home," Ash answers. "And I'm sorry if you're having second thoughts, but I'm not. We're done."

"Just like that?"

"There was no *just* about it," Ash says, voice taking on a flintier edge. "We were roommates, Nick. For a long time. Do you even remember the last time we had sex?"

Nicholas's face shutters, and he sits back in his seat, tension lining his frame.

"I'm sorry. That wasn't meant to be a criticism," Ash says softly, letting out a sigh and setting his elbows on the table. I shift my hand down to his lower back, not wanting to let go. "It's not about sex. There was no intimacy left between us, and you know it."

"So—what?" Nicholas says, tone harsh. "You just ran and jumped into someone else's bed?"

"Don't," Ash replies, his voice surprisingly calm. "We were broken up, and this"—he motions between him and me—"has nothing to do with *us*. Don't try to twist this around on me. You had your chance to ask me to stay, and you didn't."

"Would you have if I'd asked?"

"No," Ash answers simply.

I release a breath.

Nicholas looks off to the side of the bar, where a row of saddles are hung up along the wall as coat hooks. His jaw is tense, and I don't know him well enough to tell if his expression is one of stubbornness or resignation.

Virginia takes that moment to return, setting four glasses with a finger each of what I assume to be whiskey down on the table before reclaiming her seat. She toys with her glass, looking around at the rest of us.

"What's really going on here?" Ash asks, breaking the silence. "This isn't like you, coming all this way just because I didn't pick up the phone."

"You can be impulsive, but I can't?" Nicholas says, grabbing his glass. He sniffs the contents before downing it, trying to contain his small wince.

"Fair enough," Ash mutters.

"I miss you," his ex says roughly, setting his glass down with a clunk and staring resolutely at Ash. "I miss you, Ashley. The house is so...*empty* without you there."

Virginia and I exchange a glance, and I do my best not to jump in—*again*—knowing I've already overstepped. As it turns out, I don't have to do a thing. Of course Ash is perfectly capable of defending himself.

"I'm not a couch or a placeholder to keep your loneliness at bay," he says seriously. "If you want company, adopt a pet."

"I didn't mean—"

"You did," Ash says. "You always liked being needed, Nicholas, and there's nothing wrong with that. But I'm not your boyfriend anymore, or your patient, or your...your houseplant. I'm not *yours*, period."

Nicholas heaves a breath, but Ash goes on.

"Look, I'm sorry you came all this way, but nothing has changed for me. We're done, and I'm not coming back."

There's a prolonged pause before Nicholas seems to deflate. Ash sits back, too, leaning into my touch.

"I might stick around a while," Nicholas says, making me tense.

Ash only chuckles. "You always did want to vacation in the mountains. You're overdue."

Nicholas nods tiredly, wiping his hand down his face. "Yeah. This is the first time in two years I've taken time off. I assume there's a hotel in this town?"

"Right down the street," Virginia answers tightly, shooting Ash a look. He doesn't seem to notice.

Nicholas stands, hesitating. "I guess...I'll see you later then?"

Ash smiles a little sadly. "Take care, Nick."

He nods, eyes flicking to me once before he walks off. The door closes slowly in his wake, and then Virginia spins Ash's way.

"Really?" she says. "Inviting him to stay?"

"I didn't *invite* him," Ash replies, practically slumping against the table. "Telling him to get lost wasn't going to accomplish anything, Ginnie. Whatever he's doing here, it's not about me. Not really."

"Uh," Virginia says slowly. "Did you miss the part where he said he misses you and wants you back?"

Ash shakes his head, picking up his glass of whiskey and taking a small sip. "He doesn't. Something else is going on. Maybe *he's* the one having a midlife crisis."

Virginia clicks her tongue. "Well, I sure as shit hope you're right, baby boy. 'Cause otherwise, I'm pretty sure Jackson here will be showing him the door. Likely with his boot."

I try to temper my lingering scowl, but by Ash's huff of laughter, I don't think I managed it.

"Yeah, about that," Ash says, turning in his chair to face me. He wings up an eyebrow. "Partner?"

"And on that note," Virginia sing-songs, standing swiftly and grabbing her and Nicholas's empty glasses, "I'll just be, uh...watering the flowers."

She walks off, her heels clacking against the hardwood floor, and Ash waits. I reclaim my arm, rubbing my hands on the tops of my thighs.

"Yeah," I say, voice a bit gruff. "Uh. Sorry."

His eyebrow lifts higher. "Sorry?"

"About the, uh..."

"The dick-measuring contest you had with my ex?" he fills in.

"I didn't—"

"Jackson, you practically whipped it out and pissed on me."

I groan, but *fuck*, he's not even wrong. "I just thought... I don't know what I was thinking. Like I said, sorry."

"I never asked you to apologize," Ash says, downing the rest of his drink before setting his glass on the table.

"But—"

I pull in a breath as Ash shifts, bringing us closer. He takes hold of my jaw, his fingers stroking lightly over my beard hairs. "I liked it, Jack," he says, gaze holding mine, brazen and clear. "If we weren't in public, I'd show you just how much."

My breath hitches, and Ash's lips curl into a smile. He lets me go as Virginia walks back into the room.

"Do I need to water more flowers?" she asks bluntly.

Ash huffs a laugh. "What would you say to lunch, Ginnie? Jackson's treat."

"Well," Virginia says, hazel eyes swinging my way. "I'd say lead the way, cowboy."

It's midafternoon by the time Ash and I get back to the ranch. I pull the truck to a stop, tug up the parking brake, and wait, not sure what to expect now that we're finally alone.

For Ash to dress me down?

For him to jump me?

Neither happens. He hops out of the truck and looks at me expectantly. I follow him out of the vehicle, boots kicking up dirt.

"You have a few minutes?" he asks.

Technically, there's a lot I need to do today: check in with my weekend crew, assess a damaged portion of fence one of the ranchers noticed, and order some new machinery for the milking barn. But I nod, and Ash smiles in response.

We walk in silence for a minute, heading along the dirt road that leads to the petting farm.

Finally, Ash says, "Ginnie likes you, you know."

I grunt. "'Cause I know what she's capable of."

He stutters a step, looking at me with wide eyes. "What? She's not *violent*."

"No," I say with a scoff. "That's not what I meant. I don't know her like you do, of course. We were never close. But we grew up together. Went to school together, even though I graduated...what? Five years ahead of her?"

Ash nods, looking at me curiously, and I go on.

"I've seen folks underestimate your friend," I tell him. "Guys or, heck, even teachers, just because she's small and a woman. Virginia is only harsh to the folks who don't show her the respect she deserves. The respect *anyone* does. I'm not that foolish. Hence, we get along just fine."

Ash huffs a breath, shaking his head as we come to a stop in front of the petting farm. He kicks a hip against the fence and crosses his arms loosely, peering at me in a way that makes me feel like I'm under a microscope.

"Just when I think you can't surprise me any more, you go and say something like that," he says, blonde hair blowing gently in the breeze. It falls in front of his eyes, and he swipes it back, nimble fingers tucking the strands away behind his ear.

I clear my throat, pulse heavy. "I'm not *actually* an asshole."

"Never thought you were," he says easily. "But a few weeks ago, you would have brushed off my comment about Ginnie liking you, probably grumbling all the while. You wouldn't have said something so...revealing. Not to me."

He's not wrong, but admitting I've...*softened* toward him isn't an easy thing to do. So I lean my elbows on the fence and watch the families inside the petting farm enjoy their Sunday afternoon. The goats will be well fed today.

Ash shifts his posture to mimic mine, our elbows brushing. "I was fourteen when I had my first boyfriend," he says, voice quiet enough not to carry. "It wasn't anything serious, obviously. We barely even kissed. But I remember asking my mom how to tell him I liked him. She told me to be patient. To wait for the right time because I have a tendency to come on too strong, and that I might scare him off."

He huffs a small breath, and I glance over at him. There's a half-smile on his face as he watches Snickerdoodle attempting to steal carrots out of a child's hand.

"Coy is not my strong suit, Jack. It never has been, and it never will be. I don't like playing games, either. You called me your partner."

My heart pounds as Ash meets my gaze, unflinching. His pinkie nudges mine, the smallest touch. The biggest.

"You meant it," he says, eyebrows popping up as if amazed. "At least, you wanted it to be true. So I'm telling you I want that, too. I know we're just figuring this out, and we don't have to define anything if you don't want. But... I'm in this, Jack. I'm going to treat you like my partner. Because when I look at you, and when I look around at this place, I don't see temporary. I see what I want my life to be. So I'm warning you, one last time, if you want me to back off, you need to say so. Now."

There's static in my head. A whole lot of noise mixed up with the rushing of wind and the pumping of blood through my veins. There's this man standing in front of me telling me he wants to give this a go. That, out of everywhere he could be traveling, he wants to hang up his hat here. That there's something *here* worth exploring.

I don't know if I have the conscious thought or my body moves before my mind has caught up, but when I find my lips pressed to Ash's, I don't regret it. He makes a small sound against me, his hand coming up to fit to my cheek. It's not a kiss of passion or even one of lust. It's something infinitely more terrifying, and Ash accepts it with ease, his mouth soft, his sigh even softer. I feel fragile as I pull back, stripped down in a way that has never come easy to me.

As if he knows as much, Ash doesn't call attention to it. He simply gives my collar a tug and smiles. "Noted," he says, facing the petting farm again and clearing his throat. "What kind of chickens are those? The ones with the fancy head floofs."

It takes me a moment to recalibrate. "Fancy head floofs?"

"What else would you call them?"

"Feathers," I say flatly.

Ash snorts, smacking me on the chest for reasons unknown. "What are they?"

"Silkies," I answer. "Not very good egg layers, but folks love 'em."

"I can see why. They look soft."

We both watch as a young toddler tries to touch one of the chickens. The chick deftly evades them. Silkies have calmer temperaments than many breeds, and, yes, softer feathers, which makes them good pets. But even the happiest chicken knows to avoid a tottering child.

Ash turns, leaning his back on the fence as he looks in the other direction, off toward the mountains. He lets out a soft sigh before rolling his head my way. "You need to get to work," he says, not a question.

I nod.

"What's your favorite food?"

"My...what?" I ask, thrown.

"Your favorite food," he repeats, a small smile on his face. "Remi likes biscuits. Colton, as he told me—with an entirely straight face, mind you—prefers sausage that's big enough to 'really feel the weight of it on your tongue.'" Ash raises an eyebrow, and I snort. My oblivious, straight brother. "And Lawson is a fan of beef stew because it's Wendy's favorite, which is just the cutest. So how about you?"

It takes me a long moment to answer him. "Rice pudding."

I half expect him to make a joke. Maybe tease me that pudding is a *dessert*, not a *food*. But he doesn't. He only hums. "Rice pudding. Got it. Shall we?"

Feeling all sorts of mixed up in a way I'm not used to, I nod, and the two of us leave the petting farm behind. Ash splits off to head into the main house, and I turn to watch him go. When he disappears through the dining room door, it takes considerable effort to continue on my way toward the milking barn. For once, all I want is to ignore my responsibilities for a little while and do something selfish. Something that involves the man inside the ranch house. The one who grabbed on with both hands when I called him *partner*. The one who looks at home in a pair of brand-new cowboy boots, the mountains a backdrop behind him.

I don't skip work. Not this time.

But I know, in the depth of me, he'd be worth it.

Chapter 15

ASH

It's a damn fine morning.

Rain is falling in steady, fat drops. The temperature is a brisk forty-two degrees Fahrenheit. And Jackson Darling, rugged cowboy of my dreams, is standing just inside the dairy cow field, using an auger to dig a hole for a new fence post.

"Good grief," I mutter to myself, a mug of tea warming my palms as I shamelessly ogle the man before me. He's soaked, his hat doing nothing to keep the rain off his clothes, and even though he's wearing a jacket, the motion of his arms has me mesmerized. It's all too easy to imagine what he'd look like bare. The flex of his muscles. The dark hair dusting his forearms. Not to mention what those arms could do to *me*.

"Always had a strong work ethic, that one," Hank says, startling me as he appears at the edge of the deck. He walks over, no beekeeper's hat on today.

"That's one word for it," I agree. *Strong.* I mentally add a few more. *Handsome. Sexy.*

Mine.

The thought makes me shiver.

"Mind if I join you?" Hank asks, pulling my thoughts to the present.

"Of course not," I tell him. "It's your home, after all."

"Yep," he grunts, taking a seat. "But Marigold is always reminding me folks have bubbles. And it's not polite to burst one without asking."

I huff a laugh. I knew I loved that woman. "Well, I'm happy for the company."

He hums. I jolt when he shouts, "What're you doing?"

Jackson looks up, the brim of his hat nearly obscuring his eyes. "What does it look like?" he yells back.

"Looks like you're drowning," Hank calls.

Jackson shakes his head. His mouth continues to move like he's saying something to himself, and my lips quirk in amusement. "Fixing the fence," he finally shouts.

"Couldn't wait?" Hank responds.

Jackson stands fully upright, one hand on the auger, the other on his hip. "You wanna go chasing the dairy girls down the street when they get loose?"

Hank makes a *pft* sound and waves his hand through the air. The next second, Jackson does the same, and I bust out laughing. Jackson goes back to work, twisting the auger with a little more intensity than he was before.

"Stubborn," Hank says. "No clue where he got it from."

I keep my guess to myself.

"Was that rice pudding I saw setting in the fridge?" the older man asks.

I raise an eyebrow. "You didn't get into it, did you?"

"'Course not," he says with a scoff. "I know how to be patient." After a second, he adds, "It's Jackson's favorite, you know."

Oh, I know.

"His ma used to make it when he got sick. Don't ask me why," Hank goes on. "Lord knows what good cold rice is gonna do. But I swear that boy would feign illness just to get some of that rice pudding."

My heart clenches as I watch Jackson pull the auger out of the dirt. It's all too easy to imagine him as a young boy, playing in the rain, maybe, or at home, sick in his bed.

"It's not always easy to ask for the things we want," I say quietly.

Hank makes a soft sound at that. "Suppose not." With a grunt, the elder Mr. Darling stands. "I'll look forward to that pudding at dinnertime."

I give him a nod, and he heads off around the house. Sipping my tea, I watch Jackson, my mind chasing fantasies until it's time to start lunch.

The ranchers are all wet and dirty as they file into the dining room. I add a big carafe of hot cider to the table, hoping, in addition to the beef-and-lentil soup, it'll help warm their bones. Jackson is one of the last through the doors, his jeans muddy and hat dripping water onto the floor. He gives me a hint of a smile that makes my stomach swoop before he takes a seat across from me.

From further inside the house, a door opens and then slams shut. Colton's voice follows. "There's gotta be something I can do. It's *slander*."

"It's not," Remi says evenly, his voice quieter. Most of the ranchers are occupied with their own conversations, but my ears stay with the Darling brothers as Remi adds, "He didn't say anything bad about you outright."

The two come into the room, Colton snagging a piece of bread off the table as he passes on the way to an empty seat.

"He sure as heck implied it," he says, tucking the bread into his mouth and pulling a newspaper clipping from his pocket. He removes the bread to read, "'If you want the royal treatment, go King. Prime shoeing, compassionate handling, and fair prices. King Farrier Service. Better than the rest.'"

Colton looks around at me and his brothers, waiting for a reaction.

"That's not slander," Jackson says, clearly having heard the beginning of the conversation, same as me.

"The heck it isn't," Colton shoots back, crumpling the clipping in his hasty attempt to fold it back up. He tries again, smoothing the paper before folding it more carefully and slipping it into his pocket. "He implied my services are bad!"

"Eh," Remi hedges.

"I can't believe this," Colton mutters, plunking into his seat and grabbing some more bread. He drops it on his plate as he motions for the soup to be passed. "Of all the people to take his side."

"We're not taking his side," Jackson says. "We know you're the best farrier 'round these parts, Colt."

"I am," Colton says, tucking into his soup. "No one shods better than me."

I choke on my bite of food, coughing roughly.

"All right?" Ira asks, patting my back.

I nod and manage to croak, "Good."

Jackson eyes me in concern, but I wave it off.

"Fine," I say again. "Um...shod?"

"Shoe a horse," Remi fills in, lips quirked.

Right.

Colton grumbles into his soup about *Noah fucking King* as Jackson asks Remi if the Silkies are staying dry enough. Apparently, that's a concern for the breed of chickens.

As the brothers chat, my eyes stray to Jackson. It's clear he's close to his family. Protective of them, even. It's something I noticed right away, but that impression has only strengthened over time.

I'm close to my mom, too, but not in the same way. We've never been in each other's pockets, never caught up over nightly dinners together or had a large family to call our own. It's not something I thought I missed, but sitting here with the Darlings, with *Jackson*, I find myself not wanting to let this go.

When the lunch crowd disperses, I start clearing the table. I have the process down to an art now: rinsing the dishes and cutlery, loading up the dishwasher for its second run of the day, storing leftovers in the fridge, and then handwashing the bigger serving dishes and other awkwardly sized items that don't fit in the automatic wash. I fall right into the rhythm of it, humming one of my favorite Johnny Cash covers, my mind wandering as I work.

Which is why, when hands bracket my hips, I nearly jump out of my skin, not having heard anyone approach.

"Jesus," I mutter, letting my shoulders relax as Jackson's familiar body presses to mine. "Do you like scaring me, Jack?"

"Mm," he rumbles, his lips brushing the side of my head. My pulse jumps right back up. "Wasn't trying to scare you."

"What were you trying to do?" I ask, setting the final dish aside and rinsing the soap bubbles off my hands.

He lets out a breath that ruffles my hair, his crotch nudging my ass. "Dunno."

My lips twitch. *Among other things*. "Was my sitting in a chair and watching you work all morning such a turn-on that you simply couldn't resist coming and feeling me up?" I ask.

"You always turn me on," he answers.

Well, fuck.

Blowing out a breath, I shut off the tap and spin inside the cage of Jackson's arms. He's still damp, so I don't feel too bad about grabbing his ass with my wet hands and bringing us flush together. "Would you show me later?"

He groans so quietly I almost miss it.

"I hope that's a yes, Jackson Darling," I all but whisper. "But if it's not, that's okay, too. I have a hand of my own and the memory of you digging a post hole to keep me company. I'm sure it'd be more than enough to—"

I don't get any more out before Jackson's mouth is on my own. He groans again, louder this time, almost tortured, as he kisses me. His hands find their way into my hair, holding tight. I simply melt. He tastes like rain and apple cider, and he smells a little bit like dirt. I think it might be my new favorite combination.

Jackson isn't tentative as our mouths dance, not this time. He's direct, and he's uninhibited in a way I think he'd be embarrassed about if he had enough thought left to realize exactly how he's kissing me inside his family's kitchen. But considering I can't get a word in edgewise, I don't bother bringing it up. I let him pull me under, my cock hardening against his hip as he pushes me back into the countertop.

When I can finally manage a breath, I murmur his name, a small, "*Jack,*" stolen from my lips like the breath he's stolen from my lungs. He likes that. He dives back in, his mouth parting my own, his short beard hairs bristling my skin as he angles my head back for easier access. Something clatters to the floor—tongs, I think—as I reach back to steady myself. My other hand grips his jeans tight, fingers indenting into the meat of his ass as I try to pull him closer or—*fuck*—encourage him to get me off right here in the kitchen, maybe?

I'm about to suggest that very thing when a long, *"Oooh,"* pierces the air. Jackson jumps, dislodging my grip as he spins toward Colton, who's standing in the doorway with a grin.

"Christ," Jackson grumbles. "Fuck off."

"Getting frisky in the kitchen," Colton says, completely unperturbed by his brother's attitude. "Look at you, man. I'm impressed."

Colton runs off as Jackson takes a step forward, a wise decision on his part. Jackson heaves out a sigh. "He's such a shit."

I rub the back of my hand over my mouth. "Maybe. But he loves you."

Loudly, Jackson says, "A good brother would have just walked past without interrupting."

Colton laughs from elsewhere in the house, and I snort.

"Maybe it was for the best," I admit, grabbing the tongs off the ground and wincing when a muscle in my back pulls tight. "I was about to ask you to show me what else your tongue can do. Although I already know the answer to that, don't I? And it's one I like a lot."

Jackson rubs his neck, back to being adorably flustered. My chest feels almost unbearably hot at the sight, and all I want is to kiss him again. To kiss him and never, ever stop. Instead, I take pity on the man.

"Don't worry about your brother," I tell him seriously. "And for the record"—Jackson's huff has me smirking— "that kiss was well worth being caught. I'd do it again in a heartbeat."

His gaze stays on me, blue eyes bright and assessing. I'm not expecting it when he steps in close, hands almost tenderly brushing my hair back before anchoring in the strands. My breath catches when he kisses me again. Lightly. Softly. He pulls back but doesn't leave, not entirely. His nose rests alongside mine for a moment, as if he's breathing me in, and then he lets go.

Hell. The things he says without words.

Jackson clears his throat. "What were you humming when I came in here?"

It takes me a second to remember. "Oh, uh, 'I Won't Back Down.' Why?"

He shrugs, a small movement. "No reason."

He makes to leave, but I snag his jacket with the tongs. "Hold up. Where are you going?"

"Back to work," he says, looking down at the utensil. "You'll probably wanna wash those again."

"I will," I say. "Am I going to see you later?"

"I'd expect so," he says, brow furrowed.

I bite my tongue. "No, am I going to *see* you?"

Luckily, I don't have to spell it out further. Jackson shifts, eyes pinging to my lips briefly. "You wanna come over?"

"Yes. Are you inviting me?"

"Yes," he answers, voice low.

I grin, and his eyes drop to my mouth again. "Fuck, Jack, you better get out of here before this kitchen sees some real action."

"I was trying," he says, pointedly eyeing the tongs again. "But somebody stopped me."

I snort, letting him go. "Get," I say, pulling out my inner cowboy. "I'll see you at dinner."

Jackson grunts, taking a step before stopping. "It was worth it to me, too. Just...for the record."

I can hardly contain my grin. "That record keeps growing. Speaking of..."

"Oh boy."

"You never did answer my question about how you like to...*ride*."

Jackson rubs his temples, but I swear he's smiling behind his palm.

"So?"

"Nope," he says, spinning on his heel and heading out the door. "I'm not answering that. I've got work to do."

"Oh, come on!" I call, following after him. "Just give me a little something, please? Top? Side? With a crop?"

"Jesus Christ," he grumbles.

"Do you like it rough, like Shorty?"

"*Ash*."

"What?" I ask, laughing. "It's a simple question."

"There ain't no *simple* when it comes to you," he says, stopping abruptly and spinning toward me. "*Simple* is expected. *Simple* is easy and boring and routine. You are none of those things. And I can't answer your question because, frankly, I don't know how in the hell I'm supposed to choose. I'm pretty sure I'd like anything and everything with you. So no, it's not simple. Not in the goddamn least."

With that, Jackson hauls the door open and stomps out of the room. I stare after him, my smile hurting my cheeks.

"See you later, darlin'," I shout.

He grunts, the sound nearly swallowed by the rain. My pulse joins the pitter-patter.

I'm way past trouble when it comes to Jackson Darling.

Chapter 16

JACKSON

When I get back to the ranch house, I'm fully prepared to keep up my huffing and puffing, if for no other reason than on principle alone. But the moment I step inside the dining room, boots soaked and hair dripping onto the scuffed hardwood floor, I stop dead. Because there, sitting in my mom's nice white porcelain serving dish on the center of the table, is something unmistakable.

Rice pudding.

He made me goddamn *rice pudding.*

All my feigned anger floats away like dandelion fluff, my insides left bared. I feel like a child again, stripped down to nothing but pure, aching emotions and that certainty kids possess that something big and grand and exciting is waiting just out of reach. Like all you have to do is go find it.

I think I just might have found it.

"Son. Gonna join us?"

My dad's voice breaks through my reverie, and I nod in a jerk, setting my hat on the back of my chair before sitting. Ash isn't in the room yet.

"How 'bout this weather?" my dad says conversationally, cutting into his chicken as I spoon myself some roasted potatoes. It's still pouring out, the rain coming down in a dreary sheet.

"It's rain," my mom replies, her tone fondly exasperated. "What's so special about it?"

"It's a lot of rain," my dad says. "Heard there was a bit of flooding on the roads in town. This keeps up, and we could see mudslides."

My mom hums, but my attention slips to Ash as he comes through the doorway, jugs of water in hand. My gaze sweeps over him, from the sure way he walks to the strong lines of his shoulders and arms. The dark blonde hair curling behind his ear. The small lift of his lips as his eyes catch mine from across the table.

The stutter in my chest doesn't even surprise me anymore.

Ash sets down the water and takes a seat. He talks to Colleen about what the ranchers do in the winter, which is exactly what we do now. He asks Lawson how Wendy is. He even chats with my dad about the new smoker he got for his beehive.

All the while, I watch Ash and the rice pudding, which sits untouched at the center of the table. When I can't stand it anymore, I grab a small ramekin and dish some up. The texture is perfect: creamy enough it spreads some but not too thin that it loses all shape. I bring a spoonful to my mouth, and my eyes slip shut. It's sweet, and the rice has bite, and I swear he must have added something special because there's a hint of a spice I've never tasted in rice pudding before. But the recipe, otherwise, is the same one my mother always used; I'm sure of it.

When my eyes flutter open, I find Ash watching me.

"So, uh..." Colton says, trying to catch my eye from across the table. He leans so far over Ash's lips twitch in amusement. "You gonna share or what?"

Not breaking Ash's gaze, I pass the serving dish to my brother.

"Sweet," he says. And then, "You sick or something? Why're we having rice pudding?"

Ash is the first to break, his mouth turning into a wide grin. I huff my own laugh, shaking my head as I finish my dessert.

"Oh, he's fit as a fiddle," my mom says. "Although I wouldn't be surprised if he spends some time in bed tonight."

The clatter of my spoon against the ramekin is loud. "Jesus. *Ma.*"

"What?" Colton says, looking between us. "I don't get it."

At least the woman waited until I was done eating to try and ruin my appetite. She simply smiles to herself as I push out of my seat, wondering if it's too late to trade the lot of them in. Ash's eyes are practically twinkling as he watches me walk away.

"Ridiculous," I mutter to myself, swinging by the kitchen. I chug a glass of water before looking around at the countertops, trying to spot an errant spice bottle. Was it nutmeg? Cloves?

"Looking for something?" Ash asks, arms crossed as he stands in the doorway.

"What'd you put in it?"

His smile widens. "Secret."

I grunt.

He kicks off the doorframe, stepping closer. "Am I still coming over tonight?"

"Invited you, didn't I?"

He licks his lips, head shaking back and forth as he says, "Jackson Darling, you sure know how to make a guy swoon."

I refrain from rolling my eyes. "C'mere."

"Nuh-uh," he says, backing away when I reach for him. "If I do that, I'm going to kiss you again. And I'm not going to want to stop."

"And that's a problem?" I say gruffly.

The grin he gives me is so damn familiar it sets off my heart again. "If I *kiss* you," he says, still edging toward the hall, "I'm going to want to do other things to you. So no, it'll have to wait."

"When are you coming over?" I ask, my voice too damn hoarse.

"After I clean up," he answers, the many possible meanings of that setting my thoughts racing. "Better hurry home, Jack. Don't keep me waiting."

With that, Ash is out the door, and I wheel around, doing my part of the nightly cleanup as fast as I possibly can. Once the counters are spotless, I book it, passing Colton and his stacked pile of plates in the hall.

"Hey," my brother says, smile slipping as I hurry past. "Where are you—"

"Gotta go," I answer, not slowing. I pull open the front door, stomp down the porch stairs, and race home.

I shower as quickly as I can without neglecting any part of my hygiene. My pulse is firing as my hand passes over my dick, not lingering, but it doesn't seem to matter. I perk right up, all the *want* I've been trying to keep at bay taking off like a herd of goddamn horses. I give myself a slow stroke, just one, before groaning and dropping my hand.

When I jump out of the shower, I wrap a towel around my waist and check the front door. No Ash. I head back to my bedroom, drying myself on the way. My dick isn't fond of being corralled, but I tug on boxer briefs and jeans all the same, telling it to behave. I pull on a shirt next. Take it off. Put it back on again, not wanting to be too presumptuous.

Christ.

I know what this is. Why Ash is coming. The man is not subtle, and I'd be lying if I said I didn't appreciate that fact.

But it's been a long damn time since I've had anyone in my bed. Since I've *wanted* somebody there.

It's not a small thing. Not to me.

The knock at the door has me jumping. I drag my hands through my hair, over my short beard, and set off for the front of the house. My pulse is heavy, each *th-thump* a dense beat propelling me forward. Remarkably, my hand is steady as I reach for the door.

Ash's smiling face greets me, the rain still falling down behind him. "Hey," he says, a coy lilt to his words. "You made it. Hope I'm not too—"

I drag him inside the house, silencing his *early* with my mouth. He utters a *fuck*, but he kicks the door shut, him pushing or me pulling, maybe both. We end up stumbling back onto the couch, me hitting first, Ash following me down. He straddles my lap like he did all those weeks ago in my kitchen, the weight of him solid and sure. His lips never leave mine. They kiss and kiss and *kiss*, his hair tickling my cheekbones, his hands on the cushions above my shoulders. I tug him in closer, the denim beneath my fingertips rough, the bite of his teeth on my lip more so.

"Jack," he breathes, grinding down on my lap.

I know. I *know*.

I slide my hand down the back of Ash's jeans, and he groans. There's not enough space, and my grip is hard, but he doesn't seem to care. His breath hits my lips, his mouth so damn smooth and inviting I can't help but remember the way those lips felt wrapped around my cock. Ash rolls his hips, drawing a moan from the both of us. I hang onto the meat of his ass, wanting... Needing...

"What do you want, Jack?" Ash asks, breaking from my lips to kiss down my neck. My head falls back against the couch as his hand trails down my abdomen, fingers skating over my shirt before slipping under the material. My stomach clenches under his fingertips, and he makes an appreciative noise, palm smoothing up my stomach, lifting my shirt.

"Do you..." I get out before Ash nips the tendon at the bend of my shoulder and neck.

"Do I what?"

His nails skim down my stomach, and I buck upwards. Ash huffs an airy laugh as I grunt, the heft of him, the pressure against my lap making it impossible to think.

"Do I what, Jack?" he asks again, almost teasing, but there's too much heat in his words to sound remotely cruel. And he never would be. I don't think he's capable.

I sink my hand into his hair, nearly groaning from the feel alone. He stills, his hips stalling, his lips pressed featherlight to my neck.

"Do you like being rimmed?" I ask, voice rough.

He's motionless for all of a second before he sags with a moaning sort of laugh. He nips my neck again before huffing, "Yeah, Jack. I like it."

"Do you need—"

"Squeaky clean," he answers, reading my thoughts.

I tug his head back, meeting his gaze. The blue is stormy, beautiful and open. "I want you on my bed," I tell him. "Face down."

His lips part, his small inhalation audible.

"I want to eat you out until you come. And then I want to fuck you until you come again."

Ash's eyes slip shut, his groan a low rumble. "Jesus, Jack. You're gonna kill me. I had no clue you had such a dirty tongue."

"Lemme show you," I say, licking up the column of his neck.

He chuckles hoarsely, easing back. I let him go, releasing his hair and pulling my hand from within his jeans as he climbs off the couch. His pants are tented, his shirt rumpled and hair in disarray. Without waiting, he rounds the couch and heads down the hall. "You coming?"

I'm off the couch and after him in no time. Ash disappears into my room just ahead of me. When I get to the doorway, I stop still.

He's pulling off his shirt, arms raised and the long line of his torso on display. The fabric clears his head, and he drops it to the floor. He eyes me as he unzips his jeans.

"This okay?" he asks, the button going next. "Or did you want me to wait?"

I shake my head, voice raspy. "Keep going."

He eases his jeans down his legs, his cock making its presence known. It juts out against the fabric of his briefs, and my breathing turns uneven. He kicks off his jeans, holds my eye, and eases down his briefs.

I let out a breath as he stands, nude, in front of my bed. He shoots me another glance, gauging my reaction maybe, before grabbing the edge of the comforter and flinging it aside.

"Is there where you want me?" he asks, knowing damn well it is.

I nod in a jerk, and he smiles, all that smooth skin and muscle on display as he crawls, slowly, onto my mattress. It feels as if my chest is going to burst, but when Ash's mouth twists into something playful, I'm certain the implosion is imminent. He stretches his arms out, bowing low until his cheek is pressed to the sheets, his back arched, his ass high in the air.

"Like this?" he asks, holding my gaze.

I had the wind knocked out of me once. I was fifteen, riding along the base of the mountains with a mare who was always a bit flighty. A fox raced out in front of us on the trail, and the mare spooked, rearing up and depositing me unceremoniously onto the ground.

I had lain there in the dirt, staring up at the cloudy sky and the mountains towering beside me, my chest so tight I thought I was dying. And then, with a shuddering burst, my lungs reinflated. Relief. Pain. Bliss.

There haven't been many times in my life when I've felt utterly struck. Unable to breathe.

But with Ash's cheek pressed to my bed, his gaze holding mine and every piece of him bared easily and without reservation, I find myself struggling for air. It's a tight, hot thing in my chest, the pain of it welcome, the relief and bliss nearly bringing me to my knees.

It's *possibility*, that's what it is. It's the chance at something I long assumed gone. Extinguished.

I didn't think I'd want this again. But *fuck*, how I want it. *Him.*

It's him I want.

My legs are steady as I walk forward, and Ash tracks me with his eyes. He makes a small sound of surprise when I stop beside the top of the bed and grab my pillows. I ease them under his hips before climbing behind him and skating my hand over the small of his back. When I give him a gentle push, he takes the hint, settling his weight onto the pillows.

"I want you comfortable," I tell him, my body buzzing as I run my fingertips along the swell of his ass. "'Cause I'm gonna take my time."

"Fucking hell, Jack," he pants.

"Mm."

Ash groans when I skim my fingers down the crease of his ass. He's hairless there. Trimmed neatly along the base of his dick. His balls are shaved smooth, and I pull them into my hand, the backs of my fingers brushing his cock. The sight of it pressed against the pillows has my gut clenching.

"Should have known," Ash says.

I leave a kiss on his ass cheek, running my nose along his skin before doing the same to the other side. "What's that?"

"That you'd"—he huffs a small breath as I lick the top of his ass—"be a giver."

I hum, slowly working my tongue lower.

"Are you going to make me beg?" he asks.

"No," I say, swiping my tongue over his hole once before blowing. "Not make you."

"You'll just enjoy the soundtrack then?" he says, groaning when I flick my tongue. "Please, Jack."

My name, hoarse on his lips, has my eyes slipping shut. Taking hold of his ass, I lean in and drag my tongue over his rim. He lets out a whispery breath, and I do it again and again, wanting to draw more of those sounds out of his throat. He goes slack as I work him open, his body pliant and his position keeping him at my disposal.

"Jesus, Jack," he says, voice gravelly as I edge my tongue inside his body. "That's so fucking good."

The praise is simple but searing in its intensity, lighting up the long-darkened corners of my chest. I groan as I work him over harder, desperate to make him feel good. Desperate to make him come for me. My fingertips indent into the meat of his ass as I bury myself between his cheeks, wetting him, licking and flicking, my tongue dragging the most perfect sounds out of the man now humping my pillows.

"*Jack*. I need—*fuck*. Need you in me."

"Am," I say before tonguing him again.

He huffs what might be a laugh. "Your *dick*. You wanted to fuck me, right?"

"After you come," I tell him, slipping a finger inside his body.

Ash lets out a stuttered moan, pushing back against the digit. The glide is smooth, his muscles relaxed, my spit aiding the way. I have to close my eyes at the feel of him, so silky and warm. I nuzzle my nose against his ass cheek as I fuck him with my finger, my dick aching.

"Jack," Ash says, tone trembling, "I'm trying to be patient, but I'm only human. And you feel—*fuck*."

His words dissolve into a moan as I remove my finger and tongue him roughly, pushing myself as deep as I can go.

"Jack, please," he says.

I can't deny him. I tug one of the pillows out of the way and wrap my hand around his cock as Ash transfers his weight to his knees. He pushes back against my mouth, his breath ragged now as I stroke him swiftly.

"Oh God, oh God," tumbles out of his mouth as his legs start to quake. "Gonna—"

"Do it," I say. "I wanna feel you squeeze my tongue."

Ash cries out, pressing back against me as I bury myself in his body. His cock jerks, kicking up as it swells in my fist. And then he's shooting, his body clamping down on my tongue like I asked, muscles reflexively squeezing as his orgasm is dragged out of him. I pull free, licking him in broad strokes, the little jerks and spasms of his body making my chest sing in triumph.

When his cock stops releasing, I bring my cum-coated fingers to his ass, rubbing over his hole before slipping a digit inside. He groans lowly, but I keep my movements light, massaging gently, letting his muscles open back up for me. I slide a second finger in along the first and drop my forehead to the small of Ash's back.

"Did you just..." Ash huffs out a breath, his chest rising and falling. "Did you just... use my cum... as lube... to get your fingers in my ass?"

"Mm," I hum, stroking them slowly.

"You really are... going to wring a second orgasm out of me... aren't you?"

I kiss the base of his tailbone as I press my fingers a little further, seeking, searching...

"Ah, God. *Jack*."

Ash lifts up onto his elbows, looking back at me. His hair is in front of his eyes, like the surf breaking over stormy skies. His cheeks are flushed, his lips red and bitten. The muscles in his back and shoulders are valleys I want to explore with my fingers and tongue. He looks strong. Beautiful. Masculine. Delicate.

"You need to take off your clothes," Ash orders. "Because if you're going to start massaging my prostate like that, I want it to be with your dick. Not your fingers."

I plant my lips against one of the divots at the base of his spine, closing my eyes as I breathe and center myself. Slowly, I slip my fingers out of his body, sticky with his cum.

"Whatever you want, sunshine," I drawl, wiping my hand on the sheets.

Ash's responding laugh is bright and happy and familiar. I'm pretty sure I'd do just about anything to hear it over and over again.

Chapter 17

ASH

Jackson uses the sheet to wipe his face before stepping down off the side of the bed. I nearly groan, the sight stirring something primal in me. It was *my* ass he had his face buried in. *His* spit that was dampening his cheeks and beard.

Maybe that shouldn't be as sexy as it is, but sex is messy, plain and simple. And seeing the evidence being scrubbed against his sheets has me ready to make a mess of Jackson once more.

My dick isn't hard again. *Yet.* But I have no doubt it won't be long before it is.

Jackson tugs his shirt over his head as I settle on my back, the pillow with my cum on it lying beside me. My ass *aches*, all of Jackson's efforts to stretch and loosen me making me all the more eager for his cock. Don't get me wrong; the tongue-fucking was sublime.

But I need him. I need him to fill me. To spill inside my body. I need to see his face when he comes. When he finally unravels.

I've gotten a glimpse tonight of a side of Jackson that he doesn't often show. It was the same that night he knocked on my door and dropped to his knees before me. The eagerness. The desperation in his eyes that left me panting with want.

I think he needs this as much as I do. Needs the connection. Needs to *let go*.

I wanted to see Jackson Darling's stoic control shatter. I wanted to see him break open for me. I just never thought it'd be this sweet.

Jackson's pants fall to the floor, joining his shirt. His cock presses against the front of his underwear until he pulls them down, seemingly content to take his time. His eyes rake over me as he steps out of the material, and mine do the same to him. He's glorious. All hard muscle and tanned skin, his body honed by decades of work and determination and softened just so by time. His eyes are blazing, the blue looking so very bright, the coppery hints in his beard and hair glinting under the lights in his room. Even without the flannel and jeans, he looks roughened, an extension of this land. Of this lifestyle.

A cowboy to his very bones.

"Are you planning on joining me anytime soon?" I ask, giving my cock a slow stroke. It's starting to rally, firming beneath my hand and under Jackson's stare.

He grunts, making a smile twist my lips.

Raising an eyebrow, I plant my heel on the mattress and let my leg fall to the side. Jackson's eyes dip down.

"Am I still wet?" I ask him.

He groans, looking downright pained. "Not wet enough."

"Well?" I goad.

That seems to do the trick. Jackson spurs into action, walking to his end table before climbing onto the bed. He presses my other leg wide, his thumb digging into my thigh as he eyes my ass. My pulse beats a heavy drum as I wait, my hand leisurely pumping myself, my anticipation so palpable I can feel it in my toes.

Jackson flips open the lid on the lube without even looking at it.

"Fuck, you're a sight," I tell him, one arm behind my head to see him better. He's kneeling between my legs, his cock hanging low, hard and so goddamn thick. He ignores it, his focus on me as he brings lubed fingers to my ass. He slips two inside, picking up right where he left off. "*God.*"

"Good?" Jackson all but grunts.

"Darlin', you're so fucking good."

He seems to preen at that, his chest swelling and a nearly imperceptible smile tugging at the corner of his lips. His focus, however, is absolute. He pumps his fingers inside of me, spreading the lube, pressing gently against my rim to open me up.

"It's not going to take much," I tell him, my body already so languid I'm pretty sure he could get his cock in me without trouble.

"What'd I tell you?" Jackson asks, his gaze meeting mine.

"That you want to take your time with me?"

He hums a short confirmation. *Well.* Far be it from me to ruin his fun.

Jackson slips in a third finger, his strokes intentional, not efficient. He picks up my leg, bringing it close and turning his face to kiss my calf. I damn near swoon.

He tucks my leg over his shoulder as his thumb grazes my rim, his fingers rubbing inside of me. His hand trails along the outside of my leg, soothing and exploring, his fingertips on my calf, my ankle, my thigh. All the while, he plays with my ass, seemingly content to do just that—*play.*

"Your favorite color?" I ask.

Jackson's eyes flash to mine. "What?"

"I'm getting to know you," I tell him, wiggling my toes. He takes the hint and resumes fingering me.

"Gray," he answers.

"Liar."

He snorts, twisting his fingers, and *ahh*.

"Red," he says. "Like the mountains at sunset, when everything is hushed and dark and peaceful."

I hum, hand still stroking my cock slowly. Jackson's eyes follow the movement. "I like green," I tell him. "Always have. Maine was a lot of blue. The water, the sky, the crab, even. Here, there's so much green. It's expansive, like air in my lungs."

He looks pensive, and I nearly laugh at the expression because he's fucking my ass with four fingers now. I don't need it, but *fuck* does it feel good.

"I've never heard air described as green before," he finally says.

"No? Well, I've never seen someone exercise such immense control with a raging hard-on before. You ready yet? He sure looks it."

Jackson huffs as I eye his dick pointedly, but he turns his head again, kissing my leg before removing his fingers. He opens a condom without question, which I appreciate. Going without would require a conversation we haven't had. Jackson rolls the condom down his cock with quick movements, adding a decent swipe of lube after. His eyes meet mine again.

"Good?" I ask.

He nods, but still, he doesn't move. I tip my hips up in invitation. He takes a deep breath.

"Jack? Did you want me on my—"

"Like this," he says, cutting me off, his grip on my leg tightening. "I just..."

"Need a second?"

"Mm."

"All right," I say, flexing my toes a couple times. "Is this a quick-draw thing? Because if so, it's fine. If you come right away, I'm sure your tongue can—"

He starts to laugh, the sound so surprising I don't finish my sentence.

"What?" I ask, laughing along with him, that brightness in his eyes as he ducks his face making my chest ache in the best way.

He shakes his head a couple times before easing forward, the motion pressing my leg up against my body, opening me wide. His hand lands beside my shoulder, his face a foot away from mine.

"I'm not emptying my round in .2 seconds," he says, laughter still in his tone. "It's not *that*. It's a *you* thing, Ashley. A me-and-you thing."

My heart thumps painfully, my breath getting lost somewhere on the passage from my mouth to my lungs. Jackson notches his cock against me, the pressure causing me to reflexively bear down.

"It's a good thing," he adds, staring at me, the vulnerability in his eyes more shocking than anything else he's said or done here tonight.

I nod, managing a, "Yeah."

Yeah, it's a good thing. A very good thing.

Yeah, I'm ready for your cock. I've been ready for weeks.

Yeah to all of it.

Jackson presses forward, his eyes shuttering as he slips inside my body. He moves slowly, his hand leaving the base of his cock and anchoring against my leg that's still hooked over his shoulder. His fingers dig in, his lips finding my knee. He leaves another kiss there, the two of us so close his hair nearly brushes my nose.

"Jackson," I groan, the sound a whisper.

He turns his face my way slowly.

"Kiss me while you make me come," I request. Or maybe it's a demand.

Jackson's nostrils flare, his cock seating fully inside my body, hips against my ass. He lets go of my leg, planting his hand on the mattress beside my head, bracketing me on both sides. I'm practically folded in half, but I like it. The way he's pinning me to the bed. How deep he is inside my body.

When his lips touch mine, it's on an inhale. Mine. His. We breathe in, a moment of calm, a beat of stillness. And then Jackson moves.

It's slow at first, a shallow punch of his hips that has the both of us groaning. His beard bristles my face as he sucks my lip into his mouth, his tongue teasing me open the next second as his hips flex again. I find purchase against his side as we move together, my other hand wrapping around his bicep and holding tight. He punches a gasp out of me, one he quickly absorbs, our mouths all but dueling now as Jackson picks up speed, the drag of his cock feeling like heaven. A *fuck* leaves my lips, my heart pounding, the slap of Jackson's hips against my ass a filthy soundtrack over our breaths.

"Harder," I find myself saying. Another demand.

Jackson grunts, falling down to his elbow, the move causing my leg to shift off his shoulder. Our chests brush as he slams into my body. *God*, yes.

"Harder."

He curses, his teeth scraping my lip as he punches into me so hard my cock jerks from the blissful force of it. I lock my feet behind his ass, needing the leverage. My hands find the headboard, holding on, holding steady.

"Come on, Jackson," I groan, the drag of his dick lighting me up. "I'm not gonna break."

God, the near snarl he lets out. He lifts his head, clocking my expression, finding...I don't know what. And then his lips lock with mine, his hand threads into my hair, and he *fucks* me. My breath beats out of me in rhythmic puffs, Jackson's abs grinding against my cock as he ruts into me so hard the bed creaks. So hard my balls draw up. My entire body is wound tight, the pace fast and so brutally perfect I'm left no choice but to keep climbing. I must be strangling his cock with the way my muscles have tightened, and his groan confirms it.

"Gonna... come," I pant out.

He shifts in a way that hits me just right, does it again, and I'm gone. My cock jerks against Jackson's stomach, the orgasm ruthless in the way it robs me of control. My breath stutters, my muscles lock, and I come and *come*, my ears ringing with the force of it. Jackson's hips stutter, too, his pace breaking. He grinds against me, his palm slapping the side of my ass as he grabs my hip, as if he could somehow push himself deeper. He can't. He's in me to the root, his cock flexing as he empties on a groan.

My body continues to ping and buzz as my ears slowly stop ringing. I feel damn near electrocuted, my entire being sore but utterly satisfied as Jackson's weight keeps me rooted in place. The both of us are breathing heavily, his hand rubbing a slow circle against my hip now, his breath fanning over my collarbone. He feels good, *perfect*, and I inhale the scent of him, trying to store it away for later.

Man. Earth. Rain, heavy in my lungs, soothing.

"You smell like this place," I say softly, another small aftershock making me constrict around his cock.

Jackson untucks his face from my neck, blinking his eyes slowly. "Yeah? And what's that smell like?"

Home.

The thought is immediate. Strong. But I don't voice it, unsure if Jackson would even believe me.

"Horses," I answer instead.

He stares at me for the longest beat before his lips twitch. He looks relaxed. Carefree. If a good fuck is all he needs to unwind now and again, I'd be happy to oblige. *More than happy.*

Jackson shakes his head, muttering, "Impossible man," as he leans back. The fondness in his voice makes it difficult to mourn the loss of his cock as he pulls out of me. But even still, I wince slightly, the sudden cold and lack of fullness my least favorite part about anal. Jackson seems to realize. He adds a soft, "Sorry," placing a kiss on my bent knee as he sits back to dispose of the condom.

"You could always make it up to me," I say, intending to follow up my comment with a joke about kissing it better. But as I lower my arms from their position above my head, I groan instead. *Son of a bitch.*

"All right?" Jackson asks, concern in his eyes.

"Yep," I eke out, my voice tight. *And my shoulders.* Goddamn it.

"You are not," he says, all but huffing the words.

"Just need a minute," I say, laying my arms out to my sides and waiting for the spasms to stop.

Jackson grunts, getting off the bed and walking into the hall. A minute later, he returns with a hand towel.

"I'm probably going to need a shower," I point out. "But thanks, I—"

"Turn over," Jackson says gruffly.

I blink at him. "What now?"

"Turn. Over," he repeats.

Not sure what his intention is, I ease up, wincing again, and flip onto my stomach. Jackson climbs up over my legs, and then something hot is being set across my shoulder blades. The cloth, I realize.

"All right?" he asks, his hands smoothing over the fabric.

"Yeah," I answer weakly.

He grunts, pressing down. His fingers start working the muscles on either side of my spine, and I groan again, the pressure and aching pain exquisite. It's the *good* kind of hurting. The kind that means relief.

My muscles start to relax as Jackson kneads them into submission. When the cloth turns cool, he removes it, continuing to run his hands over my upper back and shoulders. It's so divine I don't ask him to stop.

"A good memory from your childhood?" he asks.

It takes me a minute to understand he's tossing me a get-to-know-you question like I did earlier to him. I hum, letting myself melt into the mattress.

"When I was eleven," I tell him, "my mom took me sailing. My grandpa had a boat, and, before he passed, we'd go out with him sometimes. But that day, it was just me and my mom. I don't remember everything, but I remember a few details. My mom's blue-and-white boat shoes. Her laughing as we caught a particularly high wake, the boat rocking as if we were far out at sea. I remember the little tuna sandwiches she made us, cut into perfect squares."

I ease out a breath, which turns into another groan as Jackson's thumb presses into a particularly sensitive spot near my neck. He massages there gently.

"That was the day I told my mom I had a crush on Mason from homeroom." The memory has a smile tugging at my lips. "She said, 'Oh, yeah? Tell me about him.' It was so...easy. I had just come out, and she made it easy."

Jackson kisses my shoulder, his scruff tickling my skin. "You love her."

"I do," I say on a sigh. "We butt heads sometimes, but my mom has always been there for me. I remind myself of that when her concern turns a little overbearing."

He hums, as if he gets it. I'm sure he does. "I came out when I was nine."

"Yeah?"

He lays kisses across my skin, from one shoulder to the next, sending a little cascade of sparks down my spine. "Mm. My mom was browsing through a wedding magazine while we were waiting for an appointment. Doctor's, I think. She asked which wedding dress I thought was prettiest, and I told her it didn't matter because I'd never be marrying a girl."

He huffs a little, and my lips quirk into a smile. "What'd she say to that?" I ask.

I can practically feel him shaking his head. "She said, 'And what if your future husband wants to wear a dress, Jackson Darling? What then?' She might as well have smacked me upside the head. She *tsked*, and I pointed to the dress I thought was prettiest. Then she gave me a big kiss on the top of my head, and that was that."

I chuckle, turning my face to the side as Jackson runs his thumb and forefinger up the back of my neck, pressing into the tendons there. He does it a few times before brushing my hair out of my face.

"Any better?" he asks.

"Yeah," I breathe. "Loads. Thank you."

He hums, easing back and making room for me to flip over. His eyes run down the dried mess on my torso as I turn.

"Hope you have spare sheets," I tell him. "And another pillow."

He grunts a little as he steps off the bed, the shifting of his ass as he walks away causing me to moan internally. "I'm not a Neanderthal," he calls from the hallway.

I huff a laugh, gingerly stepping down and following him. "No? My ex might disagree."

He groans. "We still on that?"

"Oh, we'll never be off that. *Partner*."

Jackson throws a pillow at me as I round the corner into the hall. I laugh, catching it in midair as he heads toward me, a pile of white linens in his hands. He plucks the pillow from my grasp, sets it, with the sheets, inside his doorway, and then grabs the back of my neck in a loose hold.

"You. Me. Shower," he grunts, tugging me into the bathroom.

I laugh so hard I wheeze, and Jackson's scowl tips into a smile. I don't complain as he proceeds to direct me into the shower with grunts and clipped words. I let Jackson take care of me as we wash up. And once fresh sheets are on the bed, I let him convince me without words to stay.

Chapter 18

JACKSON

"Uh-oh," my biggest nuisance of a brother says, riding up next to me on his horse, Clementine. The pair slows beside me and Starlight, joining our walk along the fence line out in one of the far pastures. The ranch house isn't even visible from here. "Should I be concerned?"

"By what?" I ask, distracted by thoughts of Ash.

Ash in my bed.

Ash's ass high in the air.

The sounds Ash made when he came. *Twice.*

Ash's hair spread across my pillow.

Ash's face as he slept.

Colton snorts. "Your *smile*," he answers. "I think the last time I saw that was when you hid all my underwear out in the horse barn. I was, what...nine?"

"I smile," I defend.

"Uh-huh," he says, sounding incredulous. "You're a regular ray of sunshine."

Sunshine. *Ash.*

"There you go again," Colton says, smacking my shoulder. "What in the hell?"

"I'm allowed to be in a good mood," I say, stopping Starlight to check a length of wire fencing that looks bowed, as if something hefty fell into it.

"Sure, I know that," he says, adding a muttered, "I just didn't know *you* knew that."

Smartass.

I dismount, grabbing a pair of pliers from the saddlebag on Starlight's back. Colton goes on as I twist the wire, making sure the line is taut.

"If it's 'cause of Ashley, I'm glad. Seems like a good guy."

I grunt.

"Has nice...legs, I guess?" my brother says.

I look up slowly.

"Arms?" he tries. "A nice ass? I dunno, what does it for you?"

Shaking my head, I finish tightening the wire before putting the pliers away and zipping up the bag. Starlight barely shifts his weight as I swing up onto his back.

"I'm not discussing my...*Ash's* ass with you," I tell my brother firmly. I'm not even getting into the fact that his ass was far from the first thing I noticed about him. It was those eyes. And his damn smile.

Although that ass...*nope*. I shut those thoughts down.

"What're you even doing out here?" I ask my brother. It's not uncommon for him to fill in around the ranch in addition to his job as a farrier, but I don't recall a reason he'd be out in the pastures today.

Colton simply shrugs. "Haven't had a chance to ride with Clementine in a while."

I nod, understanding that. These horses are more than workers or pets to us. They're family.

Checking the time, I swing Starlight back around. "Needa head back. You coming?"

Colton gives me a grin. One I know all too well. "Race you."

He doesn't give me a chance to respond before he and Clementine are off, the horse tossing her mane as her hooves dig into the grass.

I curse, kicking Starlight into motion after them. "*Ya.*"

A few of the cattle eye us warily as we pass at a breakneck pace. Starlight's head is down, his gait smooth as silk as he gallops swiftly after our competition. My ass is out of the saddle, knees bent and body low, my legs absorbing the shock as I lead Starlight sharply left, heading toward a shortcut. Colton catches sight of me swerving and swears loudly. He course-corrects, a grin on his face as he tries to head me off. He doesn't make it.

Starlight and I are first through the tree line, making it onto the narrow path that's dappled in shade. Colton breaks off, knowing he can't pass me here. He heads through the field, his laughter loud. I shake my head, urging Starlight on faster.

When we break out of the trees, I see Colton off to the right. We're nearly neck and neck, the both of us barreling toward the gate nearest the ranch house. Ira sees us coming and unlatches the big metal swing gates, one after another, since no cattle are near. My brother shoots me a glance, and I know I have only one chance to throw him off his game.

I send a silent apology Ira's way.

"It *is* his ass," I yell. "Best thing I've ever eaten."

Colton's eyes widen, his face drawn in shock. It's enough. The momentary lapse in focus gives me the chance to urge Starlight into a final burst of speed, one Colton doesn't counter fast enough. Me and my horse are first through the gates, dust kicking up around us as we slow to a swift stop.

Starlight bounces his head a few times, breath huffing out as he walks in a tight circle, his steps high and light. I give his neck a pat, praising the old man for putting up with my brother's shenanigans.

Colton comes to an abrupt halt beside us. "You *cheated*."

"Did not."

"Did so. How does that even work? You just..."

I try my best not to laugh, but *Christ*, it looks as if he's attempting string theory. "You've got a tongue. And an ass. I'm sure you could figure it out, one way or another."

I shoot Ira a thank-you as he closes the gates after us. He returns my wave, his lips lifted into a smile.

"None of the women I've been with have been into that," Colton says quietly, brow furrowed. "It feels good?"

"Nuh-uh," I non-answer, giving Starlight a gentle kick toward the stables. "I'm not talking to my brother about ass stuff."

"Aw, c'mon," he whines. "I'm curious."

I raise an eyebrow. "Are you now?"

My question flies right over his head. "Bet Remi would tell me."

"You really wanna hear specifics of our little brother's sex life?"

Colton grimaces. "All right, I see your point."

"Mhm."

He's quiet for a minute. But only until we reach the barn doors. "What's frotting?"

"Jesus fucking *Christ*. You've got Google!"

"You really think I wanna look that up?" he asks, voice getting quieter as I rush on ahead of him. "I might *see* things, Jackson."

Shaking my head, I swing off Starlight's back and lead him over to his stall. We'll be going back out, so I don't bother washing him down yet. But I do take off his gear and give him a quick brush to remove the dirt caked on his legs.

When I step back into the hall, Colton is looking at his phone, his hand partially concealing his eyes.

"Ah, fuck," I mutter, heading to the mini-fridge and grabbing a couple carrots. "Colt."

My brother looks up at me.

Pointedly, I hold up the two carrots before pressing them together from base to tip. I die a little inside as I rub them together. Committed, and wishing I wasn't, I wrap a hand around the root vegetables and give a single jerk.

"Frotting. Got it?" I ask.

He nods, eyes wide.

"Never again," I say adamantly, feeding the carrots through the bars of Starlight's stall. He chomps them down. "And we don't talk about this."

Colton's choked laughter follows me as I trudge out of the horse barn.

My brothers, I swear to God.

Pulling off my hat, I wipe the sweat from my forehead and make my way across the property. Ranching is dirty work, no matter the time of year. Sometimes, it feels as if this place is baked into my pores. I don't mind it, but it does make me wonder what Ash thinks of this lifestyle. He said he enjoys it here, but will that pass? Will the novelty wear off eventually?

I try to ignore the tightness circling my chest, but it's no use. Otto said he'd stay. He didn't.

Ash isn't Otto, I remind myself. And I let Otto go, didn't I? Even as it burned. Even as it cracked and blistered, I let him go.

What does that say about me?

My sullen thoughts come to a halt the moment I reach the petting farm, as do my steps. Ash is inside with Virginia, the pair of them spread out on yoga mats, laughing their heads off as baby goats climb on their backs and legs. Haley, the attendant, has a smile on her face as she watches them.

"Afternoon," I say to her, getting my feet into gear and heading inside the fenced corral.

"Afternoon, boss."

"What's going on here?" I ask, my pulse hopping as Ash falls onto his stomach, his back shaking with laughter.

"Yoga, I guess," Haley says in amusement.

"Jackson," Ash calls, having spotted me. He pushes upright, sitting with his legs in a pretzel and brushing his hair back. "How come you guys don't do goat yoga?"

"Is that...a thing?" I ask, heading his way.

He grins up at me, squinting against the sun. I nearly lose my breath just looking at him. "People love it," he says, absently scratching the head of a nearby goat. "Do you have anyone in town who does yoga?"

"Annabelle," Virginia answers, doing some move that has her leg sticking straight out behind her. "She runs classes out of the community center."

I hum, a little too caught up in Ash's eyes to answer. They look crystalline in the sunlight, clear blue with hints of silver-gray, like clouds reflecting off the water. I didn't understand those storms in his eyes, not at first. Not until I learned what he's living with.

Now, I can't help but wonder if he's in some pain right this minute. If that's what that subtle pinch is for as he smiles up at me.

"Jackson?" he says, head cocked.

I squat down in front of him. "You doing all right?"

His expression settles into something soft but reproachful. "Jack."

"Just gimme a number," I say quietly. "One to ten."

He lets out a sigh. But then he says, "Two, tops. I'm fine, really."

I nod, but before I can stand back up, Ash gives the brim of my hat a tug.

"You didn't say hello," he says with a grin.

Ah, hell.

I lean in, and Ash tips up my hat, inhaling as our lips come together. He hums into the kiss, and I have to pull back quicker than I'd prefer, lest I lose control.

Ash smiles, giving me a wink and tapping my hat back into place. "Hello to you, too. Now what do I get for goodbye?"

Virginia snickers.

"That eager to get rid of me?" I mock-grumble, standing up. My knee pops, reminding me of my age.

"Nah," Ash says casually. "I much prefer when you come, not go."

He ignores the scowl I send his way. "Not in front of the chicks," I tell him.

"'Scuse me?" Virginia says, pausing to lift her sunglasses. "What does my gender have to do with any—"

"He's talking about the Silkies," Ash says, barely restrained laughter in his voice.

"Not to mention the kids," I call, already heading toward the barn. "They shouldn't have to hear that."

"They're goats, Jack," Ash calls back. "They don't understand."

"Oh my God," I hear Virginia say. "Are you two...is this some weird sort of barnyard flirting?"

I snort, rounding the doorway into the barn. Snickerdoodle is inside, staring up at the loft. The cage that Remi strapped into place is just visible up in the rafters. As is the raccoon trapped inside. Remi messaged me earlier to let me know he caught the pest that was getting into our feed bins. But bleeding heart that my brother is, he left the job of *disposal* to me.

The raccoon scrambles against the wire cage as I shift the ladder into place to get it, and Snickerdoodle nickers.

"Keeping an eye on our captive, eh?" I ask the pony.

She stomps the ground, quite the fierce steed.

Snickerdoodle watches the proceedings as I put on a thick glove, retrieve the cage, and climb back down from the loft. I stow the ladder before heading out of the barn, meddlesome pony on my tail. There's a family in the petting farm now, and Ash and Virginia are rolling up their mats. Ash smiles, tucking the mat under his arm as he jogs over to me.

"Who's this?" he asks, bending down to get a look inside the cage.

"A raccoon," I say dryly.

He rolls his eyes as Virginia joins us. "Obviously. What are you doing with it?"

I glance over at the family to make sure the children aren't listening before saying, quietly, "Getting rid of it."

Both Ash and Virginia look as if I slapped them.

"What?" Ash asks. "You're not...*killing* it, are you?"

I hesitate, and Snickerdoodle kicks up her mane and whinnies, as if to say, *duh*.

"Jackson Darling," Ash says, stepping close and speaking low. "Please tell me you're not planning on killing that defenseless raccoon."

"It's a pest," I say slowly.

"It's an *animal*."

"So are you," I counter before I can think better of it.

Ash's eyes turn almost flinty. "I'm not sure if you're calling me a pest or helping my case, so I suggest you choose your next words carefully."

I flounder, opening and closing my mouth a couple times, not sure what the hell is even happening.

Virginia pipes up, a chuckle in her tone. "As fun as it is seeing a grown man's testicles retreat up his body in real time, I needa get home and wash the goat off me before the bar opens. See ya later, baby boy." She gives Ash a quick hug before turning my way. "Don't make me regret rooting for you, Darling."

With that, she's off, and I'm left staring at the stone-cold face of my *partner* while I try to figure out what goddamn hole I just dug myself into.

"Jack," Ash says, the one syllable slow.

"Christ," I mutter, rubbing over my eyes. "What would you have me do?"

"Let it go."

"It'll come back."

"Let it go *far* away," he proposes.

I groan, the sound lasting a small eternity. "Another goddamn bleeding heart around here."

"You say that as if compassion is a bad thing," Ash accuses.

I can't help it. I lean forward and kiss the scowl off his face. He makes an aborted sound, looking shell shocked as I step back.

"The things I do for you lot," I grumble, heading briskly toward the exit. A few goats smartly step out of my way.

"You're going to let it go?" Ash asks, following after me.

"I have a feeling I'll regret it, but yes, I'm gonna let it go."

He holds the gate open, blocking Snickerdoodle's path as I pass through. "You're a good man, Jackson."

"I'm a sucker, is what I am," I mutter, eyeing Ash as he keeps in step beside me. "What're you doing?"

"Coming with."

"Of course you are. Ever ridden in a UTV?"

Ash shoots me a grin. "Not unless a golf cart counts."

It doesn't.

"Can I drive?" he asks with a bounce.

"No way," I say, begrudgingly adding a, "Maybe," as Ash's eyes turn big and round.

He smiles victoriously.

Dangerous, this man.

When we get to the parking lot outside the milking barn, I head inside to grab a spare blanket while Ash waits with the raccoon. I cover the cage before loading it into the back of the utility vehicle, not wanting to stress the raccoon out more than necessary considering I'm now releasing the damn thing. Ash hops into the passenger seat, watching as I turn the ignition. I assume he's taking notes for later.

With a small lurch, the vehicle sets into motion. I drive us toward one of the trail riding paths that's widest. As we bump over dirt, I glance Ash's way to find him smiling serenely, his hand on the doorframe.

"You do know we eat the cattle, right?" I ask.

His head whips my way. "What?"

"The cattle," I repeat, talking over the low noise of the engine. "We raise cattle for beef. We can't save all the animals."

He nearly rolls his eyes. "I know that, Jack. But it's different. The cattle provide sustenance. There's no reason to off the poor raccoon."

I beg to differ, but I keep my opinions to myself, having a feeling there's no way I'd win this one. Not with those damn eyes of his armed and ready.

Clearing my throat, I let my gaze slide down Ash's profile before refocusing on the trail. "You sore at all?"

I can feel his eyes boring into the side of my head. "I already told you I'm fine."

"No, I—" A wave a hand his way. *Downward*. "Are you *sore?*"

I glance over, catching his slow spreading smile. "My ass is just fine, thank you. Very happy, in fact."

I grunt, and Ash laughs.

"But if you want to check it over later..." he says.

He laughs harder when I inadvertently step on the gas.

I'm not sure what I've gotten into with Ashley Alcott. But for once, the road ahead looks pretty damn bright.

Chapter 19

ASH

Jackson pulls the utility vehicle to a stop near the base of the mountains. Personally, I think coming out this far is overkill, but what do I know about raccoons and their travel habits?

The raccoon blinks big, black eyes as Jackson pulls the blanket off its cage. It's backed into the corner, and my chest aches for it.

"You stay here," Jackson says, pulling on thick gloves before hefting the cage.

"What? Why?"

"I don't want you in its path when I open the door," he answers, already walking away.

I shake my head, unable to decide if his concern is sweet or plain ridiculous. Either way, I stay put, watching as Jackson heads a little further down the trail. He stops before long, aiming the cage toward the trees and standing at the furthest end from the door as he raises the latch. The raccoon doesn't move, not until Jackson backs away. Then it skitters out through the narrow gap, disappearing into the woods with not so much as a backwards glance.

Jackson picks up the empty cage, heading my way. "Happy?" he calls out.

As I watch this man approach, his jeans dirty and the heavy stubble on his jaw reminding me of the roughness of Jackson's kiss, I decide that, "Yeah. I'm very happy."

He makes his usual gruff, one-note reply.

"Do I get to drive now?" I ask, holding out my hand and curling my fingers.

Jackson reaches into his pocket, slapping the keys into my palm on his way past. With a grin, I hop into the driver's seat and start up the vehicle. I wait for Jackson to join me, although it would have been a whole lot of fun to watch his face as I drove off. Maybe next time.

"What are you doing today?" I ask, getting us turned around and heading back the way we came.

"Well, I *was* doing a perimeter check, but somebody convinced me to take time outta my day to release a rabid, grain-stealing pest into the wild."

I give his leg a slap. "Guilting me won't work. And it wasn't rabid."

He grunts. "You decide what to do about your car?"

I let out a sigh, slowing to take a sharp curve. "I stopped by Ratchet's earlier. Said my goodbyes to Edna."

Jackson's brow is drawn when I glance over at him.

"What?" I ask.

"I could've come," he says, voice so low I nearly miss it over the rumbly purr of the engine.

"For what?"

"Support?" he says.

Oh, Jesus. Needing to distract myself from the heart palpitations I'm currently experiencing, I say, "You have zero sympathy for a cute little animal, but you would've come to pay respects to a hunk of metal?"

"You obviously liked that car," Jackson says. "You named it. So, yeah. I would've come."

I blow out a breath, but apparently Jackson isn't done annihilating me.

"I don't like seeing your face go all sad," he says, sounding grumpy about it. "It ain't right."

"When have you seen me sad?" I ask.

He doesn't answer for a long moment. "You were on the deck," he finally replies. "Last week. You had your eyes closed while you were, you know, doing your stretches. And you looked...*pained*. Was it physical? Or emotional?"

Fuck. For a man who says so little, he sure knows how to hit.

"A bit of both," I admit. "I, uh... It was a bad pain day. And sometimes, that doesn't bother me. I'm used to it. But other times..."

It takes me a minute to figure out how to explain it. I wouldn't even have known how before it all started because I never would've understood the way chronic pain can overwhelm you. How it can become incessant, like the buzzing of bees, so quiet at first but then, all of a sudden, loud and impossible to ignore. How you can deal with it day in and day out without issue, but then, for no discernable reason, the next day it's at the forefront of your mind and won't be shoved back again. How, at times, it can feel hopeless. How it can occupy your every waking thought, making it hard to concentrate, hard to focus on anything else.

"Sometimes I forget it's even there," I tell Jackson. "But that day, I was feeling really down on myself. Because it wouldn't let me forget, and I couldn't help but wonder *why me?* I want to remember what it feels like to stand up without wincing and to not have to put conscious thought into the way I move my upper body just so the pain doesn't flare. I'm thirty-five, Jackson, but sometimes I feel seventy. And it doesn't matter that it's not fair because what is? It's life. And I'm not going to let it stop me. But it still knocks me down every now and again."

"Pull over," Jackson says.

"What?" I ask, startled. "Where? We're on a dirt path in the middle of—"

"Just stop the damn vehicle, Ash."

I pull us to a stop and turn to face Jackson. "There. Stopped. What is it?"

I'm not expecting Jackson to take my face in his hands. Nor the seriousness is his eyes as he forces me to hold his gaze. "When you get knocked down," he says firmly, "you give me your hand, and I will pull you back up again."

"Jack..."

"I understand why you feel like you have to do it all on your own. I do. I *get* it. But you said you're in this, remember? So if you can't learn to rely on me, at least a little, then what are we even doing here, Ash?"

My breath puffs out of me. "Not fair. You're using logic against me."

"Is it working?"

"Unfortunately," I reply, grabbing Jackson's wrists. My heart is pounding. My throat tight. "It's not going to be easy for me, Jack. My last relationship felt centered around that part of my life, and I don't want that again. To feel like I'm just a list of undiagnosed medical problems."

"I don't see you that way."

"That's all well and good, but I'd still rather pretend I'm *normal.*"

"Ashley, I'm pretty sure your mother ensured that'd never happen the day she named you."

It takes me a beat, but then I'm laughing. *Hard.* "Jackass," I mutter.

Jackson looks proud of himself, the corner of his mouth hitching into the tiniest smile. It evens out when he says, "Ignoring something doesn't make it go away."

"I'm well aware," I reply pointedly.

He winces, letting go of my face. "I'm sorry. All I'm asking is that you don't expect me to look away every time you're hurting. 'Cause I don't think I can do that."

"Fuck, Jack," I groan, knocking my head back against the seat. "Why do you have to be so sweet? It makes it impossible to be mad at you."

"I'm not—"

"Sweet. Yeah, I know."

Except he is. But for whatever reason, Jackson doesn't want to show that to the world. He wears his gruffness like a shield. Protection, maybe. Innate or learned, he does his very best to hide his soft underbelly.

He's let me see it, though.

"I won't ask you to ignore if I'm hurting," I tell him. "And I'll try to speak up when I'm having a hard time. But don't push it. Don't start treating me like I'm—"

"Weak," he fills in. "Yeah, I know."

Smartass.

"And I won't," he says, the words sincere enough that I have no choice but to believe him.

I nod, let out a breath, and restart the vehicle.

When Jackson and I get back to the ranch, it's midafternoon. I pull the UTV into the same spot we left from just as my phone rings.

"Joy," I mutter, looking at the display. *My ex.* "Hello?"

"Ashley," Nicholas greets. "I was hoping we could talk."

I close my eyes, keeping my exhale quiet. His next words make me feel marginally better.

"Before I go."

"Give me a sec," I tell him. Muting the call, I turn to Jackson. "Any objections to me seeing my ex before he heads home?"

Jackson's brow furrows slightly. "Are you asking me if I trust you? Because the answer is yes."

Well, Christ on a cracker. "I'll make it quick."

"Up to you," he says, pulling me in by the back of the neck. His eyes hold mine for a moment before he kisses me. *Soundly.* I feel faint by the time he pulls back. "See you at dinner."

"Mhm," I manage.

Jackson hops out of the vehicle, grabbing the blanket and cage from the back and then heading off toward the milking barn.

"Fuck," I mutter, unmuting my phone. "Nicholas?"

"I'm here."

"I'll meet you, but I have an hour tops before I'll need to be back to cook dinner for the ranch."

He's quiet for a couple seconds. "You're cooking for them?"

"Yes?" I say slowly. "It's my job."

"Oh."

"You know I love cooking," I point out, wondering why he seems so surprised.

"Yeah, sure," he says hastily. "I just... I didn't expect it, is all. That's a lot different than..."

"Sports PR?" I fill in.

"Well, yeah."

"I wanted a change," I remind him. "I told you that."

There's another pause. "Should I come to you? If you're short on time."

"If you wouldn't mind, that'd be great," I admit.

"Where are you at?"

I rattle off the address and start making my way back toward the ranch house on foot. Nicholas says he'll leave right away, so I head around the house to the front porch to wait, watching as Marigold tends to her garden. Not fifteen minutes later, a vehicle pulls down the drive, and I stand.

Nicholas parks in front of the house before stepping out of what I assume is a rental. He's wearing a button-down and his nice wing-tip shoes, looking the same as I remember.

I head down the porch stairs to meet him. "Want to sit outside?"

"Sure," he answers, looking me over quickly.

I lead Nicholas to the wraparound porch at the back of the house. We take seats on rockers, both of us quiet for a moment.

"You're different," he finally says.

"You like the boots?" I ask, giving him a grin as I cross one foot over the other.

He shakes his head slowly. "It's not just the boots, Ashley. You look different."

I lean back in my chair, watching the dairy girls graze in the shade. "How so?"

"There's...less strain on your face. Is your pain improving?"

"It's the same," I tell him. "Minimal most days. Not gone."

He makes a soft sound. "Would you like me to do an adjustment before I—"

"Nick."

He falls silent. "I think I get it. I didn't at first. When you left, I thought... I don't know what I thought. That you were running, maybe?"

"And you don't think that now?"

"I think, maybe, it wasn't so much running away as running *to*."

I nod because that's exactly it. When I was young, I would watch the seagulls come and go as the seasons changed. I'd watch them fly away. And I'd wonder why they always returned.

I never fit in Maine, not really. I never felt settled there. For as long as I could remember, I wanted to fly away. I wanted to let my wings carry me on the wind and see where I'd land.

I don't know why it took me so long to do it. To just *go*.

"As much as I wouldn't have believed it," Nicholas continues, his voice pulling me back to the present—to the mountains and the fresh, saltless air, "this place does suit you. Honestly, I'm not sure why I'm even surprised considering all the country music you used to listen to."

I make a short sound in the back of my throat. "Neil Young isn't... You know what? It's not important. I *do* like it here. You're right about that. Darling feels like home in a way Maine never did."

He nods slowly, *sadly*, almost. "I think I was jealous, Ashley."

That pulls me up short. "Why?"

"Because you left? Because you left me? I felt..."

"Like you were missing out?" I ask.

"Well, yeah. Here you were, being brave, and I was sitting at home feeling sorry for myself. It took me over a week to stop making coffee for two people, and when I finally brewed that single pot and saw how small my life had become, I panicked."

"Your life isn't small, Nicholas," I say as gently as I can. "You have family and friends and a job you love. And I know you'll be able to find someone to enjoy it with if that's what you want."

He nods, smoothing a hand over his face. "Virginia never liked me."

I hold back my laugh. "She didn't like you *for* me. There's a difference."

He looks out over the pastures to the west. There are a few cattle far off in front of the mountains, small black dots beneath stormy peaks and a cloudy blue sky. Most of the herd is too far away to even see.

"What now?" I ask.

"I'm heading back tonight," he answers, meeting my eye. "I'll tell my mom you look good. She'll spread the news."

I huff a laugh. "Take care, Nicholas."

He nods, pushing out of his seat. "Bye, Ashley."

As Nicholas rounds the house out of view, I can't help but wonder if this is the last time I'll see him. It doesn't make me sad, not exactly. But there is an ache there. Nostalgia, perhaps, for the good times we shared. Even if Nicholas and I weren't right for each other in the end, I don't regret the part he played in my past.

I just know he's not my future.

I settle back into my seat, waving at one of the ranchers as they pass. They wave back just as a soft voice chimes from beside me.

"Are you in the mood for some company?"

I smile Marigold's way. "If the company is you? Always."

Her lips twist in amusement as she takes a seat beside me. Her hair is in a braid today, the end held in place with what looks like a piece of twine. "You're far too charming for these parts, Ashley. I bet my son hardly knows what to do with you."

Oh, he knows just fine.

I keep the thought to myself. "He's charming in his way," I tell her.

She snorts a laugh. "Mm. You're kind, too. Don't get me wrong; I love each and every one of my sons. But we're all flawed."

I can't argue that. Isn't everyone?

"Are you here to meddle?" I ask.

Marigold gives me a wide smile. "As if I would ever."

I chuckle. I might not have known Marigold for long, but I know a meddlesome mother when I see one.

"Did you know our town has a fall festival?" she asks, tone even.

I raise a brow. "Does it?"

She hums. "The Darling Autumnfest. Jackson hasn't been in years. He used to love it, you know. The distillery sells whiskey cider. One time a year only. It's his favorite."

"Uh-huh," I say slowly.

"They do moonlight carriage rides, too. For the adults. Pretty romantic, if you ask me."

"You're not subtle. You know that, right?"

"Never said I was trying to be," she counters, standing up. "Have a good rest of your afternoon, Ashley."

"Marigold."

As Mrs. Darling walks out of sight, I kick my rocker into motion.

"Trouble," I mutter, smiling to myself. "All of 'em."

Chapter 20

JACKSON

If there's one thing you can count on in Darling, Montana, it's for everybody to know your business. Regardless of whether or not you want them to.

"How's that new hire doing?" Louise asks, thinking she's being clever. "What's his name again? Arnold?"

"Ash," I answer, transferring a crate of milk out of the back of the refrigerated truck. I don't normally make the weekly milk deliveries, but our usual guy, Marshall, has a sick kid at home. Which means, today, I'm the runner.

I head into Louise's sandwich shop, the woman herself at my heel.

"Ash," she parrots. "That's right. Sweet guy."

"Mhm."

"Looker, too."

I set the crate down and stand up straight, giving her a *look*. "Really, Louise? Are we on this again?"

Louise Harper is one of my mother's oldest and closest friends. Her eldest son is my age and her youngest is Remi's.

She's always had a vested interest in our lives. For the past couple decades, that's included my *love* life.

"I'm not sure what you're alluding to, Jackson," she says, feigning innocence. The woman is far from innocent. "I'm just stating facts. Are you telling me you don't agree that he's a handsome young man?"

Young is subjective, I suppose. But there's no way for me to answer that question that doesn't land me square inside Louise's trap.

With a sigh, I decide to give her a truth. Frankly, I'm shocked the news hasn't traveled to her already. My mom is showing restraint.

"I do think he's handsome, Louise. Which is why I'm dating the man."

That's not the only reason, of course, not even the first reason. But I can tell my little bomb landed just fine. I step around Louise, who looks too shocked to manage gossip. Of course, she rallies quickly.

"Jackson Darling!" she says, storming after me. We both slip past one of her employees, who's prepping for the shop to open. "Are you telling me you went and got a boyfriend, and you neglected to mention it to me?"

"Louise..."

"I changed your diapers when you were a baby, young man."

"Oh, God," I mutter, nodding to another employee who's getting out of their vehicle. "Morning," I call.

Louise clearly isn't done. "I think wiping your ass gives me some right to—"

"Wonder why my mom didn't think to mention it," I say loudly, closing the back of my truck.

Louise stops still, eyes narrowing. *Bingo.* "We'll finish this conversation later," she threatens, wagging a finger at me before stomping back toward the sandwich shop. "Don't think this means you're getting off scot-free!"

"Wouldn't dream of it," I murmur, knowing I've just incurred my mother's wrath by poking at her dearest friendship. Honestly, the woman deserves it now and again.

Having delivered the last of the milk, I climb into my truck and get on the road. It doesn't take long to arrive back at the ranch. Our workers are out and about, a steady drum of activity I find soothing most days. It means the cogs are functioning.

Although I can't see the man, I'm guessing Ash is inside the house getting lunch ready. After parking, I head that way. It's not that I have extra minutes to spare—not on a day where I'm filling in for an absent employee—but it doesn't seem to matter. My feet know where they want to go, and I let them take me there.

As expected, Ash is inside the kitchen. I can hear him singing as soon as I step through the door, and the simple force of it hits me in the strongest way. It feels cliché to say something was missing before Ash arrived, but having him here, filling this house with life and energy, makes me realize just how quiet my existence had become. Not in a literal sense. Lord knows my family is a mouthy bunch.

But my days had become mundane. The same quiet, steady routine that led me from dawn to dusk. I wasn't...depressed. I truly don't think so. But I'm not sure I was all that happy, either.

Then this damn ball of sunshine showed up, and *fuck*. The man upended my life. And now I'm *smiling* and happy, and I almost don't know what to do with it. But I know I don't want to let this feeling go. I want to keep it—keep *him*—for as long as I possibly can.

Ash's singing stutters a beat when I step into the kitchen. He gives me a swift smile before continuing to croon softly about searching for that heart of gold. I step close and sink my face into his neck, where he's warm and soft and smells like baking bread. I inhale him down, my arms curling around his stomach.

He chuckles, turning his face slightly. "Have I become your comfort item?" he teases. "Did you have one of those as a kid? A plushie or a blanket or anything?"

I hum, not wanting to admit to Ash that my *comfort item*, as he called it, was an old, ratty horse head that fell off a stick. I used to pretend to ride it when I was a kid, until the plush head fell off. Then it came with me everywhere until it was so worn my mom couldn't sew it back together anymore.

"Just wanted to say hello," I tell him, giving his neck a quick kiss before stepping back.

He turns enough to look at me, an amused lilt to his lips. "You said hello this morning."

I grunt. "Was a while ago."

He full-out grins, shaking his head. "So sweet. You busy this weekend?"

I lean on the small kitchen table as I think that over. Ash goes back to rolling dough out on the counter. Once done, he starts cutting rounds out of it. Biscuits, I'm guessing.

"Don't think so," I finally say. I have a few small tasks to take care of, but not much. "Why?"

"Save an evening for me?" he asks, arms flexing as he finishes cutting the rounds.

"Do I get to ask what for?" I question, trying my best not to focus too hard on those arms. Or any piece of Ash. Not when I have work to get back to.

He looks over his shoulder again, grinning. "You can ask if you want to. But that doesn't mean I'm going to tell you."

I grunt, and Ash laughs.

"Like you'll say no to me," he says, wiping some hair out of his eye with his wrist. A little flour transfers onto his cheek.

Clearing my throat, I mutter, "No, not sure I can. And that's the problem with you, sunshine."

Ash's smile tells me he doesn't think that's a problem at all. I have to look elsewhere, his eyes far too transparent. Pretty sure I could see right to the heart of him if I wanted to.

"Needa get back to work," I say, pushing away from the table.

"Thanks for saying hello," Ash says, loading the biscuits onto trays to go into the oven. "See you again in"—he checks the clock—"an hour?"

"Mhm," I grunt.

"Hey," Ash calls as I step through the doorway. "Where's my goodbye?"

With a grumble that has Ash smiling wide, I stomp back into the room. I slide my fingers into his hair, tug his head around, and plant a kiss on his lips. When I let go, I swipe that damn flour off his cheek.

"Better?" I ask.

That smile never leaves his face. "Yeah, darlin'. Much better."

Ash laughs as I roll my eyes and head out of the kitchen. My lips twitch into a smile, and try as I might, the sound of Ash's happiness won't leave my head all morning.

"Hey, Jackson? Where are the signs for the festival?"

I raise a brow Colton's way, pausing as I pull off Starlight's saddle. "I dunno. Where'd you put them last year?"

"How am I supposed to remember?" he says. "That was a *year* ago."

"Yet you expect me to know," I mumble.

"They're in the loft at the petting farm barn," Remi answers, passing with his arms full of empty feed bags. "Red tote."

"Thanks, bro," Colton says, heading off.

"You going with him again this year?" I ask Remi, putting my tack away.

He shoves the feed bags into a large trash bin. "Someone has to keep him organized."

Guilt flares at my brother's words, even though I know he didn't mean anything by them. It's just that *I* was the one who used to run the Darling Ranch booth at the fall festival with Colton. Up until Otto broke the news that he was leaving right there on the side of the street while I was eating an apple cider donut.

"Remi, I—"

"Oh, don't start," my brother says sternly. "That wasn't a criticism. I'm happy to do it."

"Are you sure? I can—"

"Stop," he says, hand striking his palm in an ASL mirror of the word. "You do enough around here. Colton and I have the festival handled. End of discussion."

My lips twitch. "You're starting to sound a lot like Mom, y'know."

He throws a horse brush at me, which I catch before it hits my chest. The *fuck off* he signs my way has me huffing a laugh.

"Just lemme know if you need anything," I tell him, fairly sure at this point I can enter the festival without feeling a potent mix of rage, sadness, and grief over the end of my previous relationship.

"We won't," Remi answers, his departure signaling the end of our conversation.

I'm not sure when my baby brother went and grew up.

When I get back to the main house, it's dinnertime. I didn't have time to shower and change beforehand, but that's fine. It's not often that I do.

My mom catches me as I'm entering the house via the mudroom door, her tone sharp enough to cut glass. "*Jackson Darling.*"

"Oh, here we go."

"Did I do something in your forty years of life to make you hate me?" she asks, her hands on her hips.

My brow goes up. Slowly. "I assume that's a rhetorical question?"

"Maybe my *son,*" she goes on, "the boy I raised with my own two hands, could tell me why I had to hear he has a *boyfriend* from my friend, Louise."

All right... That wasn't quite what I was expecting.

"You know Ash and I are a thing," I point out.

"A *thing,*" she says with a scoff. "No, I certainly did not know that. I *presumed* as much, just from looking at you. I certainly knew you were doing...the horizontal hokey-pokey. But not once did you speak the word *boyfriend.*"

I catch Ash's amused expression over my mom's shoulder, his head poking out of the dining room. Belatedly, I realize it's rather quiet inside the house, which tells me all I need to know. The simple truth that, now, *everybody* knows.

It's enough to distract me from the fact that my mom just uttered the words *horizontal hokey-pokey*. I suppress a shiver.

"Well," I say, refocusing on my mother, "now you're aware. So...good?"

Her tone is wry when she says, "'Good,' he asks. No, we are not *good*. What are your intentions with Ashley Alcott?"

"Oh, Jesus," I mutter, scrubbing my face. "Really, Ma? Shouldn't you be asking *him* that about *me*?"

"Nope. Because I know that boy has good intentions sprouting outta his ass."

"Out of his—"

"*You're* the one I'm worried about," she says. "Don't you go hurting that man, Jackson Darling."

I sputter. "*Me*? Why would I?"

"'Cause you got hurt first. And we all know what hurt animals do in the face of repeated threat of injury."

Lash out.

"I won't," I tell her, getting frustrated. Ash had the good grace to return to the dining room, although I know it doesn't matter. He can hear just fine either way. Well, better set the record straight then. For *both* of them. "I have no damn intention of hurting that man. He's the purest thing to come into my life in who knows how goddamn long. And the fact that you think I'm even *capable* of it—"

My words come to an abrupt halt as I register what my mom just pulled. Because she would never truly accuse me of being careless with his feelings. And I didn't realize it until far too late.

"Are you happy with yourself?" I ask her.

She's smiling at me now. "Quite. You have a tendency to keep your thoughts balled up tight, Jackson dear. And I didn't want him missing the obvious. Or you," she adds gently.

"If I could," I tell her evenly, "I'd file for emancipation."

"You're *far* too old," she says, a happy lilt to her words as she heads for the dining room. "Now what's for dinner?"

Maybe I could move.

My dad sighs, and I jolt, not having heard him come in the front door. "You'll never win against that woman," he says, walking past. "I wouldn't suggest trying."

"You're an enabler," I call after him.

He waves a hand over his shoulder.

As I'm standing in the hallway, debating whether or not I even need to eat tonight, Ash reappears. He has two plates in his hand.

"What are you—"

"Come on," he whispers, heading for the door. "We're running."

I snort, my insides leaping at the sight of Ash's mischievous grin.

Fuck, am I in deep.

I haul ass, opening the door for Ash to pass through. Without looking back, we walk down the drive to my place. I grab two beers once we get there, and then we settle out back on the Adirondack chairs surrounding the fire pit, our bottles leaving pools of moisture on our armrests as we eat. Every once in a while, Ash's knee brushes my own.

"She's evil," he says some time later. "Brilliant and evil."

"Pretty much," I mutter, enjoying the roast beef sandwiches Ash made. "This horseradish from scratch?"

He gives me a quick grin. "Yep."

"'S'good."

He bumps my knee again. "Thanks, Jack."

We fall silent as we finish our meal, the evening sun keeping us company as it races toward the mountains. I take a sip of my beer, content to soak up the peaceful air.

"Did you mean that?" Ash asks, his voice quiet.

I look over at him with a soft grunt. "That I don't plan on hurting you? 'Course."

"No, not that," he says, setting his empty plate down and resituating to face me more fully. "I mean, that was good to hear—don't get me wrong. But no. The part about me being...pure."

Christ.

I fidget with the label on my beer bottle, feeling scrutinized and not sure I like it. Actually, scratch that. I'm *sure* I don't like it.

But this is Ash. And he's been nothing if not honest with me from the start.

Easing out a breath, I say, "Yes, I meant that. Ashley, you have this way about you that's good and bright. You remind me of that great big orb up there." I point the end of my beer bottle toward the sun for emphasis. "You make everything lighter. And maybe pure ain't the right word 'cause Lord knows you're filthy when you wanna be..."

He gives me a coy smile, and I rein in everything that smile has me itching to do.

"But I don't think there's a single piece of you capable of purposeful destruction," I go on. "You're pure of heart, and that's something I can't help but admire."

And feel drawn to.

Ash doesn't speak for the longest time. He looks out over the land, a pensive expression on his face. "I hurt Nicholas."

My chest constricts briefly. "Not intentionally. I don't think you would've walked out the way you did if he had once tried to stop you. He hurt, true. But I don't think it was your fault."

He tips his head into a nod, lips quirking slightly. "Your mom said you're not good at sharing your thoughts."

I huff. "No. Usually, I'm not."

"You have been with me, though."

I let out a sigh. "'Cause I don't know how to deny you."

Ash chuckles, the sound almost dark. "That's a lot of power to give a person, Jack."

"I'm not worried."

"Because of my pure heart?" he asks, sounding amused.

I grunt.

Ash chuckles again, leaning back in his chair and setting his ankle over my knee. I grab the skin beneath his pant leg, my thumb stroking over his ankle bone.

"You know," Ash says slowly. "It's polite to offer someone respite when they're so very far from home."

"Far?" I ask, my pulse picking up.

"Uh-huh. You wouldn't want me walking all the way home in the dark, would you?"

I glance at the still-risen sun before looking over at the man with the wavy blonde hair and eyes I'm fairly certain were crafted from the sky itself. How this warm, bubbly presence is capable of inciting such wicked thoughts, I'm not sure I'll ever understand.

I let my fingers drift up under the hem of his pant leg. "Would you stay the night, Ash? Y'know, to protect that virtue of yours."

He huffs a cheeky laugh. "So nice of you to offer. But I'll let you in on a secret."

"Yeah? What's that?"

I swallow as Ash leans closer, his grin causing my gaze to lower to his lips. "I'm not that virtuous," he whispers before dropping his leg. Empty plate and bottle in hand, Ash heads toward my house.

And I wonder why it is I was so quick to replace the word "house" with "home" in my mind.

Chapter 21

ASH

"I should've known," Jackson says, managing to sound both soft and surly at the same time. It's a true talent.

"Known what?" I ask, stepping around a child in my path. The caramel apple in their hand is nearly as big as their face.

"That you were planning on bringing me here," he answers, meeting my gaze as the two of us amble slowly past the booths and entertainment at the Darling Autumnfest. He's not wearing a hat tonight, and it looks as if he actually attempted to tame his hair. *Attempted* being the key word, seeing as the strands are stubbornly refusing to stay put.

Reminds me of their owner.

"You look nice," I tell him, realizing I failed to do so when I picked him up. "I like the ring. Is it new?"

I've never seen him wear one before, but Jackson simply grunts, twirling the metal on his finger. "It was a gift," he says a little gruffly. "From Colt."

It takes me a moment to parse through his meaning, but then I smile. "Did your brother help you get ready for our date?"

Jackson's face immediately settles into a scowl. "Not help. *Hinder.*"

I laugh at his put-out expression. "And the leather bracelet?" I ask. It's nice, but again, not something I've seen on Jackson before. He's far too practical to wear jewelry around the ranch.

He sighs, long and low. "My niece."

I bite my lip, wondering how many of Jackson's family members showed up to primp him before our first official date. It's sweet that they care. And it says a lot about Jackson that he didn't want to hurt their feelings by refusing their...*help*.

"Well, Colton and Wendy did good," I tell him. "But, for the record...you'd look nice whether covered in jewelry or wearing absolutely nothing at all."

The look he sends me is sharp, a warning perhaps because of our location. But I only grin, not above ruffling Jackson's feathers given the chance.

"What should we do first?" I ask, slowing to look at a booth full of fall-scented candles. When Jackson doesn't answer, I find him staring in the opposite direction. "Hungry?"

He doesn't respond, simply walks over to the vendor selling sugar-covered donuts. Curious, I follow.

"One," he says briskly, pulling his wallet from his pocket. I watch him exchange goods before shoving his wallet away. When he walks off wordlessly, a single apple cider donut in his hand, I start to get concerned.

"Jackson?" I ask, hastening to keep up.

He doesn't slow. He weaves through the crowd, past families and children, around pet dogs and one leashed goat.

Once he clears the rows of booths, he heads toward the trees nearby.

"Jack," I call, jogging after him.

Jackson stops in front of a big pine and, without any preamble whatsoever, chucks the donut at the tree. It hits the trunk, crumbling apart on impact, sugar and dough blasting outwards in an impressive display.

I turn to look at Jackson. "What was *that?*"

His chest rises and falls, jaw set. "Otto," he says simply.

Oh. "That donut has to do with Otto?"

He nods in a sharp jerk, staring at the specks of sugar on the bark of the tree.

"Well, then," I mutter, turning right back around.

"Where are you—"

"Be right back," I call.

I jog all the way back to the donut vendor, pay for a baker's dozen, and then return to where Jackson is still standing just outside the festival's main grounds. He looks less ruffled than he did a minute ago, but his brows still draw together when I thrust the wax bag his way.

"Have at it," I tell him, catching my breath.

He looks between me and the bag before, *slowly*, accepting the offering. Turning, he plucks out a donut, weighing it carefully in his hand as one would a baseball, and then he pitches it at the tree. Like the first, it puffs apart, pieces flying in all directions.

"Fuck," he mutters, grabbing another. Jackson tosses five donuts, one right after another, before he holds the bag out my way. "You go."

"Really?" I ask, unable to temper my grin.

He nods.

I pick a donut out of the bag and hurl it at the tree, laughing when it crumbles. "Shit, that's fun."

"Right?" Jackson says, tossing another. He huffs what might be a laugh, the tension in his shoulders starting to recede.

Jackson and I alternate, tossing the rest of the donuts until we're down to just one. Instead of throwing it, Jackson examines that donut for a long minute. Finally, he holds it out toward my mouth.

"Here," he says a little roughly. "They're actually pretty good."

Eyes on Jackson, I take a bite out of the donut. Sugar sticks to my lips as I chew, and his gaze drops, tracking the movement. He lets out a breath before popping a chunk of the fried dough into his own mouth. He offers me the last piece and then dusts off his hands.

When Jackson takes a seat on the grass, I follow suit. The festival is loud behind us, but no one is venturing out into this area, so we're afforded some privacy. Jackson crumples up the wax bag into a tiny ball.

"Was it a bad idea coming here?" I ask. Marigold mentioned Jackson hadn't been in years, but I didn't anticipate Otto being the cause. If I'd known, I would have suggested something else.

Jackson shakes his head slowly. "No. It was time. I don't..." He pauses, thinking over his words. "I've let him take from me for far too long. It's time for it to stop."

I nod, understanding that deeply. When I offer my hand, Jackson accepts it, his palm warm and fingertips callused. I have no intention of pushing him to talk about his ex, and certainly not here, but Jackson goes on, as if expecting me to.

"I'll tell you about him," he says, expression pinched. "Eventually."

A few fallen leaves crunch beneath my knee as I shift his way. "You don't have to, Jack. I don't need all the details, and you don't owe them to me in the first place. If you want to talk, I'll listen. Always. But I don't need you to lay your past bare for *me*, okay? Only if it'd help *you*."

He runs one roughened finger along the side of my hand, stroking up and down. Up and down. "I'm past it. *Him*. I swear I am, but I guess I'm still just..."

"Processing?" I offer.

He nods, eyes pinging up to mine. "I'm not in love with him anymore," he says, voice firm. "I'm not."

"Okay."

"Okay?"

"Yeah, Jack. I believe you."

He huffs again, the sound begrudgingly amused. A child laughs from somewhere behind us, and I give Jackson's hand a squeeze.

"Anything else we should smash?" I ask. "I saw some lovely candles back there."

He snorts, pushing to his feet and pulling me up with him. "I don't think that'll be necessary."

"You sure? It was kind of hot watching you go to town on those donuts."

Jackson shakes his head, drawing me in for a kiss. Or at least I'm expecting a kiss. Instead, he licks the corner of my mouth, causing a full body shiver to roll down my frame.

"Sugar," he says in explanation.

I nod weakly, my feet taking a moment to catch up as Jackson tugs me back toward the festival.

Jackson tosses the trash from our donuts into a bin as we pass. A few kids run across the path in front of us, their headbands trailing ribbons in autumnal colors. Some folks are sitting on benches nearby, eating dinner or snacking on Darling's version of homemade carnival food. Jackson leads me over to a booth for the town's distillery.

My lips curve into a smile when Jackson orders two whiskey ciders. I accept mine with a *thanks*, the paper cup warm between my palms. A band starts playing nearby, and we head that way, sipping our drinks as we stop to listen to the music. Jackson doesn't seem to have a problem with PDA because he tugs me close, an arm looped around my stomach, my back to his chest. I don't mind it one bit, and I trust Jackson to know his town's attitude when it comes to queer relationships in the open.

By six-thirty, the sun is setting, and many of the families are beginning to pack up and head home. Seeing as it's Sunday, some of the vendors are preparing to close up shop, too, displaying signs for discounts on their remaining wares. Jackson and I grab a couple maple bacon burgers, eating as we walk.

I don't think he realizes I have a particular destination in mind until it's too late.

The first moonlight carriage rides are just departing when Jackson and I arrive. He still has a bite of burger in his mouth, so all he can do is offer a reproachful look as I join the short line.

Once his food is finished, he tosses his trash and walks over. "Someone put you up to this," he mumbles.

"Why would you say that?" I ask, feigning ignorance. And *great*, now I sound just like Marigold.

"Because," Jackson says slowly, "you're not the type for grand gestures and showing off. This has my mother written all over it."

My heart beats wildly, Jackson's casual—*and correct*—assessment surprising me. I'm not quite sure how he managed to peg me in such a short period of time.

"Well, I think it's romantic," I say. *Or so I've heard.* "And it'll just be the two of us. How is that showy?"

"It's fifty bucks," he says quietly. "You realize that, right?"

"It's on me," I fire back. "And look—proceeds support the local 4-H club."

Jackson grumbles some more, but I know I have him hooked when he steps up next to me and places his hand on the small of my back to move us forward. Such a gentleman, whether or not he realizes it.

When it's our turn to board a carriage, I hop up easily. Jackson follows me, settling beside me on the small padded bench that faces forward. I'm not sure what I envisioned when I first heard *moonlight carriage rides*, but this so-called carriage is more of a buggy. It's tiny, with a top opened up to the air and a coachman sitting in a raised chair directly behind the horses. Their brown tails swoosh as we set into motion.

"Nice evening, isn't it?" our coachman says, turning his head slightly.

It only takes me a second to place him. "Earl?"

The man who first gave me a ride into town in his beat-up truck looks back, recognition lighting his eyes. "The newcomer. Ash. You're still here?"

I huff a laugh. "Still here. How's Misty?"

He hums, swaying slightly as the horses move us forward. "She's just fine, thanks for asking. How 'bout that car of yours? Did Ratchet get 'er running?"

"Scrapped," I tell him.

He makes a sympathetic sound. "That's a shame. I had a car like yours when I was a young buck. Lasted a good, long while before it went to parts. Most of the guts were rusted right through. Had to pitch 'em in the dump."

Jackson gives my knee a squeeze, mouthing the word "romantic" with an expression far sassier than I would've thought him capable of. I swat his leg, biting back my laughter. Unfortunately, one of the horses takes that moment to let out some gas. The squeak lasts for several seconds.

Jackson is shaking, his hand over his mouth, as I try my very best not to make a sound. His fingers dig into my leg.

"You folks enjoy the festival?" Earl asks, completely oblivious to the downward spiral of our supposedly romantic evening.

"Sure did," I tell him. "Donuts were great."

Jackson coughs.

Earl simply hums. "My cousin makes those. You shoulda seen the prep that went into this weekend. First, there was the batter..."

As Earl regales Jackson and me with a detailed description of the donut-making process, including the *right* way to hole a donut— *"you see, some folks stretch the hole, and others punch it"*—Jackson's hand remains on my knee, his thumb drifting ever so slightly. It's a distraction that has me missing a good portion of Earl's ramblings, but I don't think the man minds.

When we round a corner, heading back in the direction of the festival, I finally set eyes on the moon. It's big and round in the sky, beautiful, and I'm about to point it out to Jackson when our carriage comes to an abrupt halt.

"Whoops," Earl says. "One of the horses has a little business to attend to."

I open my mouth to question what sort of business a horse might possibly have when a tail lifts into the air.

Oh. Oh, no.

It's all I can do not to react when the horse's *business* plops audibly onto the concrete. I can feel Jackson's eyes boring into the side of my head, but I refuse to look.

"There we are," Earl says, hopping down to take care of the mess.

Jackson squeezes my leg again, but I shake my head, staring resolutely at the moon.

We get back on the road before long, and it only takes another minute before our carriage is slowing to a stop.

"Hope you folks enjoyed the ride," Earl says kindly, tipping his hat. "Have a fine rest of your evening."

"Thank you, Earl. It was lovely," I tell the man, stepping out after Jackson. "See you around."

Earl nods, and another couple boards the carriage behind us as Jackson and I head toward the festival.

"Not a word," I warn him. "I tried, okay?"

Jackson gives my arm a gentle tug, pulling me to a stop. When I bring my eyes up to his, the often hard lines of his face are settled into something soft and tender. "You did," he says, and unless I'm mistaken, he sounds appreciative of that fact. "Come on. I have an idea."

"Yeah? Something to salvage this disaster of a night?" I only half-joke.

"I happened to like this night," he says as we walk back into the crowd. "Talk of exes and horse dung included."

I grab my chest. "Shit, Jack. I think that's the sweetest thing anyone has ever said to me."

He snorts, grabbing the back of my neck and kissing my temple. I smile so wide my cheeks hurt.

Jackson leads me through the rows of booths, back over to the Darling Whiskey stand, where he forks over enough cash to grab a growler of cooled whiskey cider. We pass his family's booth on our way out of the festival, Remi waving at us from where he's boxing up their display. Before long, we're on the road.

Instead of having me drive back to his house, Jackson directs me down the gravel path to the horse barn.

"We're not doing a drunken trail ride, are we?" I check. "Because I'm not sure that'd be a wise decision, Jack."

He shakes his head, fighting a smile as we get out of the company truck. "No, we're not."

"Okay. So..."

"Just c'mon," he grumbles.

I chuckle, trailing after him into the barn. Jackson flips on a single overhead light that illuminates the hallway but not the horse stalls, and then he grabs a rope dangling from the ceiling. A hatch door opens as he tugs, a ladder coming down with it that Jackson settles onto the ground.

I peer up into the darkened space. "What's up there?"

"Hayloft," he answers.

I swing my gaze his way slowly. "Jackson Darling. Is your idea of romance a romp in the hay? Because that might be the most country thing I've ever heard."

He looks heavenward, as if asking for patience. "Just get up the ladder, Ash."

"Yessir," I mutter, stepping onto the bottom rung. Once I reach the top, I ease onto the platform and wait for Jackson to join me. It's too dark to see where to go.

After lifting himself up, he walks past me, his boots crunching over hay. There's a click of a lock, and then moonlight floods the loft.

"Is that a door?" I ask, heading his way. Jackson is standing beside an open space. There's nothing in front of it. No stairs to the ground or even a railing to stop someone from tumbling through.

"Mhm. Access door for the hay," he explains. "It gets lifted up through here."

"Long way to fall," I note.

"Which is why it's better not to."

"You're just full of it tonight, aren't you?" I snark, chuckling when Jackson snags me around the middle. He tugs me back toward the towering piles of hay, and we go tumbling down. My laughter gets lost in my throat when Jackson's mouth finds mine, warm and insistent. He presses into me, *grinding*, and my thoughts scatter. *"Jack."*

He eases back, sitting upright, his weight on my hips stopping me from chasing. My breath comes out in short pants as he twists the cap off the growler.

"What are you doing?" I ask.

Jackson doesn't answer, not verbally. He pushes my jacket and shirt up, his hand warm on my skin, his thumb stroking near my navel. Slowly, he tips the growler over my stomach.

Cool whiskey cider pools in my belly button, some of it spilling out when I gasp. Even though I know exactly what's coming, it still takes me by surprise when Jackson scoots back and runs his tongue up my happy trail, into my navel.

"Fuck," I mutter, hips punching up.

Jackson's grip holds me steady, his lips sucking up the liquid as I squirm.

My head plunks back against the hay as he sits up again, lifting the growler for a second time. He looks silver in the moonlight streaming through the open door, and my heart races at the sight of him, a *thump-thump* I have no hope of controlling.

"Christ, Jack," I nearly rasp. "What are you doing to me?"

Jackson tips another small amount of liquid over my belly button. "Romancing you."

Two words. Two simple words, and I know I'm gone.

With a Montana cowboy between my legs in a hayloft and whiskey pooling on my stomach, I've gone and fallen.

And I have no desire to get back up again.

Chapter 22

JACKSON

Ash looks irresistible. Incandescent.

The pale sliver of his stomach is like a beacon in the relative darkness of the hayloft, and I drag my tongue over warm skin and muscle to the hollow in the center that tastes of fall. Of caramel apples and smoke from a woodfire.

Ash groans as I lick the alcohol from his skin.

"Fuck, Jack."

"Mm."

He huffs a laugh, trying to pull his legs up. I keep my weight settled over him, smoothing my hand up his stomach to reveal more skin.

"That's... all you have to say?" he asks, his stomach rising and falling underneath my palms.

"I can think of better uses for my mouth than talking," I point out before making my way toward his nipple with my tongue.

Ash must agree because he grabs his jacket, fumbling to get the zipper open. His motions stutter when I pull his nipple into my mouth, but then he's moving again, tugging the jacket off his arm. He nearly elbows me in the face when he sets to work on his shirt. He gets it over his head and off the same arm, the other remaining clothed.

"Have you ever...had sex...in the hayloft before?" he asks me, sounding breathless.

I shake my head, brushing my mouth across his chest, knowing he likes the bristle of my beard. "Jerked off a few times when I was a teen, though."

His laughter is cut short when I suck on his other nipple, squeezing his pec to get better purchase. He groans and grinds up against me, seeking friction on his cock. I ease back, letting his nipple go with a pop and grabbing the whiskey cider.

"God, Jack. You're killing me."

I pour some of the liquid into his navel again, swooping down to lick it up before I climb up his body. The sound Ash makes when my lips meet his is hungry, near desperate. I grab his jaw, and the moment he opens his mouth, I let the whiskey fall from me to him.

He coughs, once, but then he's practically mauling me. A fist in my shirt keeps me close, a leg over mine urging me closer still. He tastes smokey and sweet as our tongues duel, as hay prickles at my hands as surely as the small of his back. I work my jacket off as Ash sucks on my lip, his cock rubbing against me through our jeans.

Ash doesn't protest when I haul his upper body into the air. I flatten my jacket down on the hay bale as best as I can and then press Ash back into it. His spine arches when I break from his mouth to work down his chest. I find sweet spots as I map his skin, places where the cider lingers. There's one on his pec. Another near the top of his belly button. Ash pants and wraps his fingers in my hair, all but pushing down on my head. I chuckle, making my way lower.

When I glance up, Ash has his other arm out of his jacket and shirt, leaving him bare from the waist up. He's looking back at me, his eyes dark and hooded. I flip the button on his jeans slowly, watching each flicker of expression that crosses his face.

"Jack," he whispers, a plea.

I rub my lips above the band of his underwear, bristling his skin lightly. He groans, spreading his legs wider in invitation. I make him wait. Just a little.

His head falls back as I place kisses above his briefs. Rub his stomach with my nose. Nip his hip bone. Finally, I ease down his zipper.

"You are the most...tortuous lover I've ever had," he says, breath puffing out of him as he gets up on his elbows for a better view.

I chuckle against his skin, kissing his cock over the fabric. "You like it," I mutter.

"Fuck it, I do," he says. "Just don't...push it. I need your lips on my cock, Jackson."

I skim said lips upwards and grab the band of his briefs with my teeth. Ash's breath catches, the sound hitching into a groan as I tug the material down.

"Fucking hell, Jack."

The moment his cock pops free, I let his briefs go and trail my lips up the sensitive skin of his shaft.

"You've wrecked me," he says hoarsely. "I hope you know that. Completely wrecked me for anyone else."

My chest balloons, so much pride and damn possessiveness hitting me with the force of a baler. I wrap my lips around his cockhead, pull his briefs out of the way, and sink down.

Ash grabs at my hair, his hips lifting off the hay. "*Fu-u-uck*, Jack. You're so damn good at that. *So* good."

I hum, slipping to the top of his dick as Ash mutters and tries to fuck back into my throat. I press his hips down with my arm, hand on his stomach as I bob my head again. He lets out a tortured moan, his cock flexing against my tongue. He tastes like man, and the tartness of the cider lingers on my tastebuds, making him all the more delicious.

There's something about bringing a man to his metaphorical knees with nothing but my mouth that has always appealed to me on a primal level. Knowing Ash is falling apart because of me? Because of how my lips feel wrapped around his cock? It's a heady fucking thing. It's base and instinctual, *intimate* in a way some acts simply aren't. I've never been good at faking my affections, but I don't even have to try with Ash. It's there in my eyes when I meet his gaze; I know it is. The same way his desperation is bared to me as he starts to lose control.

His lips are parted now, his hair a mess that casts shadows across his face. He looks like temptation personified, like the most dangerous thing I've ever set eyes on. He's beautiful, and I have no hope of resisting him. So when his breath stutters and his hips flex, I let go, letting him thrust up into my mouth.

"Jack," he gasps. He shoves his cock through my lips once, twice, and then floods my mouth.

His moan as his body locks in pleasure has my own cock throbbing. I cup myself, kneading my dick through my jeans as Ash spills again onto my tongue. His hand in my hair releases its pressure, his fingers soothing as his tension uncoils. I swallow the last of him down before letting his cock go, my breathing as labored as his.

"Are you..." Ash's words trail into a groan when he catches sight of my hand moving over my dick. He sits up, forcing me backwards, and reaches for me. "Fuck, let me touch you."

I let go, and Ash scoots up onto his knees in front of me, tugging at my jeans. The first touch of his hand on my cock, skin hot, grip proprietary, nearly has me buckling. He shuffles in close, gripping the back of my neck as he jerks me with a dry palm.

"Fuck, you're almost there, aren't you?" he whispers.

Unable to answer, I drop my forehead to his shoulder and suck in a breath. Ash's hand disappears for only a moment, and then it's back, cool and wet from his spit, the smooth glide making me buck into his grip.

"That's right, darlin'," he soothes, fingers dancing up into my hair, nails scratching. "You were so good to me. Come on my hand, and I'll show you how good my tongue can be for you."

With a hoarse shout, I release all over Ash's fist. He pumps me through it, the stickiness spreading, my cock throbbing in his grip as my lungs battle to catch air. Spots dance in my vision, the suddenness of my orgasm leaving me dizzy.

Ash kisses my ear, his hand slowing, the fingers on the back of my neck squeezing tight. He urges my head up with his grip.

"Lie back," he tells me.

I do as he says, lying down on our coats that are spread out over the hay. Ash waits until he's my sole focus, and then he brings his hand to his mouth. Slowly, he licks my cum from his skin, tongue curling around the digits one at a time. It's enough to send a shudder of renewed *want* down my spine. Once done, he bends down to lick along the length of my softening cock.

I mutter a few choice expletives as Ash's breath dances over my skin, his efforts to clean me soft yet thorough. He even snatches up a few drops that hit my shirt, bringing them to his mouth and smacking his lips when he's done.

"So sweet," he teases.

My laughter takes me by surprise. Ash, too, judging by his sudden grin.

"Liar," I mutter.

Ash chuckles, tugging the band of my underwear up over my cock. He covers himself, too, and then he falls beside me, rolling into the crook of my arm.

"Romp in the hay," he says lightly. "Ten out of ten. Who knew?"

I rub his bare arm, snorting. "All right?"

"Mhm," he hums, kissing my jaw. "Boneless, thanks to you."

We're both quiet for a moment, just our breaths and the faint sounds of the Montana wild a soundtrack for our night.

"Thanks, Jack," Ash finally says, his voice soft. "This was...perfect. A perfect end to the night."

I press a kiss to his hair, eyes slipping shut at how sincerely *happy* he sounds to be lying here inside a hayloft with me. At how easily he fits. Here. In Montana. On this ranch.

He *fits*. And it's getting hard to imagine him anywhere else.

Anywhere but here with me.

When Ash shivers, I reach around to grab his shirt. "Here," I say, giving him a nudge to get up.

Ash accepts the clothing, tugging it on as I reposition myself, sitting upright and leaning against the stacked hay bales behind us. Once done, Ash joins me, his back to my chest as we sit nestled together. He reaches for the still-open jug of cider and drags it close.

"Thirsty?" he asks.

"Not sure that'll help."

He chuckles, bringing the jug to his lips. He passes it back to me after taking a sip, his arm settling over my bent knee. The alcohol burns pleasantly on my tongue.

"My brothers and I used to play this game called 'truth or lie,'" I tell him. Although the last time was probably a good half-decade ago.

"How's it go?" Ash asks.

"You tell a truth or a lie, and the other person has to guess which. You get it wrong, you drink."

"Ah," he says. "One of *those* games. All right. You go first."

I hum, thinking for a second. "When I was younger, I wanted to be a musician."

Ash twists around, looking at me for a moment. "Lie," he finally decides. "You never wanted to leave this place."

I huff. "Did try my hand at guitar in high school, though. Wasn't very good."

"Don't suppose you were trying to impress someone?" Ash asks with a knowing smile. He laughs at whatever he sees on my face.

"We've all had bad taste at one point or another," I mumble. In my case, my brief crush was on the mayor's son. A man who, to the best of my knowledge, is still quite straight. "Your turn."

Ash gives my leg a squeeze. "I once broke my femur in three places."

I cringe. "Lie. I hope."

"You're right. Haven't ever broken a bone. Have you?"

"Luckily, no. Which is a minor miracle, considering how rough and tumble us boys were growing up."

"God," Ash says, shaking his head. "I would have loved to see a small Jackson Darling running around the ranch. I bet you were ridiculously cute, all pouty and serious even then."

My heart kicks up an extra beat. "I'm not *pouty*."

Ash laughs. "You're pouting right now."

I clear my expression, and he snorts. "I used to have an unhealthy obsession with Dolly Parton," I say, getting us back on track.

He looks me over carefully, his eyes widening. "Holy shit. Truth. Seriously?"

I nod, plucking a short piece of hay out of Ash's hair. "It was the music, believe it or not."

"*That* I believe," he says, laying his head back on my shoulder. "Considering you're a gay man."

I snort, looping an arm around his middle. His stomach is warm beneath my palm, even through his shirt. Ash's hair tickles my nose as I breathe, the earthy scent of hay mixing with *him*.

"I hate shellfish," he says quietly.

"Lie?"

"Nope. Truth. I never was a very good Mainer. Drink up."

I take a sip of the cider, fingers playing over Ash's shirt. He hums, shifting against me.

"My brother once bet me I couldn't eat ten hot dogs in ten minutes," I say. "I succeeded."

"Colton?" he asks.

"Mm."

Ash snorts. "Figures. And that's a lie. I don't think you made it."

"I sure did," I say proudly. "He never said I had to eat the buns."

Ash looks back at me, grinning. "Ah, so you're a cheater."

"Nope. Just good at outsmarting my brothers."

He huffs a laugh and curls his fingers in a *gimme* gesture. "Hand it over."

I bring the jug to my lips and take a sip.

"Fuck, Jack," Ash mutters, already knowing my intent.

Hand on his jaw, I angle his face my way. He accepts the drink from my mouth, his lips warm and tasting of apples. I let my other hand drift lower, fingers toying with the hem of his shirt as Ash's arm loops behind my head.

"You know, I have to be up in a couple hours to cook breakfast," he murmurs, letting out a breath when I shift my lips down to his neck. "We should probably...get back."

"Or," I propose, slipping my fingertips underneath the waistband of his briefs, "we could stay up here all night and take a nap after breakfast."

Ash inhales deeply when I wrap my fingers around his cock. "I think I like your ideas, Jack."

I manage a hum as Ash tugs my hair, demanding my mouth with gentle persistence. I give in easily, my hand gaining more room to maneuver as Ash pushes his still-open jeans down his hips. He hardens in my fist, soft sounds pouring from his lips as he starts to drive up into my hand.

"Fuck, you always make me so hot," he breathes.

"Truth," I mutter against his mouth.

Ash laughs, his hand in my hair almost stinging as his hips punch up off the ground. When he spins, I have no choice but to let go. "Need to feel you, Jack."

I don't object as Ash tugs down my boxer briefs. He tucks the band under my balls and picks up the jug of cider. With a smirk, he tips it over the head of my dick.

"Fuck," I gasp, the cool liquid sliding down my shaft and soaking into my underwear. "That's gonna be a mess."

"Worth it," Ash says, wrapping a hand around me. When his fist glides easily up and down, I have to agree.

"C'mere," I grunt, giving his arm a tug. "Ride my cock."

Ash stills. "Jack... I've put plenty of weird shit up my ass, but I'm not sure whiskey cider is a good replacement for lu—"

With a huff, I tug Ash forward and wrap a hand around our cocks.

"Oh," he breathes out, hands landing on my shoulders. "Oh, fuck. Yeah, I get it."

My head hits the hay bale behind me as Ash starts to move, grinding his cock against mine in the confines of my fist. For the briefest of moments, I remember my demonstration on frotting with Colton in the barn below, but the image of two carrots is quickly replaced by Ash as he drops his head back and moans. His hair is bright in the light of the moon, even as his face is obscured in shadows. It's all too easy to imagine him fucking himself on my dick with the way he's moving.

"Hell," I mutter. "You'd make a damn good cowboy."

He huffs an amused laugh before leaning forward to catch my lips. For minutes, there's nothing but this. Ash's mouth. His hands on my shoulders and in my hair. A tightness in my gut and in my chest, an ache that goes beyond the pleasure we're both so desperately chasing.

When Ash starts to come, I tighten my fist, jacking the both of us feverishly. He stutters a cry into my mouth, his body jerking, cum spilling over my hand before he collapses against my chest. I follow him not a moment later, adding to the mess on my shirt.

I run a hand through Ash's hair as his head rests on my shoulder. A few strands curl over his cheek, and I tuck them away behind his ear, that pressure in my chest back in full force.

There's one very loud truth making its presence known at the edge of my mind. It's been there all night. When Ash picked me up for our date. When he brought me more donuts to smash against the tree. When he refused to meet my gaze on the carriage ride, so certain our romantic evening had been ruined and not wanting me to see his disappointment. The look in his eye, both joy and desire, when I tackled him atop a hay bale. The way he kissed me so sweetly, tasting of autumn and home.

I never expected this man. Sure didn't see him coming over the horizon. I wasn't even looking. But now, I can't find it in me to look away.

I sift my fingers through Ash's hair again and whisper the truth that won't let go. "I think I'm falling for you."

Ash goes still, motionless apart from the rise and fall of his chest.

I tuck a strand of his hair behind his ear. "Truth or lie?"

His breath hits my neck, his palm unmoving on my chest. For once, he's utterly silent.

"Truth or lie, Ash?"

He doesn't even have to lift his head and look at me to suss out the answer. "Truth."

"It scares the shit out of me," I admit.

Ash shifts back enough to catch my gaze, his hand moving to the side of my neck, anchoring there. He strokes over my pulse point slowly. "I know."

"I don't want either of us to get hurt."

"I know, Jack."

"You can't leave me."

I don't mean to say the words aloud, but I can't take them back. It's impossible now.

Ash lets out an almost wounded sound, his nose brushing mine as he speaks. "Why would I possibly leave my home, Jack? I'm not going anywhere. Truth or lie?"

I let out a breath, hands holding tightly to Ash's lower back. No, I wasn't prepared for this man. Not his storm-lined eyes.

Not his goodness or his laugh. Not the sound of him singing in the kitchen or the smile he wears when it rains.

But he's here. He's here, and he says he's not going. So I speak the only word I can.

"Truth."

And I pray like hell I'm right.

Chapter 23

ASH

"I have a problem," I say, plunking down on a stool in front of Virginia inside The Barrel.

"Oh boy," my friend mutters. She tucks her towel into her apron before leaning her elbows onto the bartop. "Do we need drinks for this?"

I shake my head but reconsider. "Actually, water?"

Virginia nods, pushing away and grabbing a pint glass. She fills it with water and slides it over, waiting as I guzzle nearly the entire thing. "Better?"

"Yeah, thanks."

"All right, spill."

I take a deep breath, hoping the steady buzz of conversation in the bar is enough to afford us some privacy. "Jackson loves me."

Virginia is quiet for a moment. "Baby boy, you're gonna have to give me more information than that. Because I can not, for the life of me, figure out how that's a problem."

My laugh is pained. "He said it a week ago, and I haven't said it back."

"Okay," she replies slowly.

"I want to say it back," I explain.

"O-kay," she says again, even slower.

"But he told me just after we'd had this incredibly intimate evening, and he admitted he was scared I'd leave, so I couldn't say it then because I didn't want it to sound like a false assurance. And now, it's been a freaking *week*, and there's too much pressure to do it right."

Virginia lets out a breath, her head bowing for a moment. "Men, I swear to God. You're all idiots."

"Hey."

"Ash, you just need to tell him," she says seriously, hazel eyes meeting mine. They're so familiar, so comforting, even when Virginia is giving me a dressing-down. "It doesn't need to be special, and it doesn't need to be this big to-do. You love him. You tell him. Don't you think that's gonna mean more to him than you waiting just to get it *right*? Especially considering it's been a week. He's prob'ly sweating bullets."

"Well," I hedge. "He only kind of said it."

She drops her head again. "Jesus effin' Christ. Can you tell the story from the beginning?"

I groan, the sound part laugh, part desperation. "He said, 'I think I'm falling for you,'" I say, using my best Jackson impression. "After we had sex. For the second time. In a hayloft."

Virginia blinks at me.

"Say something," I moan.

"You're both idiots."

"*Ginnie.*"

"You *are*," she says firmly. "He sorta said it but didn't say it. You're too scared to say it. Somebody needs to *say* it already."

I drop my head into my palms, knowing she's right.

"And a hayloft, Ash?"

"You've never…"

"Never," she says. "That shit scratches you all up to hell. Firm pass."

"Jackson put his jacket under me," I tell her, lips twisting into a smile.

"Oh Lord. You're damn smitten, aren't you?"

"So smitten," I agree. "I want to tell him."

"Just do it. It don't gotta be complicated, baby boy."

I reach across the counter, snagging my closest friend into a hug. She squeezes me back like she's cracking a walnut.

"You're really staying, aren't you?" she practically whispers, her voice so quiet I would have missed the words had we been any further apart.

"I'm staying, Ginnie."

"Fuck, I can't tell you how happy that makes me."

"Is that why you're suffocating me?" I ask, blowing her hair out of my face.

She leans back and swats me in the shoulder. Then hugs me again. Then finally lets go. "I get to be your best man."

Virginia laughs as I spin away from the bar, on a mission.

When I get back to the ranch, it's late afternoon. The rain has been coming down all day, making the ground soggy and giving the air a misty quality that has me longing for tomato soup again. I'm surprised, when I step inside the ranch house, to find a bustle of activity.

"Grab one of the sat phones," Marigold is saying. "Just in case. You know service is spotty up there."

Colton nods, a backpack on the ground in front of him that he's shoving a medical kit into. A few of the ranchers hustle past, water bottles in hand and a frantic energy about them.

"What's going on?" I ask, coming to a halt inside the foyer.

Marigold brushes her hair out of her face. "A kid wandered off from her trail ride group and is missing. We're sending everybody out to sweep the area."

"Shit," I mutter, my gut sinking to the floor. "Is there anything I can do to help?"

"I don't think so, dear. We'll find her. We've got everybody on it, and there's only so far she could have gone."

I nod, but my stomach continues to churn. "Could I...make sandwiches or something? For people to bring in case it takes a while?"

Mrs. Darling offers me a small smile. "Couldn't hurt."

"Yeah. Okay," I mutter, heading toward the kitchen. I whip up a dozen lunch meat sandwiches as my hands shake. Marigold finds me just as I'm finishing up.

"Thanks, Ashley. Let me help you wrap those."

We slip the sandwiches into baggies, and Marigold takes them out to the lingering members of the search crew who are congregating on the back deck, Colton amongst them. The food gets split between packs as I look out toward the barn. Horses are being saddled, everyone on the ranch seemingly helping.

"Where's Jackson?" I ask.

"He was the first to ride out," Marigold tells me. "As soon as we got the call, he went to start the search. He's got a sat phone with him. Don't worry."

I nod, chewing at my lip. "How old is the girl?"

"Ten," Marigold says softly.

So young. She must be freezing in this weather. And scared.

My heart aches for her.

Mrs. Darling gives my shoulder a squeeze. "They'll find her," she says again, sounding as if she's reassuring me more than herself. "It's not even dark out yet. There's plenty of time."

I nod quickly, not wanting to add to her burden with my worry. "Right. It'll be fine."

Her smile is wan.

Once the final search crew is ready to go, Colton starts doling out directions. He's utterly serious for once, his usual smile and easygoing attitude absent. The first group left shortly after Jackson went out, taking trails to the east of where the girl went missing. Colton's group will head west.

"We ready?" he asks them.

Everyone nods, and they walk out into the rain. I watch from the porch with Marigold, feeling useless.

"I got lost once when I was seven," I tell her, a hand on my stomach. "Or so I'm told. I don't actually remember it, but my mom likes to tell the story. We were shopping. I didn't even go far. They found me inside a circular rack of clothes. But for the fifteen minutes it took, my mom was terrified."

Marigold nods, her expression pinched.

"I hate to think of what they're feeling," I admit. "The girl. Her family."

"Tara," she says gently. "That's her name."

I nod in a jerk. "Tara. We should have blankets and cocoa ready for when she's found. She'll need to warm up. And...her parents?" Marigold nods, a confirmation. "They'll want to see that their daughter is safe."

Mrs. Darling wraps her arm around my shoulder, squeezing once before leading me back toward the door. "We'll do just that."

Marigold and I pull blankets out of the cupboard, setting them on the coffee table in the living room. We don't make the cocoa yet, but we ready the mix and collect mugs. After that, she excuses herself to check in with Hank, and I pace.

I pace the living room, peeking out through the window toward the horse barn. Everyone's already gone. I pace past the couch, refolding one of the blankets before setting it back down. I pace the perimeter of the braided, oval rug that takes up most of the floor space and then head to the dining room to pace past the long windows at the back of the house.

With a stutter inside my chest, I spin and jog up the stairs. I grab my raincoat, throw it on, and head out the door.

The rain mists my face as I make my way to the horse barn. I can't say I'm thinking all that rationally, but I can't sit inside and do nothing. I want to help. *Need* to. And another set of eyes couldn't hurt, right?

I almost expect my efforts to be fruitless, but when I get to the barn, I find Shorty still within his stall. I breathe a sigh of relief. He's the only horse I've ridden, and I'm not sure I would have been able to saddle another. But I find his gear, and I lead him into the hallway, knowing exactly what to do.

Shorty waits patiently while I get him ready to ride, his hoof absentmindedly scratching at the dirt a couple times. Maybe he feels the restless energy in the air, too. The crackle of danger. The oppressive fog.

I cinch his saddle tightly, but not *too* tight, just like Jackson taught me. I adjust the stirrups to the length I know I'll need. Then I fit the bridle over Shorty's face, running my trembling hand along his nose as his breath huffs against my skin.

"We've got this, Shorty. Right?"

He huffs again.

Once he's ready to go, I check the saddle one last time. Deciding Shorty isn't holding a big breath just to sneak in an extra inch of wiggle room, I grab the reins and jump up onto his back.

"All right, Short-stuff. Let's go."

Instinct has me ducking as we travel through the door-way out of the barn, even though there's plenty of head-room. Shorty's ears flick when the rain starts pelting us. It's not coming down too hard at the moment, but it's not particularly comfortable, either. I give Shorty's neck a rub, offering him a silent thanks for his cooperation.

We head along the soft, muddy path toward the start of the trail. We're near the tree line when I finally look back at the house. There's no one running after me. No one telling me to stop. No one at all, as far as I can tell.

I lead Shorty into the trees.

My breath comes out like fog as the rain eases. It's still misting the air, but the trees take the brunt of it, sheltering us, even a little. We walk along the well-marked trails, a few fresh hoofprints in the path ahead of us. I heard Colton detailing the direction they'd take, so I set off that way, figuring it won't take long for Shorty and me to catch up. And then we can...I don't know. Help look. Help, somehow.

It's quiet as we move. Eerily quiet. And darker within the shade of the forest. The rain is like white noise, muffling everything around us. An occasional snap of a twig sounds under Shorty's hooves, but otherwise, it's silent. We're alone.

"We have to be getting close," I say, my own voice making my pulse jump. Shorty's ears flick. "They went down this way, I'm sure of it."

At least, I *was* sure. I know he said the orange trail. Didn't he?

Gathering my courage, I call out, "Hello?"

No answer. Just the rain. Just Shorty's hooves and his breath, puffing out like my own. I pull out my phone, dialing Jackson. He doesn't answer.

"It's fine," I mumble, sticking my phone back in my pocket. "I know we're on the right path. We'll find them."

Shorty keeps plodding forward.

An hour later, I'm seriously considering turning back. We're near the base of the mountains now, further than I thought the group would have gone. The trail markers are more spaced out here, and it's close to getting dark. I didn't even think to grab a sandwich myself, not that eating is at the forefront of my mind right now. Shorty is a trooper, not seeming put-out by our half-cocked rescue mission. But my legs are soaked through, my hands cold, and my fingers pruned.

"Fuck," I mutter as we come to a new fork in the road. Neither direction is marked, but Jackson told me sometimes the colored indicators get broken or covered by brush. I hop down off Shorty's back, wincing at the tightness in my back and legs. Walking around, I kick aside leaves and fallen branches, looking for the little wooden markers, but I don't find any.

As much as I hate to admit defeat, I have no clue which way to go, and if we don't head back soon, we'll lose the sun. I didn't even think to grab a flashlight.

With another curse, I hitch myself onto Shorty's back and turn him around. I shake my head as we retrace our steps back down the trail, feeling pissed and frustrated and, once again, utterly useless.

"Thanks for trying, Shorty," I tell the horse, patting his damp neck. He kicks up his head gently. "Let's head home, get nice and dry, and then I'll get you a treat. How's that sound?"

His ears flick as I scratch between them.

"Yeah," I mutter. "Sounds good."

I keep a loose hold on the reins as Shorty climbs up the short incline we came down a few minutes ago. The trail is high here, the land dipping down on either side of it. In one direction, past the trees, is the Darlings' pastureland. The cattle are probably hunkered together, finding shelter beneath the interspersed trees. On the other side of the trail, past a deep ravine, is the mountains.

I wonder if Jackson and I could explore them sometime. Surely, they have guided mountain climbs in this area. I bet there are some options for beginners. Or maybe Jackson himself knows the ropes. It wouldn't surprise me.

There's a gentle smile on my face when Shorty's head kicks up again, a little harder than before. He stutters a step, ears flicking.

"All right?" I ask. I can't hear anything but the rain.

I open my mouth to reassure the horse everything is fine, when something rustles off to our right. Shorty reverses course with a quick backwards step, and my pulse takes off like a shot, my inhalation loud as I tighten my hands on the reins. I'm about to encourage Shorty forward again when something races out in front of us.

It happens so fast.

The small animal—a racoon—freezes like a deer caught in the beams of an oncoming car. Panicked by our presence, it makes a mad dash, ending up beneath Shorty's front legs as Shorty rears up, hooves leaving the dirt before slamming back down again. He tries to back up as the raccoon scrambles underfoot, each attempting to avoid the other in the span of mere seconds that seem to last a lifetime. Shorty rears again, his back hoof slipping at the edge of the softened trail, and my gut does a nosedive, my world going temporarily weightless as I'm thrown from his back.

I don't remember the fall. Don't remember how long I'm in the air. But I remember slamming onto dirt, pain searing through my shoulder as I slide down the steep slope for what feels like an age. Rocks, branches, who-knows-what-else scrape against me as I grapple to find a handhold, unable to in time. The ground disappears right out from under me, and everything goes weightless once more.

I land with a thud, my breath leaving me. For a moment, all I can do is stare up at the canopy of trees above.

Finally, I suck in a gasping breath. And then another. Rain drops softly onto my face as I take stock of the situation. I try to sit up, but the sharp, glass-like pain radiating out from my shoulder has me flat on my back again in an instant.

"Fuck," I mutter, fighting the urge to throw up. "*Fuck.*"

I wait longer this time, cataloguing the pain as I work to slow my breathing. There are tiny, stinging scrapes all over my body. A dull ache at the back of my head. I lift my good arm to feel the area, relieved, when I bring my hand in front of my face, to see there's no blood. I let loose a breath, marginally reassured. But my shoulder is a problem.

Slowly, I press my arm against my body and hold it there, gritting my teeth and fighting back a scream as I get myself into a sitting position. After catching my breath, I stand, nearly throwing up again when my shoulder shifts.

I think I dislocated it. Hopefully it's not broken.

I look up at the steep mountain face in front of me. No help there. Turning, I find the ground I took a tumble down. It starts at eye-level, which explains the second fall. The hill is steeply sloped, the path I carved down it visible as an irregular streak through the leaves and dirt. My breath whooshes out of me when I see Shorty looking down from atop the hill. *Thank fuck.* He's still on the trail, maybe forty feet away.

"Hey, buddy," I call. "You okay?"

His ears flick, and his hoof stomps the ground.

"Yeah, okay. Let's see..."

The second I try to heft myself onto the slope, I know I'm not going anywhere. Pain sears through my shoulder, and I pant through it, my chest resting against the lip of dirt. Finally, I let myself fall, dropping the short distance back to the ground.

Using my good arm, I fish my phone from my pocket, astonished it's even still there. I swear aloud when I see the screen, cracked and clearly broken. I swear again when the phone won't turn on.

"Goddamn it!" I shout, my voice echoing inside the pit I've found myself in. Once I'm calm, I look around again. Every which way, there's a steep climb.

I don't have a choice. I have to try again.

Girding myself against the pain I know will come, I grab onto the thickest sapling I can reach on the hill I fell down and hoist myself up. Stars dance in my vision, a ragged sound leaving my mouth as I inch myself a little higher...little higher...

As soon as my hips clear the edge, I roll onto my back and suck in breath after breath, still holding the sapling tight. My arm is shaking, my other a useless weight at my side. Slowly, I wriggle upwards until my feet can find purchase. Knees bent, I push with my heels, trying to slide myself up the hill a little further.

It works. Kind of.

I grab for another sapling, smaller than the first, and pray it holds my weight. Again, I dig in my heels and push, but the ground is so wet, my feet kick out. Taking a calming breath, I try again, going slower, getting myself up another half-foot on my back before needing a new hand-hold. I arch my neck, finding Shorty watching me from atop the hill.

"Coming," I assure him.

Every muscle in my body protests as I inch myself up the incline. I'm soaking wet. Muddy. I don't have a hand to clear the moisture from my eyes. My teeth are chattering, adrenaline the only thing letting me block out, even a little, the pain radiating out from my shoulder.

Doesn't matter. I push myself up another few inches. Another few. I find another handhold, heels dug into the earth.

The tiny tree I'm holding gives.

"No, no, no," I say, frantically trying to stop my momentum as I slide down the wet earth. I grab at dirt, rocks, branches. Kick my feet...

And fall back into the pit.

I black out for a second. Spots dance in front of my eyes as I lie on the ground, my head swimming, my dislocated arm wedged beneath my body at a horrible angle.

"Shorty," I call out, voice hoarse. "Can you go back? Can you go get help? Please?"

I have no clue if he even knows what I'm trying to say, but when I get myself turned around, my jaw aching as I strain not to cry out, I can see him still up on the trail, tail swishing.

"Shorty," I yell again. "Go home? Run home?"

He doesn't, and as darkness crawls along the edges of my vision, the pain threatening to pull me under, I hear a sound. It's quiet at first, so quiet I assume I'm imagining it. But then it gets louder and more distinct, and there's no mistaking what I'm hearing.

The tinkling of a bell.

A *bell*.

In the middle of a forest in Darling freaking Montana.

Good fucking grief.

"Please, *please* don't bite me," I mumble with the last of my waning strength.

And then everything is black.

Chapter 24

JACKSON

"Fuck, that sucked balls," Colton mutters as the ranch house comes into view. He's riding beside me atop Clementine, just as wet as I am. The rain has mostly stopped, but with the sun having fallen behind the mountains, we're all cold and plain miserable.

But at least we have Tara.

She's on horseback with her dad, who joined the second search party. The little girl is in remarkably good shape, having waited beneath a tree once she was sure she was lost. It was smart of her to stay put instead of continuing to wander in a direction that might have taken her further from her group.

She's shaken and tired, but whole and healthy. And that's what matters.

"Think Ash will have whipped up something warm for us?" Colton asks, a grin on his face.

"It's his weekend," I remind my brother.

"Yeah, but you know he wouldn't care. He likes cooking for us."

"And should be appreciated for it," I grumble.

"Hey, did anything I say sound unappreciative?" he combats, not waiting for an answer before going on. "You're in a *mood*."

"Can you blame me?" I ask, sliding down off Starlight's back as we reach the stables.

"Nope," my brother answers easily. "Like I said, that sucked."

Tara's dad jumps down and helps his daughter off their horse. In the dim light, I can see the girl's mom approaching swiftly alongside my mother, both coming from the direction of the ranch house. I give the family privacy as they reunite, their soft cries tugging at my heart.

My mom beelines my way once close, her eyes sweeping the group of us who rode back with Tara and her dad. We're the last to arrive. "Is Ashley with you?" she asks, her voice shaking in a way I don't like.

"No," I say slowly. "Why would he be?"

She sets her jaw, working through something. "He's not here. I think he went after you lot."

"You think?" I ask, my heart jumping.

"I don't know, Jackson. He was here, and then he wasn't. And he didn't come back with the first group."

"*Ma*," I say a little harshly.

"Jackson Darling, I suggest you curb that tone. I'm just as worried as you are."

One look at her face confirms it. I spin around, heading into the barn.

"Shorty isn't in there," my mom calls.

I curse, my feet carrying me forward faster. The moment I set eyes on Shorty's empty stall, I spin right back around.

"You tried calling?" I ask.

"Him and his friend Virginia both," she confirms. "She hasn't seen him since earlier, before he got home."

The rest of our party is looking between the two of us now, having realized something is wrong. My mom hands me Starlight's reins as soon as I reach them.

"Go," she says. "I'll talk to the others."

I swing up onto Starlight's back, looking Colton's way. He hasn't yet gotten down off Clementine. "You got the lamps?"

"Yep," he says. "Let's do it."

I turn Starlight in the direction of the woods and kick my heels. "*Ya.*"

I can hear Colton behind me as we race back toward the trails. I have to slow once we reach the forest's cover, both for safety and because it's gotten far too dark to see. I come to a stop, waiting for my brother to catch up. Once beside me, he pulls the headlamps out of his saddlebag, handing one over.

"You really think he would've gone out on his own?" Colton asks.

I don't even have to consider it. "Yes."

For that little girl? He would've gone in a heartbeat.

The damn fool.

I shake the thought loose immediately, hating it. Hating *myself* for even thinking it. Ash isn't a fool. He's just a heart-strong man who would have wanted to help, who wouldn't have thought of the dangers to himself above those to that little girl.

"If he's not all right..." I say, shaking my head, unable to even think it.

My brother zips up the saddlebag. "He will be," he says, flicking on his lamp. "C'mon. If we didn't pass him earlier, he must be on another trail. Let's try the northwest end."

With a nod, I turn on my lamp, and the two of us take off. We shout occasionally, calling out Ash's name, stopping to listen for a reply. There is none.

No answering call. No Shorty. No Ash.

We scour the black and yellow trails along the northern border of the woods. Follow them west toward the mountains. We ride along the blue trail and then the orange.

An hour later, my worry has reached a pinnacle. We called back home with the sat phone to check in with my mom, but no Ash. A few other ranchers followed us out, but we haven't crossed paths with them, either.

When we come to a fork, Colton and I stop to regroup. We're each a little breathless, both from the riding and all the shouting. The horses have got to be tired, but they won't complain. They're used to hard work. And we won't push them past their limits.

"Thoughts?" Colton says.

I look down the two diverging trails. One leads straight west toward the mountains. The other veers south, back toward the cattle pastures.

"Fuck, I don't know," I admit.

"We'll try one and then the other," Colton says. He turns Clementine toward the southern trail when we hear something. A bray. "Is that…"

Both our heads swing toward the trail that leads west, our headlamps dimly lighting the path. I swear I hear a bell, and then…

"The Darling Donkey," I realize, my pulse jumping. "Ash is that way. He's gotta be."

"You don't know—Jack!"

"Stay with the donkey," I call back to Colton, already taking off down the western trail. "If I don't find Ash, the donkey will lead you there."

My brother swears loudly. When Starlight and I pass the donkey on the trail, he turns and trots after us, but I don't slow, knowing Colton will stay with him like I asked, even if he doesn't like it. I shout Ash's name, straining my ears, trying to listen past the pounding of my own heart. I stop after five minutes, shout, wait, listen. We go on.

We ride another ten minutes down the trail when I think I hear something. Starlight and I slow to a walk, and I listen.

"Ash?" I shout.

Again, I hear it. A faint call. I urge Starlight on, and when we come around a bend, my heart nearly falls to my feet.

Shorty.

Alone.

Starlight and I rush forward, and the moment we're close, I swing off his back, jogging a few steps to slow my momentum. "Ash?" I shout again.

"Down here."

I whirl around, sweeping my headlamp over the area. "Keep talking," I say loudly. "I don't see you."

"You came," he says, his words sounding slurred.

I swing my headlamp downward, tracing the steep hill I'm atop toward the sound of his voice. I still can't see a thing. "You all right?"

He mumbles something, and then, "Yeah. I'm conscious again."

"Again?" I call, my heart pounding. I take a step forward but pause, realizing the hill is too severe an angle to walk down. I keep my hand on a tree as I peer around, moving the beam from my headlamp in an attempt to locate him.

Fuck, where is he?

"You know that raccoon we freed?" Ash says from somewhere down below. "I think it just tried to kill me. What a thanks."

He chuckles a little. It's not a sound I like.

"What are you talking about?" I ask, freezing as I see a hint of movement.

"A raccoon," he repeats slowly, but I don't think the pace is for my benefit. All his words sound a little slow. "It ran out on the trail. Shorty threw me. It's okay, though. Not his fault."

My chest feels as if it might just split apart.

"Ash, can you wave your hand or something? I can't—*Fuck*, there you are." Everything in me sags in relief when I see his hand waving feebly. "Sunshine," I croak. "You all right?"

"Think it was the same raccoon?" he asks, not answering my question.

"Probably not," I mutter, looking at the area around me. I walk along the trail, trying to find somewhere that's not so steep where I can climb down.

"Hey, is Shorty okay?" Ash calls.

"I think he's fine," I answer, not liking the fact that Ash keeps evading my questions, whether intentional or not. "Did you get hurt?" I ask again. "Are you stuck?"

"Don't come down here, Jack," he says seriously. "The ground is too soft after all that rain. It's a painful fall."

Fuck.

"Did you hit your head?" I ask.

That would explain the slurred speech.

"It's my shoulder I'm more worried about," Ash says, almost too quietly for me to hear. "Can barely feel my fingers."

A pit opens up in my stomach. "Ashley, how injured are you?" I ask roughly, heading back in the direction of the horses. "I need you to answer me *right goddamn now*."

"I'm *fine*," he says, sounding exasperated.

"I'm coming down."

"Don't!" he shouts. "Then we'll both be stuck. And it'll hurt a hell of a lot if you fall on me." A beat passes before he says,

"Hey, did you see the donkey? I swear he was here. Unless I imagined it."

"He was here," I answer shakily, pulling out my sat phone.

Ash snorts, and then he starts to laugh.

"Why're you laughing, sunshine?" I ask, needing to keep him talking. I call Colton.

"'Cause it fucking hurts," he says, still chuckling. "It doesn't, but it does, you know?"

My hands tremble. "That bad?"

"Pretty bad," he answers. "Can you believe I fell in a pit? I was just trying to help, and look where it got me."

"You're a good man, Ashley Alcott. Hold on, all right?"

"Not going anywhere," he says. And then he's laughing again.

"Find him?" Colton asks in my ear.

"Yeah. Just up the trail. Are you close? We need rope."

My brother curses. "On my way."

I don't bother with a goodbye before I hang up.

"Hey, is the girl okay?" Ash calls. "Tara. You find her?"

"We did," I call back, walking the other direction down the trail, looking for some sort of access. I don't see any, barely even see Ash peeking out below a drop in the ground. "She's fine. Let's focus on you now. You said it's your shoulder?"

"Dislocated, I think. Can't move my arm. I passed out a bit, but there's no blood. I couldn't make it up the hill, Jack."

"I know," I say, my voice cracking. "You'll be out soon."

"Thanks for coming. Shorty wouldn't leave. Kinda figured I was fucked."

"The horses are trained to stay with their riders," I tell him. "He did good."

Ash makes a sound just as Colton rides up. My brother dismounts as quickly as I did, dropping to one knee and swinging his backpack to the ground. "He okay?" he asks, pulling out rope from his emergency kit.

"Think so," I say, keeping my voice low. "Hurt, though."

My brother looks up at me, his headlamp blinding me for a second. "One harness or two?"

"Two," I tell him. If Ash's shoulder is out of commission, it'll only hurt him worse to pull him up solo.

Colton nods, setting to work on tying the knots needed for Ash's rescue. Once done, I step into the makeshift harness as Colton secures the end of the rope to the horses. "Ready?" he asks.

I give a swift nod, go down to my butt, and start sliding down the hill. Colton keeps my progress steady, and I use my hands for balance. Relief slams into me when Ash comes into full view. He squints up at me, his face and hair covered in grime.

"Hey, sunshine," I say, voice wobbling.

He smiles. "Jack."

Fuck.

It's clear he fought hard. Dirt covers nearly every inch of his body. Exhaustion is evident in his eyes. As he said, I can't see any blood, but that doesn't mean he's not seriously injured, either.

There's about a five foot drop from where I am to Ash's position at the bottom of a pit, so I swing around to my stomach and ease my legs over the side. For a moment, I hang in the air, the harness keeping me suspended. Then the rope starts moving again, and Colton lowers me to the ground.

The second my feet hit dirt, I'm crouching in front of Ash, my hands settling on his cheeks. They shake despite my best efforts to keep them still. He looks so damn worn out. And in pain.

I kiss his forehead, and Ash's good arm comes up around my shoulder, holding tight. "Fuck, baby," I breathe, pressing another kiss to his head. "How bad?"

Ash is quiet for a beat. "Eight? Nine?"

I nod, my lips quivering. "All right. Think you can stand?"

"If you help me."

I ease back, careful to avoid Ash's injured arm as I help him to his feet. It's a struggle, his body not wanting to cooperate, the wince on his face evidence of what sort of hurt the movement is causing. But he never complains. Not once.

As soon as he's standing, I ease the harness up his legs, Ash helping by lifting his feet one at a time. Once it's in place, I walk Ash toward the lip of the hill, my arm around him tight. "Ready?"

He nods.

"Colt?" I yell.

"Hold tight," my brother calls.

There's pressure, and then Ash and I are being hefted into the air. I use my arm to keep us from rotating too much, my focus on Ash's grimace more than the hard earth scraping along my back. As soon as we make it over the lip, Ash falls on top of me, calling out as his arm gets jostled.

"I know, I know," I say, trying to soothe him as the horses tug us slowly up the hill, the rope around a tree keeping us moving in a straight line. "Just think. Once all of this is over, we'll go home, get patched up, and sleep for a good year or so. How's that sound?"

"Like heaven," Ash says, his teeth gritted.

I kiss his temple, keeping my feet braced wide so we don't spin on our way up the hill. Small debris rolls beneath my back, but I pay it no mind.

When we level out at the top of the slope, I let out a massive sigh of relief. Colton is there in an instant, untying us, helping Ash to ease off of me and stand.

"Dislocated?" my brother asks, gently touching Ash's shoulder. Ash is holding his arm to his chest.

He nods. "Think so."

Colton glances at me. "I'll set it before we leave. He can't ride like this."

"Colt..."

"Jackson," my brother interrupts. "You *know* I know how to reduce a shoulder. So let me. It'll hurt until it doesn't, and then we can go. It needs to happen."

I nod, the tightness around my chest making it hard to breathe. Colton has EMT training. He's right. I *know* he knows what he's doing, but that doesn't make it any easier when it's your loved one who'll be in pain.

"Just do it," Ash says, his voice stronger than before. "Jackson, look away if you need to."

I huff, stepping up beside him. "Like I'm gonna do that. C'mon, let's sit."

Ash nods, and in the dark of the night, in the middle of a goddamn trail at the back of my family's property, we sit across from one another on the cold hard ground. I aim my headlamp so it's not shining on his face, and Ash holds my gaze as Colton squats down beside him. My brother tells Ash what he's going to do every step of the way, getting his arm in position, something that has Ash grimacing and biting back his pain. I pretend to ignore the moisture I can see on his face.

"Here's what we'll do," Colton says. "On the count of five—"

Ash cries out as Colton pops his shoulder back into the socket. It's over fast, and then Ash is laughing, tears streaming down his face as my brother shoots me a concerned look.

"*Fuuuck*," Ash groans, hanging his head. "You didn't count at all, you dick."

"Trick of the trade," Colton says, letting Ash go so he can grab his med kit.

"You okay?" I ask, squeezing Ash's hand tight.

He nods, tears in his eyes as he continues to chuckle. One look at my face, and the sound breaks into a sigh. "Nicholas didn't get it, either. Why I'd be laughing on those days I was in so much pain. Sometimes, you just have to laugh, you know? Because the alternative..."

He trails off, wincing again as Colton starts wrapping his arm against his chest to prevent further jostling.

"I'm probably going to be pretty sore after this," Ash says, blinking slowly. "I think I've been blocking most of it out."

I lean forward and kiss his hair. It smells like earth. Like rain and dirt. Not like Ash at all. "We'll get you better, sunshine."

"Yeah," he sighs. "I want cocoa when we get home."

"Anything you want."

"With milk," he adds. "None of that watered-down nonsense. And I don't want to talk to people, okay? Not tonight. I know I was an idiot—"

"Hey," I say softly, bringing his hand to my lips and kissing his knuckles. "No one's gonna blame you, I promise. Everybody's just gonna be relieved you're all right. I—" I clear my throat and try again. "*I'm* relieved you're all right."

His lips twitch. "Worried about me, were you?"

"So fucking much," I admit, not even trying to hide the truth of it from my voice. I press my cheek to his as Colton packs up our things, my eyes prickling. "You're not allowed to scare me like that again, sunshine."

He hums, the sound light and almost happy. "I'll try my best, darlin'. Now would you kiss me? I know I'm a mess, but—"

Ash's words cut off, a soft sound pressed against my lips as I kiss him. His hand grips the side of my neck, my fingers tangle in his hair, and we breathe each other in, no words needed to express what we're feeling. The happiness. The relief.

The lingering ache.

When we pull apart, it's not to go far. We stay tangled until Colton lets us know we're ready to go. Then, oh so carefully, I help Ash to his feet and atop Starlight's back before joining him. Shorty follows behind us.

The whole way home, my arm stays wrapped around Ash's chest, my hand never leaving his heart.

Chapter 25

ASH

"All right?" Jackson asks.

I eye my overprotective partner, who's currently attempting to fluff the pillow behind my back. "Fine," I say mildly.

"Comfy enough?"

"Jack."

"Just checking," he says, letting the pillow go.

"Mhm. Get back in bed with me."

"After I—"

"*Jack.*"

He sighs, sliding into bed in his jeans. He leans against my side as we sit at the headboard, his fingers toying lightly with the material of my pajama pants. "Coffee all right?"

"It's great," I tell him before taking another sip. Luckily, I'm able to use my dominant hand. It's my left arm that's currently resting in a sling, all but useless for the time being. "What're you doing today?"

Jackson fidgets, his own coffee waiting in a thermos on his nightstand. "Figured I'd take it easy. We're not too busy right now, so—"

"Jackson Darling," I warn, setting my coffee down before turning to him. "It's been a week. I'm *fine*. You need to go back to work."

He huffs. "Everybody's always telling me I work too hard, and now I'm not working hard enough? Can't win around here."

I refrain from rolling my eyes. "You've been babying me, Jack. I—"

Jackson swings over my legs, causing my words to dry up. He settles gently on my thighs, barely giving me his weight, his hands coming to rest along the sides of my neck. His focus is absolute, eyes bright and so very blue as they ping between my own. "You dislocated your shoulder. Threw out your back trying to get up that hill one-handed. You got a mild concussion. Had scrapes and bruises all over your body."

"Most of which healed in a few days," I say softly.

He shakes his head once, lips in a firm line. "I'm talking now."

"Oh, you are, are you?" I snark.

His kisses me hard, a quick press of lips meant to shut me up. I hate to admit how well it works.

When he leans back, he holds my gaze, and I keep quiet.

"You were battered and bruised, and you're still healing," Jackson says. "I'm allowed to take care of you. I'm allowed to *care*. I get that you don't wanna be treated like a child, but you're not, Ash. You're a grown-ass man who had his ass handed to him. What kind of partner would I be if that didn't affect me?"

I swallow roughly.

"So you're gonna let me look after you," he goes on, tone unyielding. "You don't gotta like it, but you're gonna do it. We clear?"

I let out a breath, hand sliding up Jackson's side. "Yessir."

"Nuh-uh," he says, easing back. "None of that."

"Jack," I groan, trying to snag his shirt before he can get too far.

He evades me. "Nope."

"It's been a *week*."

"The doctor said you needa relax," he says, slipping off the bed and grabbing his thermos.

"Orgasms are relaxing," I defend.

"Maybe later," he says, making my pulse jump. "If you're good."

"If I'm... Oh, fuck you! That shit doesn't work on me like it works on you," I call.

Jackson simply chuckles as he rounds the doorway into the hall. A beat later, he yells, "Get some rest, Ash. I'll be back to check on you in a bit."

"All I've been doing is resting," I mutter to myself, resituating and wincing as pain flares along my spine. *And* maybe he has a point. "Fuck."

As Jackson heads off to work the ranch, I grab my coffee and my phone. There's a text from Nicholas, telling me he heard what happened and that he hopes I'm doing okay. He included a couple recommendations for physio places nearby, which, honestly, shows a lot of restraint on his part. In the past, he would have drafted up an entire outline for my recovery period.

Accepting the olive branch for what it is, I send a thank-you, not at all surprised the news of my injury made it through the country club grapevine back in Maine.

I *am* a little surprised when, a second later, I get a returned text. It's a picture of Nicholas next to...a dog? Included are the words, *"Meet Smokey, the new you."*

I bark a laugh, a smile pulling at my lips. Shaking my head, I message back, wishing Nicholas and Smokey the best before closing out the text thread. I check the early morning voicemail from my mom next. She says she booked her flight for the end of the year, and she's looking forward to seeing me. Truth be told, I'm looking forward to seeing her, too. She was worried, of course, when I called to tell her what happened. But I convinced her to wait and fly out for the holidays instead of coming now.

Hopefully, by that point, I'll be all healed up.

Letting out a sigh, I swing myself slowly out of bed. The sling on my left arm is more annoying than anything. I remove it to get dressed and replace it before washing my coffee mug with one hand. Then I slip my feet into boots and go for a walk.

The air is crisp but the sun bright as I make my way around the property, no particular destination in mind. Marigold insisted I take time off to recover, and how could I argue when I'm not supposed to be using my arm? They managed just fine for nearly six months before I came along. Surely they can manage for another week or so.

My feet bring me over to the petting farm. It's too early to be open to the public, but I let myself in through the double gates, leaning down to hand out scritches to the goats that run over. Their rectangular pupils gaze up at me, so odd and endearing. I chuckle as their ears flop around, insistent tongues running repeatedly over my hand.

"Figured I'd find you here," a voice calls.

"Ginnie," I answer, standing up as my friend comes into the pen. Her hair is in twin braids today, the brown curls semi-tamed. "Were you looking for me long?"

"Only a minute," she says. "I figured I'd either find you here with the kids or over at Jackson's. I tried here first."

I huff a laugh. "Sounds weird when you say kids like that."

She smirks at me. "Are you officially moved in yet?"

I nearly stumble. "I'm not *moved in* at all," I tell her, pulling my shirt out of the teeth of a particularly forward goat. "I've just been staying at Jackson's—"

"For the past week—"

"While I recovered, yes," I finish.

Virginia raises an eyebrow. "And you're honestly gonna tell me you plan to sleep in the ranch house again once you're metaphorically back on your feet?"

Honestly, I hadn't thought about it at all.

"I don't know, Ginnie," I say, moving my arm aside as Snickerdoodle bumps into me. I give her some attention with my good hand. "I mean, it's not like he's even asked me to stay. For good, I mean."

"Uh-huh," she mutters, walking over to look at the chickens. Most of them are pecking at the ground, head floofs bobbing as they pick up seed that fell out of their feeders. "Well, when he *does* ask, *officially*, I mean—and he will—I'll try not to gloat."

"Well, aren't you generous," I mumble.

She shoots me a toothy grin. "C'mon, baby boy. Let's go grab some lunch. On me."

"Oh, uh... I was just going to eat here."

Her eyebrow shoots up again. "You haven't left the ranch in a week. Some fresh air would do you good."

I refrain from saying *yes, Mom*, instead waving my hand around pointedly. "Sure. Because this air right here is *so* very stifling."

She examines me closely. "You don't wanna go. Why? You in a lotta pain?"

"No," I say quickly, even though *yes*, I'm in a fair bit. "It's just..."

When she crosses her arms, waiting, I huff.

"I'm the town's new Marjory Bell, Ginnie. I fell in a hole, and the damn Darling Donkey had to rescue me. Excuse me for wanting to hide away for a while instead of facing what I'm sure would be a million pitying sympathies from the well-intentioned folk of Darling freaking Montana."

Her lips twitch.

"What?" I groan.

"You said 'folk.'"

"And?"

Virginia walks over to me, placing her hands lightly on my shoulders, careful of the left side. "*And* I never thought I'd see the day when my best friend became a part of this life. *My* life. And I'm selfish, so I like it a whole lot. You're one of us now, baby."

I snort. "Where's my t-shirt?"

"I'll buy you one from the gift shop," she says wryly before letting me go. "Now be honest. How bad's the pain?"

"Everyone and their mothering," I mutter. "My shoulder joint is fine. It's my goddamn back that's fucked all to hell. It's nearly as bad as it was in the beginning."

She winces.

"I'll be *fine*," I say. "I've done this song and dance before. I can do it again."

"I'm sorry that you have to," she says seriously. "And it's okay not to be *fine*, Ash. No one would think less of you for admitting that you're hurting."

I scowl, *hating* that very thing, and Virginia chuckles.

"Christ," she says. "You look just like him."

I don't even have to ask *who*. But I do ease up on the scowl.

"If you wanna stay and hide for now, I'm not gonna stop you," Virginia says. "Just... Once you're ready, I'll be here, okay?"

"I know that, Ginnie. You've never not been in my face, and I love that about you."

She snorts. "Love you, too, baby boy. Now get some rest. Go relax or something."

"Relax," I say with a huff. "Everybody wants me *relaxed*."

And *great*. Now I sound like Jackson, too.

Virginia leans in to give my cheek a kiss, and then she heads out of the petting farm. I stick around a minute longer, petting the goats and stopping Snickerdoodle from eating my pocket. I wonder if she's used to a certain someone bringing her treats.

When I get to the ranch house, the eleven o'clock lunch hour is already underway. I slip into the kitchen, not wanting to be seen. Everyone has been perfectly nice since the...*incident*, but I still feel like an ass. I shouldn't have gone out on my own like that. All I ended up doing was causing everyone—and myself—a world of trouble.

It's a mistake I won't be making again.

The soft sound of feet approaching alerts me that I'm no longer alone. Remi looks surprised to find me lurking in the kitchen.

I offer him a small smile. "Hey, I was just..."

He holds up a finger and presses a button on the device behind his ear. "Sorry, go ahead."

"You didn't have to turn it on for me," I tell him. I wouldn't have minded typing on my phone like I've seen some of the ranchers do when Remi doesn't have his CI on.

"It's no problem," he replies easily.

Still... "You prefer not to use it, though?"

At least, that's the impression I've gotten.

Remi tilts his head back and forth. "It's...complicated. The implant has its uses, that's for sure. But people seem to think I can't exist happily without sound, and that's just not true."

I can't begin to imagine what that's like, but it's clear Remington doesn't view his deafness as a deficit.

"I, uh... I'm trying to learn ASL," I admit, smiling a little sheepishly when Remi's eyebrows fly up. "I'm only on letters, so it might take some time."

He looks at me for a long moment, lips finally lifting at the corners. "Most people don't bother."

"That sucks," I say plainly.

He huffs a laugh. "Kinda. You hiding in here?"

I groan. "Am I that obvious?"

"Little bit. Wanna join me in the studio?"

"The...what?" I ask.

Remi laughs again, walking over to the pantry. He grabs a box of crackers and a bag of chips and then waves me forward.

Curious, I follow the youngest Darling brother down the hall, past the bustling dining room and up to the second floor. He opens the door at the end of the hallway, and we climb up a narrow set of curving stairs. My mouth falls open when I see what I assumed was an attic but is in fact a wide-open room beneath the pitched roof of the house. Canvases of all sizes are stacked around the space, paint splotches dried *everywhere*.

"An art studio?" I ask.

Remi nods, setting the snacks on the floor before walking forward. "Keeps me busy when I'm not with the animals. You can hide up here if you want."

Awed, I take a seat as Remi pulls a canvas away from the wall and sets it on an easel. Seemingly unbothered by my presence, he starts uncapping paint bottles. I open the box of crackers, snacking as I watch him work. There are a few small windows running along one wall of the room, right beneath the sloped ceiling, so the space is plenty bright as Remi starts painting. He hums to himself every once in a while, his movements fluid and relaxed.

I'm so caught up in watching him that I don't realize how much time has passed until Jackson suddenly crouches down beside me, startling me as he sets a plate with fruit and a ham sandwich on the floor.

I give him a smile as my heart rate comes down. "Hey," I say quietly. "I'm guessing I missed lunch?"

Jackson hums. "You did. Had to track you down. Wasn't expecting to find you up here."

"Sorry."

He shakes his head. "Nothing to be sorry for. You doing all right?"

I pop a grape into my mouth and nod.

Jackson assesses me for a moment before nodding back. "All right, then. See you soon."

With that, Jackson stands, kissing the top of my head before walking out of the room. I pull the plate of food closer, eating my lunch as Remi paints a field of dandelions beneath a light blue sky.

When Remi heads back to work, I go for another walk around the ranch. I amble up and down the bank of the slow river, which is so shallow in places I'd almost call it a creek.

Then I walk the fence line, looking at the cattle and the occasional rancher who passes by.

By the time I get back to Jackson's house, I'm sorer than I want to admit. I wince as I bend to get my boots off, abandoning that plan and kicking them off instead. After getting a drink of water, I decide to take a soak in Jackson's tub, hoping it will help relax my muscles.

And that's exactly how Jackson finds me a good half hour later, the water I'm lying in having cooled to warm instead of piping hot. He squats down beside me, arms on the side of the porcelain tub, his eyes roaming over my naked body for only a moment.

"Need help?" he asks.

"I'm fine," I tell him, pushing upright. I brace my hands on the edges of the tub, and Jackson reaches for me. "I'm *fine*."

"Ash—"

"I got it," I snipe.

Jackson doesn't back off. His hand wraps around my bicep to help me stand, and I snap, just a little.

"Goddamn it, Jackson, I said I'm *fine*."

He lets go, but he doesn't back up. He stands there, watching as I clumsily get myself to my feet, and then he continues to stand there as I step out of the tub and grab my towel. I wrap it around my waist, pulse racing.

Jackson trails after me like a quiet sentinel as I head to the bedroom, grabbing the same pajama pants I took off this morning. Trying not to show my discomfort, I get them on, followed by a t-shirt. I maneuver the damn sling into place and head toward the kitchen.

Jackson follows.

I open the fridge, looking inside. "I can cook us something. What sounds good?"

"Ash," he says softly.

"I'm not useless, Jackson."

"Ash," he says again, his hand curling over my own on the handle of the fridge.

I close my eyes, unable to stop my breath from puffing out of me as Jackson's body heat lines my back. He feels good. *Too* good. All I want is to lean into him.

Jackson closes the fridge door, and I let him, the both of us standing still inside his kitchen as the quiet wraps around us. He sets his chin on my shoulder, his arm around my stomach. He doesn't say anything, just holds me, and it's too much.

It's too damn much.

"I'm sorry," I whisper.

His lips brush my cheek. "I know."

"I didn't mean to yell."

He nuzzles into my neck, his beard bristling. "I know, sunshine."

"It's just fucking hard sometimes. To think," I tell him, leaning my weight back against his chest. My limbs feel heavy. *Everything* feels heavy. "When all I can feel is how sore I am, there's no place in my head for anything else. And I pushed myself too hard today because I didn't want to admit I'm not okay. I didn't want to acknowledge the fact that it's going to take months to feel better again. I've been here before, Jackson, and I hate it. I hate how I feel."

His arms never leave me. Neither does he. "What do you need?" he asks, his voice a quiet whisper.

I pull in a breath. Let it out. "I need to rest."

He kisses my cheek again and spins me slowly. "C'mon," he says, his arm around my back.

I let Jackson bring me to bed. I let him grab dinner for us from the ranch house, the both of us eating with our plates resting on the sheets. I let him handle the cleanup alone.

And when he comes back to bed, I ask him to keep me warm.

Chapter 26

JACKSON

"He's looking better," my mom says, twirling a sprig of dried lavender between her fingertips. "He's got his glow again."

I grunt, watching as Ash kneads a large ball of dough inside the ranch house kitchen. His sling is off, finally, and per his physical therapist's instructions, he's back to regular activity, barring any discomfort. His posture isn't as loose as it was before the accident, but my mom is right. He looks happy again.

It's an immense relief, even though I know he's far from recovered. And even then, he may not ever be without some pain.

I try not to let the thought get me down, knowing Ash doesn't want my pity. Never that.

"Just don't go working him too hard," I tell my mom, turning away from where we were spying in the hall.

She makes an amused sound as she follows me back into the dining room. Lavender is spread along one end of the table like a blanket of purple, and my mom returns her sprig to the pile. "Jackson dear, pretty sure out of the two of us, I'm not the one who's at risk of *working* him too hard."

"Oh, gross," I mutter, picking up my hat.

"There's nothing gross about sexual intercourse," my moms says. "It's a perfectly natural—"

"*Ah, ah, ah,*" I say, willing my ears to close up. I hold up a hand, suppressing the shudder that wants to roll throughout my entire body and soul. "What's gross is talking to *you* about it."

My mom plucks up another lavender sprig, opening her mouth to say something I'm sure would be scarring, when my dad walks into the room.

"Hey now," he says, snatching the lavender from her hand. He starts collecting the rest, handling the dried buds carefully. "Did anyone say you could play with my *Lavandula?*"

Hands full, my dad walks out, and my mom glances my way.

"He is the strangest man," she says simply.

"You married him."

She sighs, sounding happy about that. "I did. Twice." As I reach the back door, she calls out, "You're glowing, too, Jackson. It's a damn good sight."

I grumble, waving my hand over my shoulder as my mom laughs at my retreating back. Shaking my head, I put on my hat and head for the horse barn.

My brothers are inside when I arrive, Remi sitting on a crate outside the tack room and Colton leaning against the wall, feet crossed at his ankles. He pushes upright when I walk in and holds out his arms.

"Let the secret meeting of the brothers commence," Colton proclaims loudly.

Ignoring my brother's ridiculousness, I grab another crate and plop down across from them. "Thanks for coming."

Colton drops his arms. "Yeah, yeah," he mumbles, clearly sore about me not playing along. "What's going on?"

I rub my jaw. "Lawson."

Colton nods as Remi hums.

"He's been off," our youngest brother says.

"He has," I agree.

Colton looks between the two of us, brows drawn. "His wife announced she wanted a divorce and had him move out the next day. Of course he's *off.*"

I shake my head. "It's more than that. He's going through something, and he won't talk to me about it. Has he talked to either of you?"

They exchange a glance, each shaking their head.

"What do you think it is?" Remi asks. "Being apart from Wendy so much? That's gotta be hard."

"Might be that," I agree before shrugging. "But I dunno."

"Well, what do you suggest?" Colton asks, grinning before I even have a chance to answer. "Brotherly intervention?"

"Brotherly intervention," I concur.

Colton pumps his fist. "I'll bring the mallows. And the whiskey. *Ooh.* Strippers?"

"No strippers," me and Remi say at the same time.

Colton pouts. "Y'all are no fun."

"Will you invite Ash?" Remi asks.

I grunt. "'Course."

He smiles, a knowing thing. *'You love him,'* he signs, watching me closely. Maybe because he knows how hard it might be for me to see those words. Or it would have been. *Before.* Back when I was still bitter. When I was hurting over Otto and didn't want to put my heart at risk again.

Now?

Now it's not so hard at all.

Remi's smile widens, but he doesn't push. Colton looks between the two of us, having missed Remi's unspoken words.

"What?" he asks.

"Nothing," I answer, standing. "Bonfire tonight. I'll make sure Lawson's there."

Colton claps his hands together, he and Remi discussing marshmallow options as I head out of the barn. A smile lifts my lips when I think about the man inside the ranch house making bread. The one with the perpetual hum and a fierce sort of resilience I can't help but admire.

I think, quite possibly, he might be the strongest person I know.

"Okay, so tell me again why none of you have simply *asked* your brother what's wrong?" Ash says, pulling on his boots. It's dark out, the fire already going out back. When I don't respond, Ash pauses, looking up at me. "Jack?"

His hair is falling over his cheek, eyes wide and stormy blue. All I can do is shake my head, not knowing how to articulate the random rushes of affection I've been feeling for him. For months, really, but especially these past few weeks.

"Not the way we do it," I mutter, distracted as Ash tucks that hair away. It falls again, and there goes my chest, feeling as if it's being wrung in a vise.

Ash huffs a laugh. "No, you Darling brothers just throw bonfires and use whiskey as an excuse to air your feelings. Which, look, I'm not opposed to your methods. But do you have stock in the town's distillery or something? 'Cause I swear you guys go through more—"

"Move in with me."

His eyes whip my way.

"Move in," I repeat, my heart thudding. "You've been staying here every night anyhow. Just...move your stuff here. Stay. With me."

He drops his head forward, muttering a, "*Fuck.*"

My gut sinks. "You don't wanna—"

"Yes, I'll move in with you, Jackson Darling," he says, pushing to his feet. My heart races as he steps forward, coming to a stop right in front of me. "I'm going to owe Virginia lunch thanks to you. You mean it? You want me here?"

My breath leaves me in a rush. "More than anything."

Ash's eyes run over my face. "Christ, Jack. You're too good to be real."

"Not all that good," I assure him, knowing the thoughts I'm having about Ash are far from virtuous.

He smirks, as if he knows as much, but a series of loud knocks on the back door interrupts us.

"You guys coming?" Colton calls, voice muffled through the wood. "If you're fucking, hurry up and finish."

"*Jesus goddamn Christ,*" I grumble loudly. "I'm gonna disown 'em. All of 'em."

Ash only laughs. "Coming," he calls. And then, to me, he says, "Jack? For the record, you're wrong. You're *so* very good. And I'll let you prove it to me later."

Before I can come up with *anything* to say to that, Ash smacks a kiss against my lips and heads for the back door.

Fucking hell.

Taking a breath, I follow him.

My brothers are settled around the bonfire when Ash and I get outside. Colton has a bag of jumbo-sized marshmallows on his lap, and he's loading four of them onto a stick. Remi is leaned back in his Adirondack chair, legs crossed in front of him. Lawson is gazing out into the night, pensive, as he's been ever since Laura asked for a divorce. It's cool tonight, but between the fire and our coats, no one seems to mind.

Ash doesn't bother with his own chair. He waits until I'm settled in mine and then claims the spot between my legs. With one foot kicked up on the slanted wooden stool in front of us, he leans his back to my chest, utterly relaxed like there's nowhere else he'd rather be. I wrap an arm around his stomach.

"*So*," Colton says, missing casual by a mile. "What's been going on with everyone? Law?"

"Hm?" our older brother says.

"How's, uh, your classes at the school?" Colton says, wincing slightly.

Lord.

Remi shakes his head.

"Fine," Lawson answers before taking a sip from his whiskey tin.

Colton looks around for help.

"Wendy doing okay?" I ask.

"Mhm," Lawson hums. And that's it.

Colton stuffs a giant marshmallow in his mouth.

"Oh, for fuck's sake," Remi says, sitting forward. "Law, are *you* doing okay? We're worried about you."

"Me?" Lawson says, sounding genuinely perplexed. "Why?"

"Because you seem..." Remi trails off, looking to me.

"Not yourself," I finish.

Ash gives my leg a squeeze.

Lawson is quiet for a moment, looking at the fire. "I am myself. Just...a little sadder than usual, I guess."

Remi and I exchange another look.

"Anything we can do to help?" I ask.

"Don't think so," our oldest brother says. "I think it's okay to be sad sometimes, you know? I don't want to rush through it just so I can avoid feeling this way."

No one quite knows what to say to that, least of all myself. I've never been particularly good about broadcasting my feelings, but Lawson has never had that issue. He's always been open about his emotions in a way I used to think naive.

Now, I think my brother might be a lot braver than I ever gave him credit for.

"If there's anything we can do," I tell him, "just give the word."

Lawson nods, but we all go still when the sound of a motorcycle cuts through the night.

Colton sets his roasting stick down slowly. "Is that..."

The engine roars louder until the sound ceases entirely. There's the thump of boots on gravel, and then a man comes striding around my house. The dark obscures his features, but I still recognize him instantly. As does Colton, who jumps to his feet.

"Colton," the man barks.

"The fuck are you doing here?" Colton snarls back.

Noah King doesn't stop moving until he's within the circle of our bonfire. His scowling face is lit by the flames, his head shaved short along the sides, the dark hair on top a mess. "You fucking kidding me?" he growls. "You told Marie Doherty my work was shoddy. She dropped me as a client. Thirty fucking horses on that farm, Colt."

I cringe, even as Colton puffs up his chest. "You can't prove anything."

Noah takes a step closer, shaking his head. "I've never, not *once*, told someone you did shoddy work," he says, prodding Colton in the chest once, twice. "That was low."

My brother bats Noah's hand away. "Sure have hinted at it plenty, though, haven't you? Every other week, it's in the paper. *King* this and *King* that. Best goddamn farrier in these parts!"

"It's called advertising," Noah shoots back. "What you did is downright dirty."

"Maybe Marie just knew if she wanted quality work, she should go with someone trusted," Colton says, crossing his arms.

Noah works his jaw. "Right. 'Cause Colton goddamn Darling can do no wrong."

"You said it, not me," Colton responds.

Noah shakes his head again. "You're a real piece of work, you know that? Stop fucking with my business."

"Stop fucking with mine!" Colton shouts after him. Noah is already halfway across the yard.

"Whoa," Ash whispers, turning his head my way. "*That's* Noah King? Dude's hot."

"Hey," I grunt, tightening my arm around him.

He laughs. "What? He is."

"He's an asshole," Colton puts in, dropping back into his seat.

"How'd he know where you live?" Remi mumbles.

"He thinks he's *so* high and mighty," Colton goes on. "Well, one of these days, he's gonna fall off his damn perch. Just you wait and see."

"Colt," I say softly. "Did you really tell Mrs. Doherty he does bad work?"

He winces. "Not on purpose. And not in those words, not exactly. I just..." He groans, falling back in his chair. "I was flapping my mouth. It was an accident."

"You need to make it right," Remi says. "Apologize to him. Talk to Mrs. Doherty."

"I can't do that," Colton moans. "I'd never live it down."

"Well, maybe you deserve to deal with the consequences of your actions," Lawson says in that calm teacher voice of his. "Your happiness shouldn't come at somebody's else's expense, Colt."

"I'm not *happy* about it," Colton defends.

Lawson doesn't argue with him. He just stands, setting down his tin. "I'm turning in."

"You sure you're all right?" I check.

He sighs, a tired sound. "I'm fine, Jackson. I'd just like to be alone for a little while."

I watch him walk off, my chest tight and aching.

"He'll be okay," Ash says, shifting around to face me. "I get it, you know? His life threw him a major curveball, and he needs time to process. To wallow a bit. Sometimes the best thing we can do is let ourselves feel. It's healthy that he's not shoving it all down."

"What if it doesn't get better?" I ask, voicing my worry aloud.

"It will. And if it doesn't, you guys will be there to help him."

"I wish Oakley were still here," Remi says. "He always had a way with Lawson."

"Who's Oakley?" Ash asks.

"His best friend," Colton answers, popping another few marshmallows on his stick. "Two of them were thick as thieves. Until Oak moved away."

Ash hums.

"Colton," I say, getting my brother's attention again. "Remi's right. You needa fix it."

He groans. "*Fuck*. I hate doing the right thing."

"No you don't," I reply, knowing my brother well enough to be certain of it.

Colton just shakes his head. "Noah fucking King. No one has ever poked at my frog like him."

Ash coughs. "I'm sorry, what?"

Remi tries to hide his amusement, but it comes through in his voice when he says, "It's part of a horse's hoof. On the underside."

"He's a *thorn*," Colton says. "Right under my skin."

Ash gives me a *look*, his eyebrows raised. I shrug because I truly don't know what the deal is between Noah and my brother. Colton is easygoing with just about anybody.

Anybody but Noah fucking King.

Ash purses his lips and turns back around, settling against me. "Maybe you two just need to bang it out."

Remi chokes on a laugh as Colton's head lifts, slowly. The mallows he was roasting tip down into the fire.

"Bang my archnemesis?" Colton says, face scrunched up in disgust. "I'd rather go brim over boot than touch a hair on Noah King's gold-plated ball sac."

"Oh my *God*," Remi says, dropping his face into his hands.

Ash is outright laughing now. "Brim over boot?"

"He means falling off a horse," I mumble, lips twitching.

"Not what it sounds like," Ash mutters back.

I can't disagree.

Colton shivers, a full-bodied thing, before he scrubs his burnt marshmallows off the end of his stick. He loads a couple new ones. "*Ugh*. Bang Noah King. Can you imagine? It's not even that the dude has a dick, I just hate the guy."

Remi gives me a smile, looking so amused I can't help but smile back.

Maybe this family of mine gets on my nerves from time to time, but I suppose they're not so bad. I might even call them pretty great.

Pulling Ash back against my chest, I settle in as Colton and Remi argue the logistics of gold-plated body parts. The fire crackles in front of us, smoke floating up into the air. Stars dot the sky, and the smell of dried leaves mixes in with the burnt wood from the bonfire.

I can't remember the last time I felt this calm. This settled. I'm still worried about Lawson, that's true. But we'll have his back should he need it. Ash was right about that.

The man himself shifts, turning his head to look up at me, fingertips brushing my jaw. "You good, Jack?" he asks, voice quiet.

"Yeah," I say, meaning it with every fiber of my being. "Never been better."

Chapter 27

ASH

"I honestly wasn't sure if they were going to kick each other's asses or kiss," I tell Jackson, shucking off my boots once we're inside the house. "Did you see that tension between Noah and your brother? Whew. I mean—"

Jackson's arm slips around my middle, and I go still, turning my face to see him better.

"Hi there," I say, sliding my hands over his. "What'cha doin', partner?"

"You working on your country?" he asks, nose skimming my cheek.

My lips curve into a smile. "Reckon I have a little country in me. Or I *will* in—"

"I'm not little," Jackson grumbles.

I bark a laugh, pushing his hands lower on my abdomen. "You have intentions, Jack?"

"Lots when it comes to you," he says, beard and lips skimming my neck.

My head falls back onto his shoulder as his hand covers my cock. He kneads me through my jeans, and I let go of his arms so I can grab his ass, pulling him tighter against me.

"Want you, Jack."

He hums, kissing down my neck. "Lemme take you to bed, Ash. I wanna kiss every inch of you. Slow and sweet."

Fuck, that does sound good. But there's something else I want, too.

"*Or*," I say, spinning and grabbing Jackson's waistband, fingers slipping beneath the denim, "we could test out that theory of yours about me making a good cowboy."

Jackson doesn't grin like I expect him to. Instead, he frowns almost thoughtfully. "I don't know if that's such a good idea."

"What? Why—" I scowl as it hits me. "My back is fine."

"You're still recovering," he says.

I pop the button on his jeans, raising an eyebrow. "I'm feeling good today. I know my limits, Jack."

"I just don't want you hurting," he says, voice choking off as I slip a hand inside his pants.

"And I appreciate that," I tell him, stroking him to full hardness. "But I want to ride my partner's cock. Are you going to tell me I can't do that?"

"Fuck," he mutters, hands tightening on the outsides of my arms. "Why can't I ever say no to you, Ashley Alcott?"

"Because you're a very smart man," I answer. "Now sit."

He looks affronted. "I'm not a dog."

"*Please* sit," I amend. "So I can suck your dick."

Jackson backs his ass up, all but falling onto the couch. I chuckle, following him and dropping to my knees. I spread his legs wider, palms running up his thighs.

"Now who's a good boy?" I coo, smirking up at him.

His glower is immediate. "Don't start."

"No?" I ask, tugging his jeans open and getting a hand on his dick. I pull him free from his underwear, stroking up and down.

"I'm not..." His head falls back. "Not one of your pets."

I lean in, swiping my tongue over the head of his cock. "You don't want to be good for me, Jack?"

"Ah, fuck," he mutters, eyes latching back onto mine. I lick him again, tongue swirling over his head before my lips brush against him in a light kiss. "Christ, I can't think when...when you..."

His words dissolve into a groan when I take him into my mouth. It's satisfying, rendering this man speechless. I think I could worship him for the rest of my days if it meant seeing that look in his eyes that tells me I've captured him, wholly and without regret.

I pop off his dick, hand stroking again. "I think you like being good for me, Jack. Knowing you've pleased me."

He grunts, hips hitching off the couch.

"And what would please me right now," I go on, licking just beneath his glans, "is for you to let me climb on your lap, sink down over this beautiful cock of yours, and ride you so hard I come all over your chest. Would you let me do that?"

His breathing is labored, cheeks flushed and dick hard in my grip. "So long as I still get to kiss you."

The fluttering in my chest has me pushing upright, meeting Jackson's lips as I suck a breath in through my nose. He tastes like whiskey and sugar, like fresh air, somehow. There's never been, and never will be in my lifetime, anyone like Jackson Darling.

"Get naked, Jack."

Jackson starts tugging off his clothes as I get up and round the couch, heading toward the bedroom. I grab the lube and a condom, and then, just for good measure, a second condom. Best to be prepared.

When I get back to the living room, Jackson is spread out like royalty, stark-naked and magnificent as he sits sprawled over the blanket he tossed on the couch. I hand him the supplies and tug off my shirt. As I shuck my pants, I watch Jackson roll on the condom and lube his shaft, anticipation sweeping through me.

Jackson grabs my hips as I straddle him, my knees landing on the cushions to either side of his legs. His hands slide down to my ass, fingers dipping into my crease as he tugs me closer. I go willingly, bracing myself on the back of the couch as Jackson all but swallows my dick in one go.

"*Fuck*," I groan, adjusting so I can get one hand into his hair. I hold on, hips shifting as he bobs his head. "You're not trying to distract me from my goal, are you?"

His tongue curls along my shaft before he slides free. "Just getting you wet," he answers. "And enjoying you."

"Well, by all means. Enjoy away."

Jackson's smirking mouth covers my cock again, his lips warm and tight, his tongue talented as hell. He doesn't protest when I start controlling the pace, fucking into his mouth. His hands leave my ass for a moment, but then they're back, one palm on my cheek as wet fingers press against my hole.

"Fuck," I mutter again, pace stuttering as he eases a finger inside of me. "*Christ*, that's good."

Jackson hums, the sensation pulling another groan from me. His fingers work to loosen me as I take pleasure from his mouth, the sight of him swallowing my cock almost too much for me to bear. The way his lips are stretched, the hollowing of his cheeks, the shine in his eyes as he looks up at me in rapture.

"Okay, okay," I breathe, giving his hair a tug. "I'm ready, Jack."

He eases off, and I drop down to claim his lips with my own. A taste. A thank-you. A promise, even, that this means more. That all of this is so much more.

Jackson's thumbs dig into my hips as I reach back, grabbing his cock. I line up, and, with an exhale of pure relief, I sink down enough for him to slip inside my body. Jackson's face is set in a stoic mask, but I know it's a measured thing. He's working hard to control himself, to control everything he's feeling.

When my ass comes to rest on his thighs, his fingers tighten against my skin.

"Good?" I check.

He nods, his Adam's apple bobbing as he swallows. "Giddyup."

With a bark of laughter, I lean forward to kiss that soft smirk, and then I start to ride. My head falls back as I move, the glide of his cock perfection and then some. The way he fills me up, pressing against the deepest parts of me, the pressure and stretch like nothing else. One of Jackson's big hands covers my ass cheek, his other anchored tightly to the side of my thigh. His eyes never once leave mine as I work myself over his cock, taking, giving in equal measure.

He looks beautiful. Rugged and hard. Soft in all the right ways. He looks honest. *Earnest.*

This man has never tried to play games with me. Even in the beginning, when he was closed off, he never lied. Never wanted me to hurt. He cares in a way that's so very big. It's immense but not boastful.

I don't know if it was the wind I followed here. My friend, Ginnie. My heart.

But I've never in my life been more grateful to have ended up exactly where I am.

Jackson's hand wraps around my cock as I lean forward to kiss him again. I'm still wet from his spit, and his work-roughened palm grips me just right. He jerks me as I bounce on his cock, his hand brushing my lower abdomen, his kisses bristling my lips. All hard and soft, every piece of him.

I stutter out a gasp as he shifts, lifting his hips to meet me. "*God*, yes, there," I encourage, my hand flying to the couch again, my entire being buzzing, the new angle driving against my prostate just right. "*Jack*."

"C'mon, sunshine," he mutters against my lips, hand twisting over the head of my cock. "I need you to come 'cause I'm barely holding on here. You feel too fucking good. Need you to—*fuck*. Need you to come on my cock like you promised."

"You could always...suck me off," I huff between breaths, "if you come first."

Not that he'll have to. I'm two seconds away one way or another.

"Not. Coming. First," he grunts out, the stubborn, wonderful man. He grabs my hip, slams me down on him as he jerks my cock, and I'm done.

I cry out, my groan mixing with Jackson's sound of aching relief. He continues to pump my cock as my body pings and releases, everything in me tight and expansive all at once. I suck in a breath, the height of it going on and on and *on*. Jackson jerks against me as I'm lost in it, his face buried in my neck, his fingers tightening almost painfully on my hip as his cock floods the condom. I can feel it. Not his cum. But the kicking. The throbbing of his dick as he finds his release.

Jackson's grip loosens as he catches his breath, me doing the same. I inhale the smell of him, the scent of sex and wilderness and *home*.

"Yee-fucking-haw," I mumble happily.

Jackson snorts a laugh against me, his arms wrapping tightly around my back. I chuckle with him, so ridiculously smitten I can't stop my words, not that I want to.

"Did you mean it?" I ask, my fingers drifting up into Jackson's sweaty hair. "When you said you might be falling. For me. Did you mean that?"

Jackson lets out a breath, a soft sigh of sorts. "Yeah. I meant it."

"Do you still feel that way?"

"No," he says. "I don't think. I know."

My inhale feels shuddery as I lean back, catching Jackson's gaze. There's only good there. Nothing but absolute good.

"I am so incredibly in love with you, Jackson Darling. I know it in my heart, in my new boots, in the parts of me that led me here to you. I love you, *fiercely*. Fully. I love you, Jack."

His lips press together tightly for just a moment before lifting into a shaky smile. "I know."

I bark a laugh, and his smile turns almost shy. "Really? That's all you have to say?"

"Well," he says, those hands on my back running up and down, "are you done talking?"

"Yes?" I hedge.

"Then, no, that's not all I have to say." His palms lift to my face, thumbs ghosting over my cheeks before he tucks my hair away, his gaze following the motion.

God, the way he looks. So open. So sincere.

"Ash," he says, voice hoarse. "From the moment I saw you standing in our kitchen, I was struck. I knew you were something. I just wasn't sure what. Turns out you're the love of my life."

My breath leaves me.

Jackson only smiles. "And it's bigger than I ever thought it could be, you know?"

I nod. Because I do.

"I love you, Ashley Alcott. And I'll keep on loving you as long as I can."

"And how long is that?" I ask shakily.

He grips my face, hold gentle. "Long as those mountains stand, I figure."

"That's a long damn time."

"Mhm."

"Longer than we'll be alive," I point out.

"Sounds about right."

Fuck.

"You're one smooth talker, you know that?"

He kisses the corner of my mouth. "Can't say anyone's ever accused me of that before."

"Then they weren't paying close enough attention."

He snorts lightly. "Ease up."

I groan. "Do I have to?"

"Afraid so," he says, gripping the base of the condom as I slide off his cock. I watch him tie it off.

"We could ditch them," I propose.

"You wanna?"

"Yes," I say simply, desperate to feel Jackson inside me without barriers.

His lips twitch. "All right."

"Just all right?"

"Very all right," he amends.

I snort, a ridiculous smile on my face.

"And maybe next time," he adds slowly, voice sly, "I could be the one on top. Show you how a real cowboy rides."

My outrage battles with my arousal. "You *asshole*," I say, slapping his chest. "I ride just fine. But yes. Yes, let's do that."

He chuckles, snagging my hand. The sound quickly eases away, his eyes soft as they gaze at me. "Would you let me take you to bed now, Ashley? I'd like to kiss you for a while. Love on you."

Fucking fuck.

"Yeah, Jack," I answer, the only one I can give. "Take me to bed."

He does, leading me down the hall and kissing me like he promised. My lips, my body, anywhere he can reach. We lie tangled together for a long time, until the early morning hours. I fall asleep sated, warm, and utterly content.

The next day, when the sun is high in the sky, I pack my two meager bags of belongings and walk the quarter mile back to Jackson's house. To my home. I put my clothes in the dresser, my shoes by the door.

And the little cowboy figurine? I set that on my nightstand, right beside the bed.

Looks like I was right. I got to keep my cowboy close after all.

Chapter 28

JACKSON

"Now we'll ease into plank," Annabelle says, her back straight as she balances on her toes and forearms. "Try to keep position, even if you get some company."

The class mimics her, some chuckling as goats climb on their backs or try to nibble their fingers. The kids of the goat variety love it, happy to dance around the class and get attention.

Ash seems to love it, too. He's right in the middle of the group, stretched out along his blue yoga mat. There's a wide smile on his face and a laugh at the corner of his mouth as he tries to flick his hair away from one of the goats without breaking his pose. The little bugger goes back in for another chomp.

Virginia comes to Ash's rescue, giving the goat a gentle nudge until it hops away.

"I like this," my mom says, leaning on the fence beside me.

I grunt, glancing her way. "What's that?"

"Growth," she says simply. "Forward momentum. It's good to see. Both for the ranch...and for my sons."

"Sentimental," I mutter.

My mom laughs. "Takes one to know one, Jackson dear."

She ignores my grumble.

"What did I used to tell you, hm?" she asks, nudging my arm. "When the days seemed dark..."

I sigh. "I just had to wait 'cause the sun was coming."

"That's right," she says firmly. "And look. Here he is."

My eyes seek out Ash again. He's lying on his back now, grinning up at the sky. I'm not sure I've ever seen anything as lovely as him.

"You here to gloat?" I ask my mother. "Take credit for the two of us coming together?"

She huffs a short laugh. "I can't take credit for that, much as I want to. It wouldn't have happened if it weren't right."

I can't argue with that.

"*But*," she says.

"Oh, here we go."

"I *would* accept a thank-you for giving y'all a nudge. If you were so inclined."

I clamp my teeth together. "I'm not thanking you for keeping him here against his will."

"It was hardly against his will. He was happy to stay."

"You tricked him."

"Did no such thing," she says. "I only offered him a room."

"Instead of a vehicle."

"Are we gonna go around and around again? I'm happy to dance, Jackson, but you'll never out-step me."

"When you get old," I say slowly, "I'm gonna stick you in a home."

"You never would," she says easily.

No, I wouldn't.

"Come on," my mom says, looping her arm with mine. "Walk me back to the house."

I eye her as we turn around. "*Are* you getting old?"

She snorts. "I'm not a day over forty-five and never will be."

My laughter is loud. My mom pinches my arm.

When we get back to the house, my dad intercepts us at the door, looking downright giddy. My mom appraises him with a wary eye, as she should.

"What's going on, Hank?" she asks.

"Come, come," he says, waving us toward the kitchen.

At a loss, the two of us follow.

My dad picks up a small plate from the table. On it is a biscuit cut in half and smothered in what looks like honey. He holds it out toward my mom. "Here. Put this in your mouth."

My mom, *rightfully*, doesn't move a muscle. "What'd I tell you about making demands, Hank Darling? You want something in my mouth, you ask nicely."

"Oh, Jesus," I groan, rubbing my hands over my face. "I want that gone. I want that memory gone."

"*Please*," my dad says, sounding contrite. "Just trust me, Mari."

I let my hands drop in time to see my mother accept the offering. She picks up the biscuit and takes a bite, her eyes widening in surprise.

"Is that..."

"Lavender honey," my dad fills in. "Did I get it right?"

My mom looks absolutely stunned. The plate lowers in her hand as she stares at my dad. "Did you get a colony of bees, take up beekeeping, of all hobbies, and spend an entire evening in the hospital after you forgot to wear your gear just so you could source your own honey?"

"Grew the lavender myself, too," he says proudly. "Took three seasons. I would've had a better honey yield, but it's only my first year. We'll get more next time. I think they like the pink hive. It's got a good energy, y'know? Pink makes folks happy. Suspect it's the same for bees."

"Why?" my mother asks.

My dad cocks his head. "You said you liked lavender honey. Couldn't find it anywhere around here, remember?"

"That was four years ago," she nearly whispers.

"It was. Took a while to get everything right, but I think it tastes pretty good. What d'you think?"

I leave my moon-eyed mother with her ex-husband, dutifully ignoring the sound of my dad's surprise as he gets the stuffing kissed out of him.

None of my business.

It's surprisingly warm as I finish out my afternoon of work. Snow will be here before we know it, but fall isn't quite ready to go. It seems to have gifted us with the perfect day before it's gone, too. The leaves have all but fallen, the ground littered in gold and brown. But the sky is blue and the air a pleasant whisper against my forearms as Starlight and I head back to the stables.

I'm just shutting the door to his stall when I hear a bell. A rather *familiar* bell these days. Letting out a sigh, I pull a date from my pocket.

"This is the last time," I grumble, holding it out as the Darling Donkey trots happily over. He snags the treat from my palm, teeth grazing a little too close to skin for comfort. "I mean it. No more."

He sniffs at my pocket, and I offer him a tentative pat.

"Thank you," I add a bit begrudgingly, not for the first time.

The donkey tries to take a bite out of my jeans, and I curse, pushing him gently away before heading out of the barn.

I have time to shower before dinner, so I walk the short way down the drive to my house and do just that. It's as I'm sifting through my closet, looking for a fresh shirt, that I find something I'd all but forgotten was here.

I tug the sleeve of the flannel out from the very back of the rack. The shirt is buffalo plaid. Brown and orange. It was Otto's—the one thing he left here, forgotten or by choice, I'm not sure which.

I let my fingers run over the fabric for a moment, trying to drum up even a hint of those feelings that used to swamp me every time I thought of my ex. But there's nothing. No lingering regret. No anger. No pain. There's just an empty space, a box where memories used to live. It's aired out now, full of nothing but dust.

In my head, I close that box. Push it aside. I don't need it anymore.

Warm arms circle me from behind, hands landing flat on my chest. Ash leans his chin over my shoulder, his palms giving me a cheeky little squeeze.

"I like finding you naked," he says.

"I'm wearing a towel," I point out.

One of his hands slips down, giving the edge of the towel a tug. It falls to my feet. "Naked," he says.

I huff a laugh, letting the sleeve of the flannel go. "You get everything squared away with your new truck?"

"Edith is parked out front and happy to be here," he answers. "She's such a pretty red."

"Just like Edna."

"Mhm," he hums, hands back on my pecs, lips pressing a quick kiss to my neck. "You were staring at that shirt for a while. Is something wrong with it?"

I let out a sigh, curling one of my hands over Ash's wrist. "It was Otto's."

He's quiet for a moment. "What do you want to do with it? Burn it? Make a pincushion?"

I snort before sobering. "I wanna let it go."

He gives my neck another kiss. "I have an idea," he says, bending down to grab my towel. He backs slowly toward the doorway with it in hand.

"And what would that be?" I ask, turning to watch him.

"It's supposed to be a full moon tonight," he says, lips lifting at the corner. "Want to make it a triple?"

It takes a second for his meaning to compute. "Ash..."

He tosses the towel over his shoulder and unbuttons his jeans. "Come on, Jack. You said that night was because of him, right? So let's take it back. Let's make it our own."

My heart thumps as Ash drops his pants and underwear down to his feet. He tugs off his shirt next and then wraps the towel around his bare neck.

"Go skinny-dipping with me?"

I shake my head, even as I'm smiling. "What do you think?"

"That you're not going to say no to me."

"You'd be right," I admit.

Ash grins, a big, beaming thing, as I walk toward him. He starts backing up again, naked as the day he was born.

"It's not dark yet," I point out, not that I think that'll stop him.

"It will be soon," he says, reaching the back door. He twists the handle. "Race you?"

Against all common sense, I find myself running next to Ash as we head toward the river. It's ridiculous, beyond reckless, but neither of us cares. The grass is brittle underfoot, the occasional leaf crunching, and even though the sun has started to set, anybody looking our way would see two grown-ass men streaking across the ranch.

Ash makes it to the river first, dropping the towel and then yipping when his toes touch water. "Oh, fuck," he says, doing a little dance that has me gasping for breath after the run we took.

I follow him in, cursing as the cool water flows up to my ankles, my knees, my cock. I cup myself on instinct as my balls try to recede into my body.

"Fucking fuck," Ash says, his ass peeking out over the water. "I didn't know it'd be so damn cold."

"It's nearly winter. Of course it's cold."

"Fuck," he says again.

I laugh, a sound that takes Ash by surprise, if his grin is any indication. He walks over to me, arms out at his sides for balance, the base of his cock visible as he tries not to sink too far into the water.

"So what now?" he asks, beautiful and wet and so very mine.

"We look at the mountains and contemplate life," I tell him.

"Is that what you did?" Ash asks, turning to the west and leaning against my side.

I nod, the both of us shivering. "It is."

"All right, then."

We're quiet for half a minute before I say, "My mom used to tell me this story. About the sun. And the mountains."

"Yeah?" he asks.

I nod, watching the color that's bleeding across the sky. The sun is a small sliver of gold now above the mountain's peak, casting everything in coppers and reds and even dusky purple. "She said the sun loved the mountains very much. Had since the beginning of time. But the mountains were stuck, you see. Forged in stone and bound to the earth, no matter how hard they tried to reach up into the sky. So the sun had to chase them. Every day. Every night."

Ash hums, looking over at me, and I go on.

"So that's exactly what the sun did. It flew across the sky, every day, every night, without fail, until it could be with the mountains again. When the world went dark, the sun and the mountains were together. They were one."

Ash slips his hand into mine, his fingers chilled but his grip sure.

"It was just a bedtime story," I say. "Meant to make me less afraid of the dark. But when I was scared or when I was sad, my mom would remind me that the sun was coming. That good things were ahead."

I let out a breath and look to my side. Ash is watching me steadily.

"*You* are my sun, Ash," I tell him seriously. "My sunshine. My good thing ahead. Thank you for chasing me, even when I was being a stubborn ass about it."

"Fuck, Jack," he says quietly, tightening his grip in mine. "I..." He cuts off, huffing what might be a laugh and shaking his head. "When I came to Darling, I was singing this song. I remember because my car had just broken down, and Earl picked me up on the side of the road, and I was fairly sure I was going to die."

My chuckle is hoarse, and Ash smiles, a gentle thing.

"So I remember that moment pretty well. It was Cat Stevens, the song. It felt fitting. Because I'd traveled west on the setting sun. And I never, not once, wanted water. I didn't want that place I came from."

He eases out a breath, and I swear I hold my own, my lungs needing his words like oxygen.

"I think I was born for this life, Jack. Maybe even born for you. Maine was never home for me. And I didn't know what home was until I came here and saw those damn mountains. Until I found you."

"Ash."

"So if I'm your sun, then you're my mountains, Jackson Darling. Any running I do will be to come home to you."

My eyes prick, and I blink rapidly, that promise something I didn't know I needed. It's hard, sometimes, to let go of our hurt. To move past it. But Ash has made it easier. Whether it's him or simply him at the right time, I don't know. I don't think it much matters.

He's here. He's not going. Won't ever go. I trust that. I just do.

I bring his hand up to my lips. "I wouldn't have let you go. Not like he did."

His eyes soften, understanding there. Ash isn't my ex, no. And neither am I his.

"I would have fought for you," I go on. "I will *always* fight for you."

His lips tremble as I kiss his knuckles, my hands doing their best to keep his warm. His voice is almost amused when he says, "I can't believe we're doing this with our dicks out while we freeze our balls off in a river. First the hayloft, now this?"

My laughter is a raspy thing, sharp almost in the quiet night.

Ash leans against me, pressing a kiss to my shoulder. "We'll both fight for this. It's what you do when you're partners."

"Partners."

"Yeah, Jack. That's us." He hums before adding, "Look."

The sun is barely visible now, the smallest hint of gold above the mountains. I sigh as it sinks fully away.

"I like that story," Ash says softly.

"Me, too."

He loops his arm through my own, the both of us huddling together for warmth as the river laps at the tops of our thighs. "So…" Ash says slowly. "How long do we stay out here? Not that I'm complaining, exactly. But I'm starting to lose sensation in my dick."

I snort through my nose. The sound turns into a chuckle and then a full-out belly laugh. Ash laughs with me, the two of us clinging to one another as we freeze. It takes me a moment to hear the *other* noise coming from behind us. The hooting and hollering.

"Oh, hell," I mutter.

"Is that…" Ash turns his head, looking over my shoulder. "Yep. That's everyone, isn't it?"

He lifts a hand and waves at what is surely the entire dinner crowd at the ranch house having caught us in the nude. I decide if I don't turn around, I can pretend it's not happening.

"They're just standing there," Ash says, still waving. "Shit. I think Colton took a picture."

"I'm gonna hide every single piece of his underwear in the damn milking barn," I grumble.

Ash laughs even louder. "I'll help."

Huffing a breath, I point out the obvious problem we're now facing. "You realize we only brought one towel, right?"

"What does that have to do with… *Hey.*"

I take off, and Ash runs after me, both of us splashing through the water as we race toward shore. I hold one hand in front of my junk, but honestly, if folks are still watching, it's their own damn fault if they get a peek. I make it to the side of the river first, snatching up the bathroom towel and holding it out wide.

Ash is puffing when he catches up to me, immediately sinking against my front. I wrap the towel around us. "Thought you were going to leave me here," he says, a little out of breath.

"Considered it," I admit.

He huffs, and we turn as one, heading for my house as someone lets out one final wolf whistle. It's a little clunky holding the towel around our midsections, but I manage, keeping our dignity somewhat intact.

"Everything ready for your mom's visit?" I ask. Ash's arm is around my waist, his body brushing against mine as we walk.

"Yep. She'll stay in my old room."

"*Your* old room, is it?"

He chuckles. "It was mine for a little bit. I'm excited for her to see this. To meet everyone."

I give Ash a squeeze. "You realize my mom's gonna have her mucking stalls by the end of her stay, right? It's how she shows she cares. By roping folks into manual labor."

Ash grins my way. "Remind me to take a picture."

I snort.

By the time we reach the house, we're a pair of icicles. We jump into the shower, setting it to scalding, both of us huddling under the spray to warm up. Once we get out, we dress and wander into the kitchen, Ash grabbing some leftovers to heat up while I warm some cider on the stove. He brandishes a container my way I hadn't noticed earlier.

"Rice pudding," he says happily. "Stole some earlier to keep here. I'm glad I did. I doubt those hooligans would have saved us any."

I watch Ash as he sets the rice pudding on the table, rambling all the while about how *although I suppose we're the hooligans, huh? Considering we were the ones that went streaking. They just watched. But honestly, they're a bunch of troublemakers. You can't deny that.*

He cuts off, looking at me with a curious tilt to his head, those stormy eyes bright. "What?"

"Nothing," I say, drawing him close and running my thumb over the dimple in his chin. I tip his face up, bringing our lips together in a short, soft press. He hums against me, arms encircling my waist.

I feel...*overwhelmed*, but not in a bad way. I'm swamped by my emotions. Grateful for everything that's found its way into my life.

Grateful for *him*.

"Would you sing me that song later?" I ask. "The one from when you arrived in town?"

His arms tighten around me, his hair brushing the side of my head as he leans his cheek against mine. I close my eyes, heart feeling so damn full I'm not sure how I can withstand it.

"Yeah, Jack," he says softly, his lips near my ear. "Don't you know? There's not a single thing I wouldn't do for you."

Epilogue

ASH

Three Years Later

"Oh, honey. You look so handsome."

I glance at my mom in the mirror. She's wearing a light blue lace dress, her hand over her mouth as she looks at me. "Yeah? You like the white?"

She lets out a breath before walking my way. "It's perfect. Just like I'd always imagined."

"You thought about my wedding day?" I ask curiously.

She straightens my lapel, even though the fabric is already perfectly pressed. "You're my son. Of course I did. I never wanted to pressure you, but I hoped you'd have this some-day. I think it's any parent's dream for their kid to find happiness."

My lips turn up into a smile. "Even if that means them being thousands of miles away?"

"Even then," she says seriously. "Are you ready?"

"More than," I admit.

"Such a handsome groom," my mom says softly, shaking her head. "Come on. Let's head outside."

Arm looped with mine, my mom accompanies me out of the spare bedroom of the ranch house. The halls are quiet as we make our way through the house to the back door. It's a beautiful fall day, the temperatures just warm enough to keep our guests comfortable but not so hot as to be swel-tering. The foliage has started to change color, oranges and yellows mixing in with greens, and the cattle, like usual, add small dots of black-and-white to the landscape. Everyone is waiting for us near the river, so we head right that way.

When I catch sight of my soon-to-be-husband for the first time in hours, I can't help but bark a laugh.

Jackson has donned more jewelry than I've ever seen on him. Rings cover fingers on both hands. Leather and beaded bracelets peek out from below the hem of his suit jacket. I wouldn't be surprised if a few necklaces are hidden beneath his shirt and tie, too.

It's clear his family got to him, the sweet nuisances.

I expect Jackson to be scowling when I meet his gaze, but he's not. He's watching me with an expression that has my feet stuttering, even as my heart takes off at a gallop.

"I'll wait with the others," my mom says, giving my cheek a quick kiss before walking off, leaving me with Jackson.

"Hi," I say quietly, closing the distance between us.

He swallows roughly, his gaze running up and down my form, my white suit in direct contrast to his black one. "Hi," he finally replies.

I huff a laugh, running my fingers through Jackson's hair. Like usual, the strands are refusing to stay put, but damn if I don't love them that way.

Love *him* that way.

"You look handsome, Jack," I tell my fiancé.

"Too much jewelry," he mutters.

"Nah. I think it's just right."

Jackson tucks a strand of my hair back. "You're stunning."

Pretty sure my heart is trying to fly out of my chest. "You like the boots?"

He looks down, a smile on his face. "Sure do. They're a perfect fit."

Somehow, I know he's not talking about the size.

When Jackson's gaze returns to mine, my breath catches, the same way it did the first time I locked eyes with this man. And many, many times since then.

"Can I marry you now, Ashley Alcott? It feels like I've been waiting a lifetime for this."

"And what if I'm getting cold feet?" I tease.

"You're not," he says, so sure. "You'd have run far before now if that was the case. You're not going anywhere."

He's absolutely right about that.

I take hold of Jackson's hand, giving him a squeeze. "Yeah, Jack. Let's get married."

My mom gives me a nod when I signal to her that we're ready. Neither Jackson nor I cared much about custom when it came to planning our wedding day. We're not the flashy types; Jackson was right about that. Our ceremony consists of a small gathering, just our families, friends, and the folks from the ranch. Everyone takes their seats now in front of the mountains, the river snaking along our left.

I couldn't have dreamed up anything better.

The officiant waits up front, with Jackson's brothers standing off to one side and Virginia on the other. My heart swoops in my chest as our music starts to play, and my hand tightens on Jackson's.

"Ready?" I ask.

Bright blue eyes meet mine. "Ready for anything with you."

Damn sentimental man.

Jackson and I walk down the grassy aisle together as Cat Stevens's "The Wind" plays softly from speakers nearby. I never would have guessed years ago when I was dragging my suitcases behind me, the mountains waiting ahead, that I'd find my home right here in the small town of Darling, Montana. I wouldn't have guessed I'd find my own cowboy, that I'd fit here with him.

But sometimes our trajectory in life isn't what we expect. And I think that can be a good thing. I haven't once regretted my decision to up and travel west without a solid plan.

Not when it led me here.

When we reach the front of the aisle, the music that will forevermore remind me of the sun and the mountains comes to a close. Colton shoots Jackson what I assume is supposed to be a surreptitious thumbs-up, and I huff a laugh, meeting Virginia's gaze on the opposite side of the officiant. The tears in her eyes have me pulling in a shuddering breath.

Jackson and I separate to stand opposite one another, the breeze blowing gently and rustling the taller grasses at the edge of the water. For just a moment, everything is still and hushed, Jackson's eyes holding mine.

I wish I could say every moment of our wedding is one that gets seared into my memory, locked away timelessly for me to revisit again and again. But that's simply not the truth. Jackson fills my vision, leaving everything else hazy in my periphery.

I remember the important moments, though. Like our vows. I remember the way Jackson's eyes begin to water as he speaks. I remember how his voice trembles.

"Ash," he says hoarsely, his emotions already overwhelming him. "When I was a little boy, I used to run around this ranch, exploring every nook and cranny. I never got sick of it, and I remember thinking surely there was nowhere on Earth as perfect as this. And then...then I met you."

Ah, God.

Jackson takes in an uneven breath, composing himself. My own smile wobbles.

"They say love is like falling," he says. "But I don't think that was the case for me. Loving you is as easy as breathing. It's the way you smile and how your eyes brighten when you're excited, which is often. It's how comfortable it feels to be in your arms after a long day, and how, no matter what, your strength of spirit never wavers. You're as big as this place. As expansive. You're in my lungs, Ashley Alcott, and loving you was never a question. It was simply a matter of fact."

I hastily swipe my cheek as Jackson grabs my hand in his, bringing us closer together. His next words are nearly a whisper.

"As long as these mountains stand, I will love you. That I promise, sunshine."

I pull in my own shaky breath as Jackson smiles at me in that way he does, all humble and sincere. I never stood a chance against that smile.

"Jack," I say, my voice barely cooperating. "I used to pretend I was a bird. A seagull, to be precise. I imagined my wings taking me wherever I wanted to go. I never knew, exactly, where that was. I just knew there was *something* out there. I was sure of it. When I finally listened to that voice, I found *you*."

I wipe my cheek again, although it's a losing battle. Jackson's grip is tight in mine, and it grounds me. It makes it easy to go on.

"What I found was a man with a heart of gold. Someone good and kind, with the cutest scowl." I huff a laugh as Jackson attempts one now, rather unsuccessfully. "I found someone hard-working and protective. Someone stubborn about doing what's right. I found the sweetest man I've ever known."

Jackson shakes his head, but his eyes are wet, glimmering like the river beside us.

"I found the place I'd been searching for," I tell him honestly. "I found *who* I'd been searching for. There's not a day I don't love you, Jackson Darling. Not an hour, not a second. It's in every beat of my heart, in the iron that runs through my veins. You're a part of me, cowboy, and, as surely as the sun sets day after day, I will keep on loving you."

I can feel Jackson's inhale in my own chest, feel the way he aches with it. Because I ache, too. The best sort of pain.

It's a blur again after that. Snickerdoodle comes down the aisle with our rings, a sight that has our wedding guests laughing. Smooth metal is slid onto my finger, and another ring is added to Jackson's current collection. There's steady blue eyes and words spoken—soft and solemn *I dos*. There's the whoop of a particularly rowdy Darling brother as the officiant pronounces us husband and husband.

And then there's Jackson's lips on mine, tasting of home.

Our family and friends clap as we walk down the aisle, hand in hand. Virginia lets out a piercing whistle. My cheeks hurt with how hard I'm smiling.

It's early evening when our celebration moves inside the dining room at the back of the ranch house. Lights are strung along the beams in the ceiling, more hanging from the awning over the back porch. For once, I didn't cook dinner, but everyone enjoys the sandwiches Marigold's friend Louise provided and the glasses of Darling Whiskey being poured.

Jackson and I take a moment for ourselves out on the deck, the air a little cooler now, our jackets on a chair inside. Music plays from within the dining room, and I catch sight of Marigold and Hank dancing with one another, Hank's head resting on Marigold's taller shoulder.

"Should we take the horses out this weekend?" Jackson asks. "We could pack some lunch. Stay out all afternoon."

My lips twitch, my arms wrapping around his back as his hands settle on my hips. "Jackson Darling, are you asking me on a date?"

He grumbles something I can't quite hear before saying, "And if I am? I'm allowed to take my husband out on dates, you know."

This man.

"Yeah, Jack. That sounds perfect. Maybe your mom could pack us a picnic."

Jackson stills for a second before tucking his face against my neck, his teeth nipping. I bark a laugh, the sting and subsequent soothing of his lips making me eager to get home to our bed. Or, heck, even the couch would do.

"I'll pack our own damn food," Jackson rumbles, sounding put-out.

I smooth my hands up his back, hugging him to me. "Sweet, sweet man," I murmur.

He shakes his head, beard bristling my skin. "I don't know why you keep calling me sweet. You're the only goddamn person who thinks that."

I huff a laugh, pulling back enough to see Jackson's face. "Because you *are*. You, Jack, are sweet like whiskey."

His brow creases. "Meaning what? I come with an abrasive kick?"

A smile curves my lips, and I bring my mouth close to his ear. "*Meaning* you put up a rough front. But under all that bite is a sweetness that lingers on my tongue."

Jackson sucks in a breath as I tug his earlobe between my teeth, his eyes darting down to my mouth as soon as I lean back. "For the record," he says hoarsely, "I think you're full of it."

"I can be full of *you* later if you want."

He groans, tucking his face against my neck again. "Fuck, sunshine. How long do we needa stick around our own reception?"

I glance inside. At my mom talking to Jackson's parents. At Remi animatedly telling Lawson about the new Silkie chicks at the petting farm. At all the ranchers, our extended family, and Virginia, my dearest friend, the reason I was drawn to Darling in the first place. Even Colton, who's stacking a pile of bacon-wrapped sausages onto his plate.

These people, they're ours.

"I think we've paid our dues," I tell my husband, snagging his hand. "C'mon, darlin'. Bring me home?"

His smile is comfort, his voice familiarity. "Happy to."

Jackson and I walk beneath the setting sun as the mountains turn red, his hand linked solidly with my own.

And I know I'm already there.
Home.

The End

About the Author

Information about Emmy Sanders and her complete list of works can be found on her website. Subscribe to her newsletter, join her Facebook reader group, Emmy's Enclave, and connect via email or social media:

www.emmysanders.com

Find online:
www.facebook.com/emmysandersmm
www.instagram.com/emmysandersmm

9 798989 542055